A DISTANT HOPE

ALSO BY ELLIN CARSTA

The Secret Healer
The Master of Medicine
The Draper's Daughter

A Distant Hope

ELLIN CARSTA

TRANSLATED BY GERALD CHAPPLE

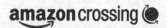

amazon crossing

Previously published as *Die ferne Hoffnung* by Amazon Publishing in Germany in 2018. Translated from the German by Gerald Chapple. First published in English by AmazonCrossing in 2019.

Published by AmazonCrossing, Seattle

www.apub.com

Amazon, the Amazon logo, and AmazonCrossing are trademarks of Amazon.com, Inc., or its affiliates.

ISBN-13: 9781542042284
ISBN-10: 1542042283

Cover design by Shasti O'Leary Soudant

Cover photography by Richard Jenkins Photography

Printed in the United States of America

A DISTANT HOPE

Prologue

Looking around the table and at the seemingly happy people chatting over that day's dinner, he smiled contentedly. Though everyone lived in the villa, it was not a given that they would take their meals together. But today everyone was gathered in Peter Hansen's honor: Georg and Robert, his two eldest sons, along with their wives and children, as well as Karl, his youngest son, who at twenty-nine still hadn't managed to find a wife, let alone start a family—which caused Peter some worry. At times he thought maybe something wasn't quite right with Karl.

His gaze fell on fourteen-year-old Luise, his youngest granddaughter. He couldn't explain why Robert's second daughter was the dearest of his three granddaughters. He didn't quite know how to deal with her sister, Martha, two years her elder, or with Georg's daughter, Frederike, the same age as Martha. Even his grandson, Richard—the only male descendent so far—was for him merely his son's son. Richard was seventeen, and his parents wanted him to graduate from high school a year early. Hansen doubted his grandson could do it. He saw him as a young man lacking in ambition, who must certainly have some talents, though his grandfather was unable to discern what they might be.

Frederike and Martha resembled their respective mothers too much for his taste; the girls felt that their purpose in this world was to lead a comfortable life at the side of a wealthy husband who would support them financially.

His own wife, Marie, had been cut from a very different cloth. During their almost forty years of marriage, she had been more of a partner to him, until an illness spirited her away two years ago. Not a day had passed since then that he hadn't contemplated her meaningless death and his now equally meaningless life.

He surveyed the room again, only vaguely following the conversation. He put down his silverware, removed the linen napkin from his lap, and stood up holding it in his hand.

"I would like to thank you again for finding time for me on this day. It means a great deal to me. Now, I ask you to excuse me." He laid the napkin on the table and walked slowly to the door. Passing Luise, he paused and gently stroked her cheek. His granddaughter smiled and nuzzled against his hand. A moment of indecision, and then he continued on his way.

He felt his family's questioning gaze as he closed the sliding door behind him. He calmly climbed the stairs to his study. After closing the door, he leaned against it for a moment and took a deep breath. He considered this room the most beautiful in the house. Marie had furnished it with her impeccable taste. If only she were here! Everything would have turned out differently—of that he was certain.

He took out a sheet of paper printed with the company letterhead and laid it before him on the desk. *Peter Hansen & Sons. Coffee Merchants since 1850.* He smiled. The curved letters seemed but a wonderful, slowly fading memory. He picked up his fountain pen and searched in vain for the right words. Then he placed the pen on the sheet of paper, took a deep breath, and opened the bottom drawer. Taking out a mahogany box, he set it on his desk, closing the drawer before opening it. The pistol was cushioned on a bed of red velvet. It felt good to lift it and place it to his temple. He saw the loving face of his wife before him as he pulled the trigger. Peter Hansen's life ended on his sixty-fifth birthday—with a loud bang.

Chapter One

Hamburg, 1888

She'd lost track of the time. Mother would be frightfully angry. Luise hurriedly placed the bunny back in its hutch and closed the little wooden door. She came here more often since her grandfather died. She missed him so very much! She quickly wiped the rabbit hair from her pale-pink dress and brushed away the dirt its little paws had left. She really should wear an apron when she held the bunny. Her mother had scolded her often enough. She was sure to be punished, and not only because of her dress.

She threw a parting glance at the three rabbits. Only one of them was hers, the white one with black spots. She'd named it Caesar. The others belonged to Martha and Frederike. Grandfather had given them to the girls three years ago, cautioning them to take good care of the animals. Cousin Richard had received one as well, but after a few days, it was dead in its cage. Luise didn't know the cause of death. She would have cared for it; the other girls hadn't evinced the slightest interest in their responsibilities. Luise was grateful for the present and sincerely delighted with the rabbits, but the other two girls seemed to find them a burden.

Just a few days after making the gifts, their grandfather had summoned them to his study and warned them again, individually, to take seriously the responsibility they bore for the little creatures now in their hands. The next day Richard's rabbit died. Luise was reluctant to connect the animal's death with Grandfather's rebuke, which had obviously annoyed Richard. But if she was honest, she got chills remembering how Richard had delighted in the creature's sudden demise.

Luise ran as fast as she could along the path to the villa, gravel crunching beneath her soles. Then she tripped, twisted her ankle, and fell onto her knee. Pain shot through her whole body. She struggled to her feet and wiped the bloody cut on her knee. A bit of gravel was stuck in the wound; she picked it out, forcing herself not to scream or burst into tears. With a little spit on her finger, she tried to clean her knee, but the blood and spittle mixed with the dirt, making an even bigger mess. Luise felt sick to her stomach. Not from the pain or the blood, but because she knew what to expect from her mother's "disciplinary measures," as they were called.

Luise thought about sneaking into the house and running to the bathroom. Maybe her mother wouldn't notice, and she could at least clean up her wound and make herself somewhat presentable. But she rejected the idea: it was too late to look like a proper girl from a good family, with her dirt-stained dress, her bloody knee, and her mussed hair. She could expect at least five afternoons under house arrest.

She ran up the five steps to the towering villa with its white and sunshine-yellow trim. Luise loved the house she'd lived in with her family since she was born. She took a breath and pressed down on the latch, pushing open the heavy wooden door. There was no one in the vestibule, where she'd expected her mother would be waiting for her. Voices sounded from the dining room, and Luise took a few steps, near enough to hear Uncle Georg talking. Her father responded, but she couldn't make out his words. She drew herself up, knocked, and poked her head through the partly opened door after hearing her uncle's "Come in!"

"Please excuse me for being late, Mother."

Her mother waved as if shooing a fly.

"Not now, Luise. Go upstairs with the other children. Wait until you are called."

"Yes, Mama," Luise said meekly, ducking her head and closing the door. Her heart was beating wildly. The tension in the room was almost tangible. She had seen her parents; her uncle Georg and aunt Vera; her other uncle, Karl; Dr. Lampert, the family lawyer; and a man she'd never met. What did it mean?

She ran upstairs to the room she shared with her sister. Martha sat on her bed, Richard and Frederike opposite her on Luise's bed.

"There you are," Martha said. "Whatever happened to you?" She pointed to Luise's bleeding knee.

"What's going on downstairs?" Luise asked, sitting next to Martha, who didn't answer.

"We're broke, that's what," Richard replied with a sarcastic smile.

Frederike poked him in the ribs.

"You don't *know* that."

"But I heard it. Lampert said so."

Luise swallowed hard. She couldn't believe that they had run out of money. How was that possible? And what would that mean for the family?

"Who's the other man downstairs?" she asked.

"His name's Reidel, from the bank," Richard said.

"It still doesn't mean anything," said Frederike.

Luise gave her sister a questioning look, which elicited a shrug.

"All I know is what we heard. Something about Grandfather's estate and how it's to be divided up."

"If there's anything left to distribute," Richard argued. "That's why the old man blew his brains out."

"He did not!" Luise protested immediately. "Grandfather had a heart attack while cleaning his gun, and it went off."

"You're such a silly cow." Richard rolled his eyes.

"Mother told us that's what happened, and I believe her," Luise insisted.

"Believe what you want. But we were all there when he shot himself. Father told us not to tell the truth about it. But that doesn't change the facts one bit."

"I don't think there's no money left." Frederike toyed with her braid. "Maybe there isn't all *that* much money, but enough." She swept her hand around the room. "Just look around. I could buy ten new dresses from the furnishings alone."

"And why do you think that Reidel fellow turned up here right after the will was read?" Richard asked, turning to his sister and then to the other girls.

"But our fathers have been working at the office for such a long time," Luise objected. "They would have noticed if there were business problems."

"The old man kept a tight grip," said Richard.

"Oh, our fathers will sort it out," Frederike remarked blithely, just as there was a knock at the door.

"The ladies and gentlemen wish for you to come downstairs," Anna, the housekeeper, announced.

"We're coming," Richard said, and they got off the beds.

"Could you just wait a minute?" Luise pointed to her knee.

"Yes, but be quick," said Martha.

Luise rushed to the bathroom at the end of the hallway. She grabbed a towel, wet it, and wiped the blood and dirt from her knee as best she could. She brushed back her blond hair, adjusted her dress, and hurried out. The others were waiting at the head of the stairs.

"Thanks," Luise said.

Their parents and Uncle Karl were waiting in the dining room. Dr. Lampert and Mr. Reidel were gone.

Georg Hansen invited them to sit down. As the eldest he had taken his father's seat as the new head of the family.

They sank into their seats without a word, staring at Georg expectantly; he wore a three-piece suit, as always, and not a single strand of his dark hair was out of place.

"Your grandfather's will has been read. He made some dispositions regarding personal belongings that are to be passed on to you. Your parents"—he looked over at Martha and Luise—"and Vera and I will see to it that the objects are collected in the coming days."

"What's with the money?" Richard asked unceremoniously, making his mother hiss angrily.

"Richard!" she scolded.

He shrugged. "One should be allowed to inquire at least?"

"Since you are not an adult, Richard, as you just demonstrated yet again," his father reprimanded him, "you have the right neither to ask nor to expect an answer." He looked daggers at his son. "We will continue to carry on your grandfather's business. For the time being, nothing will change for any of you. That is the sum of what you need to know. Are there any questions?"

"Good." He went to the door and called, "Anna, you may serve dinner."

Luise, who had kept her eyes lowered throughout, raised them as she sensed her mother's gaze.

"And what do you look like today, Luise?" Elisabeth addressed her daughter with an angry look. "Like some vulgar little girl—you ought to be ashamed of yourself!"

"Please forgive me," Luise said submissively, lowering her eyes again.

"You were with those disgusting rabbits again, weren't you?"

Luise nodded guiltily.

"I was feeding them." She refrained from saying that she was the only one who took care of them, after all.

"Robert, those rabbits must go!" Elisabeth demanded.

"No!" Luise looked at her in horror. "Please, Mama, don't do that! They were a present from Grandfather!"

"They're the only thing from him they have left," Robert objected.

"Just look at your daughter," Elisabeth hissed at her husband. "She's filthy. Not at all presentable."

"Please—I promise to take better care," Luise begged. Tears sprang to her eyes. She threw her sister a pleading glance.

"Let's do keep the beasts," Richard interjected. "If times don't get better, we'll at least have some meat for dinner." He emitted a loud laugh as Luise blanched at the idea.

"Pay more attention to keeping yourself clean, Luise," her father said—the only blond one in the family besides Luise. "Otherwise there *will* be consequences. The rabbits can stay for now."

Luise breathed a sigh of relief.

"Thank you, Father. I'll be more careful from now on." She peeked over at her mother, who seemed displeased with her husband's decision, though she kept quiet.

"Richard," Robert addressed his nephew. "Karl and I will be leaving for Vienna first thing in the morning on business. Your father would like you to join us."

"Me? Why?"

"Your vacation begins the day after tomorrow. Missing the last day won't kill you," Georg suggested.

"But why go to Vienna?" Richard persisted.

"You must learn how business is done," Georg explained to his son. "When I was your age, I knew more about the coffee trade than you, and about what to watch out for. It's time you became involved with the logistics of the firm."

Richard pouted. "But I want to recover during vacation. Why should I have to go from one kind of work to another?"

Georg took a deep breath and exhaled forcibly. He wished he could take his son to another room and give him a good talking-to, the way his own father had with him. But if he let Richard get away with his disrespect in front of the others, it could weaken his position.

"Recover from *what*?" he asked, raising his eyebrows ironically. "From an excess of learning? Not for you, given your poor grades."

Richard stared angrily, seeming to weigh a rejoinder. His eyes met Luise's; she shook her head almost imperceptibly. Richard's eyes narrowed to slits, but he kept quiet.

"Good," Georg remarked. "That's settled."

The housekeeper, assisted by a servant girl, brought in trays of various dishes, ending the conversation. Richard was obviously seething, but the subject was closed during the meal.

Robert, Karl, and Richard had been gone for almost five weeks, and the family longed for their return. School had begun two weeks earlier, but Georg had seen to it that his son was excused, arranging for Richard to make up the time by doing extra work when he returned from Vienna. Moreover he hinted at the prospect of a financial contribution to the institution—without any idea where the money would come from. He pinned his hopes on his brothers' success. If they were to return empty-handed, he didn't know how long Peter Hansen & Sons would stay in business. The mood in the household was tense—grueling for all its members.

Georg always walked to his office in the warehouse district, where the beans were stored and bagged. The offices were on the top floor of a redbrick building, and the smell of coffee permeated the place. Luise noticed that her uncle left the office earlier each day. And although she would have liked to see more of him, she worried about the anxiety inscribed on his face.

Aunt Vera and her mother, Elisabeth, grew closer, which made Luise all the more suspicious, because they had often fought bitterly before. If, after so many years of antipathy, the two women suddenly got along, Luise reasoned that they must be worse off than she expected, or than Uncle Georg wanted to admit.

At mealtimes when her uncle was usually absent, Vera, Elisabeth, Frederike, Martha, and Luise spoke very little; if something *was* said, it was always their collective hope that Robert, Karl, and Richard would be back from Vienna with good news soon. If that were not the case . . . nobody wanted to think about that, let alone discuss it.

Outside of attending Catholic school, Luise was either with the rabbits or reading in her room. For her birthday her grandfather had given her Theodor Storm's novella *Immensee*. He had told her that she should take the book as a call to action—it was a plea to live her life for herself so she wouldn't later mourn for missed opportunities.

Luise had read the book but didn't really understand it. After her grandfather died, though, she read it again and again. She hadn't seen until then what her grandfather might have meant to say through Reinhard and Elisabeth's story, and she wondered whether he, like Reinhard, recalled an unfulfilled youthful love later in life. Her grandfather had, to be sure, found his great love in his wife and had not let her go, as Reinhard had in the novella. Still, both he and her grandfather had lost their lover, in one way or another.

Luise dearly wanted to ask her grandfather if he regretted anything about the way he'd lived his life. Did he have different plans when he was young? Did he want to live somewhere else with his wife? Not work in the coffee trade, or even have had no children? If so, Luise wouldn't be in this world either. Questions like these bothered her time and again—questions her grandfather could no longer answer.

And just like Reinhard in Storm's novella, she'd started to put her thoughts down on paper. She kept the loose pages in a little portfolio and made a firm promise to herself: one day she'd buy a little book and write down everything she felt and thought.

"What are you writing?"

Luise was startled. She hadn't noticed Martha come into the room. She quickly shut the portfolio.

"Nothing at all."

"Let me see it!" Martha demanded, holding out her hand.

"No, this is mine." Luise held the portfolio to her breast.

"If I tell Mother, she'll make you give it to her."

"Please, Martha, don't do that!" Luise clutched the portfolio tightly. "It's nothing improper—you've got to believe me. It's just . . ."

"What?"

"My thoughts."

"About what?"

"About school, our family, the coffee business. Anything at all."

"Anything about me?"

Luise shrugged. "No, not really."

"I want to read it to be sure."

"And you won't tell Mama?"

"No, I won't."

Luise handed Martha the portfolio, which she took to her bed.

"*Immensee*?" Martha shot Luise an inquiring look.

"A novella by Theodor Storm. It's about two lovers who knew each other as children and promised to be together. But Reinhard had to go elsewhere, and Elisabeth stayed where she was. They write to each other and . . ." She stopped when she saw the boredom in Martha's face. "I've got the book. You can read it if you like."

"You're writing about a novella? Whatever for?"

"Because I thought their story was moving." Luise shrugged.

Martha looked at her sister without a shred of understanding and flipped through the pages, reading a passage here and there.

"You only write about boring things."

"I write what I think," Luise said apologetically.

Martha snapped the portfolio shut and handed it back to her sister.

"Here, nobody's going to want to read it."

Luise slipped it under her pillow.

"I hate vacations," Martha sighed. "My friends planned to go on picnics together, but I was the only one they wouldn't let go along. And that stupid cow Annegret used the picnics to make eyes at Ferdinand, though he's been interested in me for six months. I hate Annegret."

"I thought you were friends?"

"Friends? Bah. Nonsense! She was always jealous of me in dance class when somebody showed interest in me. And now she's trying to get Ferdinand for herself."

"Why don't you try to get his attention?"

"How? He only has eyes for that witch. And she doesn't even want him. She only wants what others have. She just doesn't want me to have him."

"Maybe she'll lose interest soon," Luise said, trying to soothe her sister.

"Oh, and then I'm supposed to be happy being his second choice? What does he think, that I'll wait around pining for him?"

"I don't think he's so great, anyway."

Martha looked at Luise and shook her head. "You're still too young to understand. Ferdinand's parents have one of the largest trading companies around. His wife could have anything she wanted."

"But you've got enough pretty dresses," Luise objected.

Martha rolled her eyes. "You're just young and have strange ideas about things. You don't understand how women feel."

Luise was at a loss.

"I'll go find Frederike. She understands. She'll help me think of a way to get back at Annegret."

"Do that," Luise said indifferently, relieved when Martha closed the door behind her. Luise thought her sister was right about one thing: Luise would never understand her.

Chapter Two

It was exactly six weeks and two days until Robert, Karl, and Richard returned to the Hansen villa. They received a warm welcome from the family, though with an undertone of anxious curiosity about the fate of the trip.

"I must get out of my travel clothes," Robert said with a smile. "But we bring good, no, excellent news. We'll tell you all about it at dinner. I'm starving."

Karl patted his brother on the shoulder. "You took the words right out of my mouth." He looked around. "Where's Georg?"

"Still at the office. He's been working long hours lately," Vera answered.

"Send a boy to tell him to come home as soon as he can," Robert said.

The housekeeper had been watching their arrival and curtsied. "I'll send someone at once, sir."

"Thank you, Anna."

"Are you all right?" Luise asked Richard, who hadn't said a word and looked worn out to her.

He shrugged.

"It's fine" was the only thing he managed to say. Then he followed his uncles out to freshen up.

"Now tell us!" Georg exclaimed. He had arrived home just before dinner and greeted his brothers exuberantly. Anna had managed to prepare a modest feast on short notice, and the mood at the table was more relaxed and joyful than Luise had seen in a long time.

"Did you get our letters?" Robert asked his brother.

"Yes, both of them. And did you get the deal you hoped for?"

"You received letters!" Elisabeth interrupted, as amazed as she was annoyed. "The least you could have done was to tell us!"

"Forgive me, Elisabeth," Georg said. "Of course, you're right. I've had so much occupying my thoughts recently, I simply forgot."

Elisabeth nodded, but her anger at her brother-in-law was obvious.

"I'll summarize what we wrote," Robert said. "As you guessed, the company's in a precarious situation." He put up his hand when Georg was about to object. "We shouldn't keep them in the dark any longer."

Luise had a question on the tip of her tongue, but she suppressed it. She hoped she'd have the chance to talk with her father privately. Maybe she'd find out whether her grandfather did commit suicide.

"You're probably right," Georg conceded. "Before Robert tells us about their stay in Vienna, let me tell you how this came to pass." He had some wine, wore a thoughtful expression on his face. "As you all know, Father did not like anyone to interfere with his business matters. And there was never any reason for Robert, Karl, and me to doubt his judgment." He shrugged. "Presumably his judgment was lacking, however, when he made the decision that put us in this situation."

Georg took another drink before continuing. His father had summoned them into his office nine months before his death and told them that the merchant trade with German East Africa had become more difficult because of customs duties and more frequent raids by the native Africans. This made it urgently necessary to find new suppliers, because the company was no longer able to keep its contracted commitments. So Peter Hansen, on the recommendation of a friend, contacted a trader in Bagamoyo, the capital, who had a reputation for delivering large quantities of coffee at a good price. The problem was that each shipment was so large that Hansen had to use all his available funds and borrow more money from the bank. Nevertheless, this would eliminate the supply problems facing their company. Hansen thought he was one of the few merchants who could meet the constantly rising demand for coffee and hoped it would strengthen his company's position even more.

"Father put all his eggs in one basket," Georg explained. "But he was cheated. By the time he realized it, it was too late."

Georg said that the alleged coffee dealer had only temporarily assumed the position from an ailing overseer of a coffee plantation. He was selling coffee that had long been promised elsewhere, but all he had to do was convince buyers that those huge amounts of coffee beans were for them.

"Did they catch the wretch who cheated Grandfather?" Richard asked.

"They're still looking for him. The German colony is still being founded. It's far easier to swindle someone there than it is in Hamburg. It wasn't just Grandfather, but six other merchants we know about as well. The minute he had the money, he went into hiding and hasn't been seen since. He probably bribed one of the captains and absconded to God only knows where. With all that money, he can go anywhere."

"If only he hadn't gotten involved with those lumpen Negroes," Elisabeth sighed.

"The man's name was Hans Müller, and he's German, Elisabeth," Robert said, cutting her off.

"At any rate the money's gone, and now you know why," Georg said. "So tell us what happened in Vienna. Were you able to get our customers back?"

"Yes and no," Robert replied. "You can understand their aggravation. The name Peter Hansen & Sons always meant reliable, reputable business dealings. When we couldn't deliver anymore, our partners suffered losses and had to find other importers. They've signed contracts and don't need our coffee now."

Georg looked at him grimly. "If you told us about the *successful* part, I wouldn't be opposed."

"The coffee trade is on slippery footing," Robert replied, raising a finger, "but not the cocoa trade."

"Cocoa? You never said anything about it in your letters."

"Because I know you so well, dear brother. Karl and I agreed it would be better to discuss it with you in person."

"The Hansens have been in the coffee business since 1850!" Georg shouted.

Karl laughed loudly. "Robert predicted that's exactly what you'd say."

Georg looked from one brother to the other. "Robert, you wrote that a business opportunity had opened up?"

"That's correct. We were in every café in Vienna. Yes, the demand for coffee is high. But it won't take long for cocoa to catch up and be just as popular. People there are wild about chocolate. They eat it; drink it; decorate food, cakes, and pastries with it. In a couple of years, the demand for cocoa will outstrip the demand for coffee," Robert said euphorically.

"Robert's right," Karl agreed. "The cafés are so crowded that you often have to wait for a seat. And many customers are having chocolate."

"We found seven cafés that would be delighted to have a good source of cocoa, if we could deliver it."

"But we don't have any suppliers," Georg argued.

"We don't have any suppliers *right now*," Karl said. "And so we come to the opportunity Robert mentioned in his letter."

Everyone turned to Robert with anticipation.

"Even if you think we're mad . . . Karl and I have put our minds to this. And Richard, too, of course," he hurriedly added. "We were gone for so long because a café owner told us her supplier from Cameroon would be meeting with her shortly. He comes regularly to see his mother in Munich and takes the opportunity to look in on the cafés in Vienna and other cities he sells in. His name is Johann Meyerdierks, a German who went to Cameroon three years ago. Since then he's owned a plantation."

"And you met this man in Vienna?"

"We did," Karl said.

"Can he only deliver cocoa, or coffee beans, too?"

"Only cocoa. But that's not the whole story," Robert answered, and took a deep breath. He apparently anticipated resistance to what he was about to say. "He wants to sell his plantation as soon as possible."

"He wants to sell?" Georg echoed. "So he won't have much of anything to sell for very long."

"He's looking for somebody to take over the plantation," Karl explained.

"Then we should keep in touch with this man Meyerdierks so that he introduces us to his successor when the time comes," Georg said.

"That won't be necessary," Robert said. "We already know his successor."

Georg looked from Robert to Karl, reading the looks on their faces. Then he shook his head violently. "You two are mad! There's no way. No way at all!"

"No way for what?" Vera looked at her husband. "I don't understand."

"Neither do I," Elisabeth said.

"Robert and Karl are considering buying the plantation," Georg explained to the women. "Or am I mistaken?" he asked, turning back to his brothers.

"That's exactly what we intend to do," Karl confirmed.

"Think about it, Georg. We'd be our own supplier! No more losses, no money trickling off to somewhere. We could get a strong hold on the cocoa business before others do."

"Or fail and lose everything." Georg grimaced.

"We won't fail," Robert replied, "because we'll deploy on a broader basis. You will stay here in Hamburg, run the office, and sign new contracts according to how much we can deliver. Karl will go to Vienna to open a new office so that the beans can be stored *in situ* for delivery to our clients. And I"—he glanced over at Elisabeth—"will go to Cameroon and run the plantation."

Elisabeth gasped audibly.

"You're not in your right mind, Robert Hansen! There is no way I will go and live among Negroes who might cut your throat at any minute. And neither will my daughters."

"Elisabeth, you don't understand. The German colony is still being founded, yes. But there are German churches, a German school, German families, and communities."

"And ferocious, dirty savages." Elisabeth put down her knife and fork and folded her arms across her chest.

"You'll have more servants than you have here," her husband said. "And if we believe Meyerdierks, the landscape there is exceptionally beautiful, more than anywhere else in the world."

"I think Hamburg is very beautiful, and I don't need savages for servants."

"You don't have the slightest idea about cocoa growing." Georg looked at Robert thoughtfully. "Do you think you can do it?"

"That's beside the point, because we won't be going there!" Elisabeth kept on.

"Meyerdierks says that the crucial advantage is the plantation's location." Robert ignored his wife's protests.

"And it's a good one?"

"So it seems." Robert nodded. "There are two harvests a year. Last year his plantation produced ten thousand tons."

"What's that you say?" Georg asked. "Ten thousand tons?"

Robert grinned. "I tell you, it's a gold mine. He's increased the yield since he took over the plantation three years ago. And he says even better yields are possible."

"It only took him two of those three years to get rich. And by rich, I mean *really* rich," Karl added.

"So why does he want to sell the plantation?" Georg seemed unpersuaded.

"Because his mother is ill, and he wants to take care of her during the last years of her life. Meyerdierks himself is going on fifty. You can guess how old his mother must be." Robert looked at Georg earnestly. "This is a real opportunity for us, Georg! I have a good feeling about this."

Georg looked as if he were mulling it over. "Even if we wanted to, we don't have the money to buy a plantation."

"That's the best part," Karl spoke up. "We don't have to pay Meyerdierks until after the next harvest, *and* not the whole sum at once. He's giving us six years, though he says we'll need less than half that to make enough to pay it all."

"Sounds almost too good to be true, doesn't it?" Georg said.

"Maybe it was destiny, I don't know," Karl said.

"How did you leave it with Meyerdierks?"

"We told him we'd come home to talk to you. He's on the way to Cameroon. He's expecting us at his plantation within the next six weeks. If nobody comes, he'll know we're not interested and will offer the place to someone else."

"I will *not* go to Cameroon," Elisabeth repeated.

"Maybe you do have the wrong impression of the country. After all, it's very beautiful there," Vera stepped in, trying to mediate.

"Then *you* go there with *your* family, and *we'll* stay here in Hamburg," Elisabeth retorted.

"Let's sleep on it and discuss it again in the morning," Georg suggested.

"I've slept on it for several nights, and Karl has, too. And Richard knew our plans in Vienna and likewise sees the potential, in spite of his young years. Sleep on it for a night if you must, Georg. Cameroon is our future—I feel it in my bones."

"You're definitely going ahead with this?"

"Yes, Georg, I am. And I hope to do it under the name Peter Hansen & Sons."

"And if I say no?"

"Then it will go under the name of Robert Hansen, and I'll assume all the risk."

"You can*not* do that," Elisabeth said spitefully.

"We don't want to leave you out, Georg, but we're afraid the opportunity will be lost if we wait too long," Karl added. "If you're not convinced, Robert and I will leave the Hamburg office to you and help pay off the bank debt. We'll still be brothers, as we've always been. But we may be going separate ways in our future businesses."

The children exchanged uneasy looks. Everyone in the room sensed that a course into the future was being fixed at that very moment.

Georg looked at Robert, then Karl. "You're that sure about it?"

Robert nodded. "No doubts whatsoever. I'll go to Cameroon and would be pleased if you'd come with me on this first trip, Elisabeth, and see your new home along with me and the children."

"Not under any circumstances!" Elisabeth replied vehemently.

"Well, then you won't see it until we move."

"I don't want to go to Cameroon either," Martha said clearly. "All my friends are here."

"You'll make friends there if you want to," Robert said.

Luise, unsure, looked first to her mother and then to Martha before finally turning to her father. "I would love to go with you to Cameroon on the first trip."

"You shall *not* do that!" Elisabeth threatened.

"She's going to be living there soon, Elisabeth. You'd be well advised to follow our daughter's example." Robert smiled at Luise. "Then go pick some light clothing, my little girl. It's warm in Cameroon." He winked at his daughter, raised his glass, and waited for the others to do the same. "To new times, and the hopes that they bring!"

"To new times," the others echoed—except for Elisabeth, who didn't give her husband so much as a glance. She pushed her chair back noisily and stood up.

"Excuse me," she said angrily. "Come, Martha. We won't find a sympathetic ear here."

Martha stood up, casting an uneasy glance at her father. Then she followed her mother out the door.

Luise's eyes followed them. She felt bad about how things had gone. It wasn't right for her father to simply ignore her mother's concerns the way he had. But he had final say in their family, just as Georg did in his. And Luise was excited about being en route to Cameroon in just a few days.

"May I be excused for a moment?" she asked.

Her father looked surprised. "Certainly, Luise. Where are you going?"

"I'll be right back," she replied. She returned momentarily with the large globe, which normally stood on a wooden pedestal in the study. She lifted it with some effort onto the little sideboard at the end of the room. Then she asked, "Where's Cameroon?"

Robert stood up with a smile, went over, and turned the globe. The others were curious, too, and stood up to see better.

Robert put a finger on a spot.

"Here, little one, is Hamburg." He drew a curved line downward. "We'll take a ship past here to West Africa. And here," he said, tapping on another spot, "here is Cameroon. Our new home."

Chapter Three

Cameroon, 1888

The journey to Cameroon took exactly twenty-eight days. Luise used the time to review her final hours in Hamburg. The gulf between her and her mother seemed to have widened. Elisabeth had hardly spoken to her since that dinner when she decided to go to Cameroon with her father. Luise had often felt she couldn't do anything right in her mother's eyes, but it had gotten considerably worse.

Every time she went to see the rabbits, she wore one of Anna's aprons so she wouldn't get dirty. She did her chores diligently and didn't ask for her mother's help in preparing for the trip, to avoid reopening the wound. It was all for naught. If Elisabeth paid attention to her at all, it was only with disgusted looks and angry comments. Luise didn't know what she'd done to deserve them, apart from agreeing to go with her father.

She had begged Martha to take care of the rabbits, feeling a bit guilty, though her sister should have shared in looking after the rabbits. She hoped Martha would keep her promise. Just to be sure, she asked Anna to feed them regularly. The housekeeper's assurances relieved Luise far more than the promise she'd wrung from her sister. Though

Anna's responsibilities at the villa left her little free time, Luise knew the rabbits wouldn't starve during her absence.

She wrote all these things down during the voyage. And she experienced new things daily; Luise was bursting with thoughts during the trip and worried she hadn't brought enough writing paper. She'd never been away from Hamburg before and had seen her cousin's trip to Vienna as a grand adventure. She could scarcely believe she was heading for an infinitely more distant place by her father's side. For all her excitement, she felt a little anxious about what to expect in this new world, which would be her home for the next few years.

"Look over there!" Her father pointed out something as their ship glided into the bay. "The German flag."

Luise nodded and smiled. She sensed he was trying to share a feeling of their homeland. She did *not* tell him that it was precisely the sense of the foreign, the unknown, that amazed her. Everything looked completely different, and yet, as the steamer anchored some distance from shore, she had the feeling that everything was strangely familiar, as if she'd been there before.

Several wooden huts stood on the left, above a long bay and beach that culminated in a huge forest. In Hamburg, ships moored directly against the imposing quay walls, but here passengers and cargo had to be ferried to land in smaller boats. From the beach a road led up into an interior that remained obscured when seen from the water. A distant mountain towered behind the forest, its highest peak touching the clouds.

"Is that Mount Cameroon?" Luise asked her father.

"The *great* Mount Cameroon," he corrected her. "The local people call it Fako. It's an active volcano."

Luise nodded and craned her neck landward again. Several smaller mountain ranges covered by tropical jungle crisscrossed the landscape in front of Mount Cameroon. The trees were 150 feet high or higher. She'd never seen anything so beautiful, not even in the picture books about foreign lands her grandfather used to show her. She felt, no, she knew that she wanted to belong here. Right here, in this faraway place, she would find home. The feeling overpowered her, filling her eyes with tears.

"What's the matter, little one? Don't you like it?"

Her father put an arm around her shoulders and gently drew her to him.

"I can't describe it," Luise began in a small voice. "But it's . . . it's so . . ." She stammered. "It's as if I've been here before. Everything seems strange and yet familiar." She looked up to her father. "I know that's nonsense, I'm sorry."

"I don't think so, Luise." He drew her toward him more closely as he looked over the railing at the land spread before them. "I feel the same way. Maybe where we ought to belong in the world is right here."

"Yes," she whispered, then swallowed. "That's the way it feels to me."

Several small, brightly painted boats approached to ferry them onto land. All the dark-skinned men were naked above the waist, which Luise found disconcerting. She'd never seen a man like that at home, certainly not in public. They climbed into the boats and were on the beach a few minutes later. Luise was somewhat shaky on her feet after the long voyage, but she climbed out of the little boat, taking the hand a man offered to steady her.

"Thank you," Luise said, nodding at him. He let go of her hand when he saw that she was firmly on the ground, and paid her no further mind. Luise wondered if she'd done something impolite, and wanted to apologize if so. But the man had already turned away and picked up a package that another boat had brought from the ship.

"Do you understand my language?" her father asked another native, who was busily unloading the boat.

The man gave him a brief look and resumed his work without answering. People swarmed everywhere, unloading, but nobody seemed to notice Robert and Luise Hansen standing helplessly on the beach watching the commotion. Robert spoke to several more people but got no response.

"Where want go?" a voice asked suddenly, and Robert turned around.

"Good day. My name is Robert Hansen, and this is my daughter Luise. We'd like to go to Johann Meyerdierks's plantation."

The man nodded and called to two other men, who hurried over and picked up Robert and Luise's luggage.

"Walk," the native said, turning away.

"We're supposed to follow them. Come on, Luise."

The two men with their luggage waited uphill and indicated that the Germans were to get onto a kind of stretcher—a piece of cloth between two poles. Four men stood ready to carry them to their destination.

"I would prefer to ride," Robert stated. "Horse!"

He waited, then pointed at a half-dozen horses he'd spotted and made a whinnying sound. One of the men gestured toward the stretcher again, but Robert shook his head, pointed again to the horses, and tapped his chest. The man understood and soon returned leading one of the horses by the reins.

"Thank you." Robert mounted the horse and motioned to Luise that she should sit on the stretcher. Two men immediately lifted her up. For a moment she was afraid she'd fall, so she clutched the cloth. She quickly regained her balance, though she felt uncomfortable being carried by the men. But she kept the thought to herself. Her father had repeatedly told her during the voyage that everything would be different in Cameroon. And he said she should try to adapt to the people and understand their way of life. They would be dependent on the labor and experience of the locals for growing cocoa. Luise promised to do her best to learn, but even without her father's request, she would have done the same.

The stretcher swung back and forth as the bearers walked along the uneven path. The rocking of the ocean had bothered her much less. They'd been traveling for a good hour when the men shouted to each other and lay down the stretcher. At first Luise thought that they were taking a break; after all, they'd been carrying her the whole time without rest. But the men ran ahead, and Luise saw that a tree had fallen across the path.

The two men tried with all their might to push the trunk away, but it didn't budge an inch. Then one of the men came back, pointed to the horse, and said something to Robert that neither he nor Luise understood. But it quickly became clear that he wanted to use the horse to help drag the tree off the path. Robert dismounted, and the man skillfully tied one end of a rope around the trunk and the other around the horse's neck. As the animal pulled, the men tried to shove the trunk aside. Robert hurried over and pushed as hard as he could, too, and together they managed to clear the path enough for them to be able to pass. The native in charge bowed several times before helping Robert remount, lifting Luise up again, and continuing on their way.

Perhaps an hour later the path widened into a road that turned toward a stone house and farmland. Luise was overcome with amazement as they approached the buildings. The house was built wider than higher. The main building—a white stone two-story house—was flanked by single-story extensions. It had three bay windows on the front and a bright-red tile roof; the additions were covered with straw or something like it. A wooden veranda ran around the entire building, and the front was lined with square pillars that appeared to support the roof. She gaped at everything until the bearers set her down directly in front of the main house. Robert dismounted, and a white man in light-colored clothing emerged from the building.

"What a welcome surprise," he said in a friendly voice.

"Herr Meyerdierks—how very nice it is to see you again," Robert said, shaking the man's hand. "May I introduce my daughter Luise?"

The plantation owner offered her his hand. "Welcome! We Germans here in Cameroon all go by our first names. Please call me Johann."

Luise smiled, but avoided addressing him by his first name so soon. That was not how she was raised.

"I'm Robert." Luise's father's face reflected his pleasure at seeing the plantation owner again.

Meyerdierks reached into his pocket for a few coins and said something to the bearers that Luise interpreted as a thank-you.

"Come and sit on the veranda, and we'll have a drink. Was it a good trip?"

"Time passed faster than we expected. And the view here is really overpowering."

"This way, please." Meyerdierks led the way and gestured to a table and some woven chairs.

As they sat down, a servant quickly appeared and put a glass carafe and three glasses on the table, while another man watched.

"Thank you, Mojo," Meyerdierks said. Then he nodded toward the man standing behind Mojo.

"That's Malambuku, who's been with me from the start. He's the overseer and supervises the servants. You won't find a better man if you decide to settle here."

"Thank you, *sango*." Malambuku nodded and left the veranda.

"He speaks German well enough, and he understands it entirely. His son, Hamza, is exceptionally gifted when it comes to cocoa trees. He's just turned sixteen but is already so skilled that I couldn't do without him."

"You've chosen a very beautiful spot to live," Robert marveled.

"When you've freshened up a bit, I'd like the pleasure of showing you around the plantation." Meyerdierks gazed out across the land. "It will be hard to leave all this behind—the breadth of the landscape, the people, the climate. It's like . . ."

"Like a melody," Luise chimed in for the first time and finished his sentence.

Meyerdierks looked at her in surprise, and the girl immediately apologized. He smiled.

"Yes, that perfectly describes Cameroon. Thank you, Luise. You've summarized my feelings for this wonderful spot in a single word."

Luise smiled, somewhat embarrassed. "Thank you, Herr Meyerdierks."

"Johann," he corrected her. "Even if you're younger—that's the custom here. There are just under two hundred Germans living in Cameroon, and we all use first names."

"Two hundred?" Robert seemed surprised. "And are there regular meetings?"

"Church on Sunday is as important here as it is in Germany. After the service we get together and discuss current events, and of course catch up on the latest gossip. Not very different from home."

"And yet you want to sell?" Robert swung his arm around. "We'd be satisfied to lease it for a time."

Meyerdierks shook his head.

"If I'm finished with something, then that's the end of it." He took another look at the surroundings. "I may come back to Africa someday." He took a sip. "My mother won't live forever, and I've grown to love this country. But in my experience, either you do something with all your heart or not at all. I can't go back home to take care of Mother and leave part of myself here. I'd do neither very well."

"A courageous decision," Robert remarked. "And the conditions we discussed in Vienna are still acceptable?"

Luise's pulse sped up when Meyerdierks paused.

"Not quite," the plantation owner finally said.

"What do you mean?" Robert asked, with more of an edge than intended.

"We didn't discuss the labor force in Vienna, which was an omission."

"Which means?"

"I would be prepared to give you more time to pay off the plantation if you would agree to keep all the workers in your employ."

Robert breathed a sigh of relief. "That is certainly possible. Unless you hire people to lay out your socks in the morning."

Johann laughed heartily. "No, no. You'll need every last one of them. But there are rumors about other plantation owners, and there's no way I'd want that for my people here."

"What sort of rumors?"

Meyerdierks grimaced. "They show no respect for the locals, and some treat them worse than animals."

Robert shook his head. "That won't happen when I take over the plantation. Never!"

"That's just how I sized you up. That is why I want you to guarantee to keep all my people and not force them to find work elsewhere."

"How much do you pay your men?"

"They get room and board and ten marks a month as well."

"German marks?"

"Yes. The currency was introduced here last October."

Robert reflected for a moment. "I admit that's more than I'd expected. But back in Hamburg an employee makes a hundred marks a month and has to pay for rent, clothing, and food out of that."

"People don't need much here. They live in huts, a bit away from the house and near the cocoa trees. Food costs are almost negligible, scarcely worth mentioning."

"How many do you employ?"

"Twelve men and four women, that's a firm number. But of course the women aren't paid. Malambuku gets twelve marks a month. Hamza and the other men ten marks. Malambuku's other children are thirteen, twelve, ten, and eight and are unpaid as well. The same for children of the other workers. They're given food, that's all."

"What are the total expenses?"

"If you reckon two hundred marks, that should be sufficient."

Robert quickly calculated that he could hardly take care of his own family with that amount.

"And how much time would I have to pay off the plantation?"

"If you take over all the workers and don't cut their wages, I'll offer you eight years."

"And the ten thousand marks you asked for in Vienna still stands?"

"Agreed," Meyerdierks confirmed.

Robert leaned forward. "We will have to put it in writing, but a handshake can confirm the deal right now."

Johann leaned forward as well.

"I feel reassured that I'm placing the plantation in the best of hands." He grasped Robert's hand and shook it. Then he stood up. "We should drink to this with something stronger," he announced, and went into the house. He returned with a crystal carafe containing a copper-colored liquid and two glasses. "I assume you won't join us, Luise?"

She laughed and shook her head. "Most assuredly not."

Johann poured and gave a glass to Robert, who got to his feet.

"Here's to success!"

"To success!"

Chapter Four

Hamburg, 1888

It had been nine weeks since Robert and Luise left for Cameroon, and Elisabeth awaited their return anxiously. Not a day passed without Elisabeth praying that her husband would return with disappointment written all over his face, having found the plantation unsuitable. Elisabeth didn't want to imagine anything else. She did *not* want to go to Cameroon! She did *not* want to live anywhere but Hamburg. Unless her husband decided to run the office in Vienna and send her brother-in-law Karl to Africa in his place. She'd heard that society in Vienna was like Hamburg, so Elisabeth would be comfortable there. But Cameroon? With those Negroes, and surrounded by dirt, dangers, and wild animals? No, absolutely not!

She sat at her dressing table and contemplated herself in the mirror. It had been a mistake to marry Robert—she knew it now more than ever. She'd only accepted him because Georg, whom her father had introduced her to at a reception and who seemed to be her perfect match, was already engaged to Vera. He was considerably more like her than her husband was. Robert had something impetuous about him, definitely not respectable. And furthermore, she recognized him too much in their daughter Luise, though she'd taken pains to raise both children to be well-bred girls from a good family. She'd succeeded with Martha. But Luise? No, something of her father's love of adventure had won out there, which she loathed beyond measure. Admittedly, she'd been irked, but not surprised, that Luise had traveled with her father despite Elisabeth telling them in no uncertain terms what she thought about it.

Still, he was her husband; though she had to resign herself to it, she certainly did not have to acquiesce in his decisions without protest. If the worst were to happen and Robert returned still wanting to run the plantation, she'd have to come up with something to keep herself in Hamburg with Martha. But what would life be like after that? She couldn't imagine herself going to events in Hamburg society without Robert by her side. What would people think? Maybe she wouldn't even be invited. And it would all be Robert's fault!

The thought brought a flush of anger to her face. Damn that Robert Hansen! She'd given him two children and almost lost her once-impeccable figure. How dare he behave like some impulsive adolescent determined to have whatever he wants, no matter the cost! She clenched her fists, raised her eyes, and studied her image in the mirror. She was still a beautiful woman and could attract men very different from Robert. But what would that do to her reputation?

Her reverie was interrupted by loud voices outside the room. From the window, she could see a carriage, and Karl embracing Robert. Hidden behind the curtain, she tried to read her husband's face. Was it joy or sorrow, triumph or disappointment? She couldn't tell. She turned away with a sigh.

"Mother!" she heard Martha shout from downstairs. "They're back! Father and Luise are here!"

Elisabeth went into the hallway and put on a smile. "I'm coming," she called in as friendly a voice as she could muster, lifting her dress so she wouldn't trip on her way down the stairs. Robert and Luise were already in the vestibule.

"Robert! Luise!" she cried out in delight. "How fortunate! You're back safe and sound!"

Her husband embraced his wife on the bottom step. "It's so nice to be home."

Luise was flanked by Martha and Frederike, who peppered her with questions: What is Cameroon like, what did she see, and what could she tell them?

"Let her arrive home in peace, for heaven's sake," pleaded Vera, who approached her niece and hugged her briefly.

"You must be exhausted," Elisabeth said. "Do you want to freshen up first or tell us everything right away?"

Robert and Luise exchanged glances.

"We do have a lot to tell," Robert said, and Luise nodded in agreement.

She asked Anna to find something for them to eat and took her husband's arm, and everyone went into the dining room. That he chose not to wash up after his trip was another mark against him, but she smiled as though she were truly happy to have him home. His relaxed demeanor, however, was a bad sign.

"Well?" Karl asked the moment they sat. "Have you good news?"

Robert was about to answer when he heard Georg's steps in the hallway. He stood and went to meet his brother.

"You're back!" Georg embraced him enthusiastically, slapping him on the back. Elisabeth thought it absurd for two grown men to behave like that just because they hadn't seen each other for a few weeks.

"You're just in time. I was about to begin my report."

They went into the dining room, where everyone looked happy, except Elisabeth, whose displeasure showed despite her effort to put on a brave face. Georg and Robert sat down.

"Now don't torture us any longer, Robert," Karl urged.

"How did you like Cameroon, Luise?" Georg asked, thanking Anna for his glass of beer.

"Cameroon is indescribable." Luise's face was glowing. "It's so incredibly beautiful that it's beyond imagination!"

Her eyes sparkled as she recounted events starting with their landing in Victoria Bay. Richard listened with some indifference, but Frederike and Martha hung on her every word.

"And the plantation?" Karl asked, turning to Robert.

"Huge, beautiful, and in impeccable condition." Robert took a swallow. "You have to see it with your own eyes to believe it. Everything runs like clockwork. Meyerdierks has the most capable and industrious workers."

"You mean Negroes, don't you?" Elisabeth asked disdainfully.

"Yes, the natives, Elisabeth." Robert sent her a cautioning look. "Blacker than you've ever seen in your life." His words dripped with scorn. "Hardworking men and women who deserve a great deal of respect."

Elisabeth lifted her chin. She obviously had a response on the tip of her tongue but swallowed it.

"Meyerdierks and you, you've come to an agreement?" Karl asked.

"Yes," Robert said with satisfaction. "He kept his word as expected. The only change was that we must keep his workers on and continue paying them. That will be in the bill of sale. There're some Germans, and British and French in other colonies, who enslave Africans."

"I hope you made it clear that our family would never do such a thing," Georg said.

"Goes without saying."

Robert then detailed how much a worker earned monthly and how the cost of food was calculated.

"That's appreciably less than here," Georg said.

"Why should people there need any more money?" Elisabeth remarked pointedly. "Being so far from civilization, they hardly have the opportunity to spend money, unless I'm mistaken."

"Indeed you are," Robert replied. "Trading is very lively in Cameroon. And young men save for the 'bride price' so they can marry, as Meyerdierks told us. That's an important aspect of their culture."

"A bride price?" Elisabeth repeated mockingly, but refrained from saying more when she saw her husband's angry look.

"How did you leave it?" Georg asked, returning to the central topic of discussion.

"Meyerdierks gave me all the necessary dates so I could have a bill of sale drawn up. You and Karl will still have time to consider whether you'll come in on it or not. After that I'll tidy up my affairs here and leave for Cameroon with my family. The main cocoa harvest goes from September to February. The secondary harvest has been coming in since May. It will be August before I've put everything in order, so we'll be in Cameroon by the middle of September at the latest. Meyerdierks will stay for a month after we arrive. We'll date the sale September 15. Until then the harvest belongs to Meyerdierks, everything after that is ours."

"That means we'll start with some revenue?"

"Exactly."

Georg looked relieved. "On that point, I'd like to talk with you and Karl alone later."

Robert could tell that Georg's news was not going to be good. But for the moment he didn't want to spoil the mood.

"Right."

"You might as well discuss it here and now," Elisabeth objected. "After all, all our futures are at stake."

"Your husband, Karl, and I will handle it," Georg said, sweeping his sister-in-law's remark aside.

"Are you ready for dinner?" Anna knocked sharply before opening the door and peeking in.

"Yes, Anna. Luise and I are famished, aren't we, Luise?"

Luise's nod corroborated his words.

During dinner it was mainly Luise who regaled them with her impressions of Cameroon and its people. It was a high-spirited evening until Georg, Robert, and Karl excused themselves and went to the study to confer about the future. Elisabeth was annoyed that she wasn't part of the discussion. Maybe she could have sown some doubt and destroyed that idée fixe of her husband's. But she was consigned to an observer's role, which infuriated her.

Georg closed the study door and poured three glasses of cognac from a carafe.

"As good as your news is, mine is just as bad," Georg announced, looking at Robert. "Karl already knows: the bank will withdraw our credit if we don't pay our loans in two weeks. We've liquidated all the stock in the warehouse. But it isn't enough."

"Damn it! We just need a little time." Robert looked from Georg to Karl. "Did you tell the bank about our plan?"

"Yes," Georg replied. "And I'm not sure it didn't make things worse."

"How so?"

"I don't think they trust us to pull it off. Perhaps they even got the idea that we were all going to abscond to Africa." Georg shook his head. "But you can't talk to them. We won't have anything left for a down payment to Meyerdierks."

"I hope I didn't go too far, but I shared our financial situation with him. That is, our coffee losses in German East Africa," Robert explained.

"How did he react?"

"Kindly." Robert looked at his brothers. "He told me he'd heard similar stories. Everything in the colonies is still confused, and swindlers have easy pickings. He showed sympathy for our situation. For that reason he repeated his offer to have us start with the installments *after* the first harvest."

"You couldn't wish for a better business partner. But we won't be able to hang on until then," Georg lamented.

"So what will we do?" Robert studied Georg most earnestly.

"We must sell the villa."

"No!" Robert jumped to his feet. "Mother and Father loved this house, and we grew up here, and our children. Absolutely not!"

"Do you think it's easy for me?" Georg stood up, too, went to the window, and looked out.

"Let's try for another mortgage."

"Robert, mortgages go right up the flue. We won't get any more money."

"Nevertheless, there must be a better way than selling the villa." Robert thought feverishly.

"If you think of one, I'd be glad to hear it." Georg went back to his chair and sank down in it helplessly.

"I'll talk to the bank." Robert sat down as well.

"I was at the negotiations," Karl piped up. "Georg and I tried everything—believe me."

"And the warehouse?"

"Empty, as I said."

"I mean the building. What are the liabilities?"

"Just as high as the villa's."

"What would the building get us?"

"Too little," Georg estimated.

"But it would buy us some time. And that's the thing we need."

"No. It wouldn't get us any time. Besides, I doubt we'd even find a buyer. For the villa, we could. And we could sell it ourselves, but if we don't, if the bank takes it over, we'd get significantly less for it."

Robert squinted at Georg. "It sounds as if you already have a buyer."

"Yes," Georg confessed. "I have."

"I didn't know that," Karl exclaimed. "Since when?"

"The notary organized a meeting three days ago. He's prepared to pay one hundred thousand marks for the villa. We'll never have an offer like that again. It would pay off all our debts in a single stroke, and we'd have enough to start again."

"You should hear yourself talk—it's as if you'd sell our parents' memory." Robert shook his head.

"You're being unfair," Karl chided his brother. "Georg is looking for a way out just as you and I are."

Georg held back the words he wanted to hurl at his brother, keeping a calm tone of voice instead. "Robert, you're taking your family to Cameroon, Karl's going to Vienna. I don't need a villa for Vera, the children, and me—there's room here for four families. And we have no choice. Either we sell or the bank takes the villa from us and we realize a fraction of what Frederiksen is offering."

"August Frederiksen?" Robert jumped up again, fists clenched.

Georg looked down. "Yes."

"That dirty swine will never have the villa!" Robert snapped. "Father hated him!"

"There was a time when they were friends," Georg corrected him. "Sit down."

"I won't!"

"Sit down and be reasonable!"

Robert snorted several times, then sat on the couch again. "Father must be turning over in his grave."

"That's enough, Robert," Georg said, looking as if he meant it.

"What do you think?" Robert turned to Karl.

"What can I say? That I'm not pleased with the idea? Obviously not. But I don't see any other way out."

"But Frederiksen of all people," Robert said again. "You know very well what Father thought of him. Frederiksen cheated him, and that's why we're in this position."

"I know. But if Father hadn't made those bad decisions, we wouldn't be discussing it now."

"Don't speak ill of him!"

"I'm not. You know how much I respected him. But he took his own life because he couldn't see any way out. And we're stuck with his mess."

Robert began to say something, but stopped when Karl laid a hand on his arm.

"Georg is right, and you know it."

"I still want to talk to the bank," Robert said.

"All right." Georg gave in. "Shall I go with you?"

"Yes. Let's all of us go to show we're united. The bank's done good business with Peter Hansen & Sons. They owe us some consideration."

"I hope you can convince them." Karl frowned, pressing his lips together.

"I'll make an appointment with Herr Reidel first thing in the morning," Georg said.

"Not with Reidel," Robert responded. "He's not the real decision maker. We have to speak with Palm in person."

"Fine," Georg said. "I'm sorry we don't have better news. But I'm sincerely happy that you're back here safe and sound."

Robert gave a mirthless smile. "Are you two still on board with the Cameroon business, or do you want to look elsewhere?"

"I am by all means," Karl answered immediately.

"I think we don't have much of a choice," Georg said after a momentary hesitation. "Our reputation will suffer if negotiations with the bank fail and the villa has to be sold. But we'll cope. We wouldn't be the first businessmen this has happened to."

"And not the last either," Robert said. "But we're not there yet."

He stood, took the glasses off the table, filled them again, and gave one to each of his brothers.

"Let's drink to the fact that Peter Hansen & Sons will not go under. We three will make it flourish again and will return to this villa when we've gotten through all this."

Georg and Karl leaped to their feet.

"I'll drink to that." They clinked their glasses.

"To Peter Hansen's sons!" Karl said with a smile. But fear of not pulling it off, and of uncertain times ahead, stood in the room with them.

Georg, Robert, and Karl waited silently in the ornate chairs outside the bank manager's office. The tension was palpable.

"The Hansen brothers."

The manager, Herr Palm—a gray-haired, rather stocky man about sixty whom they'd first met at their father's funeral—came out to greet the brothers with a handshake.

"Please come in. May I offer you something? A coffee?"

"Delighted," Georg replied. "I hope it's from our company?"

Palm smiled at him. "That's a bank secret," he joked, and asked his secretary to bring some coffee. "Do be seated, please." Palm gestured toward the conference table.

"Thank you," Robert said, and they all sat down around the mahogany table that exactly matched the color of the paneled walls.

"And how are you today?" the manager began informally. "I hope the family's well?"

"Yes, fine, thank you."

"I've heard that Richard wasn't in school for a long time a while back. Hopefully he wasn't sick?"

"How did you hear that?" Georg was surprised. "No, Richard was with my brothers in Vienna, learning more about the trade."

The secretary brought in a tray of coffee, cream, and sugar and placed the little containers in the middle of the table.

"Thank you very much, Fräulein Handtke." The manager nodded to her. He waited until she'd left before resuming. "I heard it from my grandson. He's the same age as Richard."

"Really? I didn't know that."

"He's my daughter's son. His name isn't Palm but Köhler. You wouldn't have known."

"Köhler . . . Alexander Köhler? That name is familiar."

"Yes, indeed. That's my grandson."

Georg had heard Richard speak of an Alexander Köhler often, but there was nothing kind about it. Köhler was an outsider and hardly had any friends, but on the other hand, he was one of the best students. He bored Richard to death.

"My son has nothing but good things to say about your grandson," Georg lied. "He's an excellent student, isn't he?"

"Yes, he is," Palm added after some reflection. "But unfortunately a little unworldly. I'm afraid my daughter was overprotective, since she only has one child." He sipped his coffee. "It's worthy of you to initiate Richard into the world of business this early. The sooner young people learn how the world works, the better."

"That's exactly how I see it. And I see that everything is not always simple. That's the reason we're here," Georg said.

Palm nodded. "I know about your situation," he said. "Reidel briefed me thoroughly. Regrettable, the whole thing. Truly regrettable."

"Our father was a customer at this bank his entire life. He trusted you, just as this bank could trust him," Robert reminded him.

"That's right," Palm agreed. "Your father was a marvelous businessman, and I had boundless respect for him as a person as well. I was very sorry when he passed away."

"Then you also know that a Hansen's word can be relied upon," Robert pursued.

"Yes, I know. And I do not believe this bank has ever refused to take your word."

"Well then," Georg observed. "We've asked for a postponement, but your colleague refused."

Palm raised a finger and waggled it. "That's not exactly right. You have asked as of now for a third extension. We granted your request twice. But we have our own obligations toward our clients. Herr Reidel was following regulations, his actions are beyond reproach."

"Of course," Robert calmly noted. "We learned from our father that we can always trust your bank. And we have come now to ask for your trust one more time."

Palm shook his head. "I really do not see how that's possible."

"Not yet." Robert seemed sure of a win. "Because you don't know yet about the superb business deal we just concluded."

Palm leaned forward. "Really? You have prospects?"

"More than that," Robert assured him, and then told him about purchasing the plantation in Cameroon. "Johann Meyerdierks knows so certainly what the profit will be that we won't begin paying installments—which are spread over eight years—until *after* the first harvest," Robert concluded.

"A genuine vote of confidence, indeed," Palm applauded. "But what if the plantation suffers losses?"

"Meyerdierks has worked his property for three years, expanded the cropland, and was able to increase his income. He can be generous with us because he's earned more money from it than he can spend in his lifetime."

"Hear, hear!" Palm grew thoughtful. "I'll be frank: I don't support Bismarck's exploitation of the Dark Continent. We've plenty of trade opportunities here in our own country. Let the French and the English and the Belgians seek their fortune in Africa. That has nothing to do with us Germans." He took a sip from his cup.

"Oh no?" Georg rejoined. "Do you like your coffee, Herr Palm? The beans might well have come from that very continent you don't think is significant."

The bank manager put his cup down.

Robert threw Georg a stern look. They didn't need lectures at this point, and Robert thought Georg's remark was counterproductive.

"What my brother means to say, Herr Palm, is that the Dark Continent has already been part of the German Reich for a long time. Whether it's coffee, cocoa, cotton, or palm oil—you can't conjure those commodities out of our lives. And consumption's rising. That's exactly why the step we're taking is not only a bold one, but it points to the future."

Palm looked at him, pondering.

"Father always told us that you're a man who understands what his clients envision. That's why we are here. We need six-months' grace period. Then we'll be able to pay back every last mark."

"Half a year?" Palm gasped. "Impossible."

"Herr Palm, we are speaking to you as our father's trusted friend. Maybe you considered the relationship between you two differently, but that's exactly how he saw you: as a friend. What do you think he would have said if *your* daughter had asked *his* help in some matter?"

Palm rubbed his chin in contemplation. Robert sensed that he must keep up the pressure.

"He was a man who liked to help others. If he had one hand climbing up the ladder of success, he always held the other below to help those who hadn't come as far as he had."

"Yes, I know," Palm said. "Did you know I do have something I'm very grateful to your father for? That's the reason I agreed to have this meeting today."

"Really?"

"Yes. Your father was already a good client of the bank when I was a new employee. I made an error, and your father, who had every reason to lodge a complaint, did not. It even cost him some money. It wasn't much, but his silence made it possible for me to get a promotion, which would have been out of the question after my mistake."

Robert smiled. He sensed that recollecting those past events could nudge Palm into changing his mind.

"I thanked your father, but he didn't want to hear of it. He told me that one should never forget to be a mensch."

"That sounds like our father," Karl commented.

Palm shook his head. "I wouldn't have called us friends, but now that you say the word . . ." He smiled to himself. "We knew each other over thirty years, always sharing our mutual trust. He was probably a better friend to me than I was aware of." He sighed, then raised his eyes. "Nevertheless, my hands are tied. I'd like to help you with all my heart, believe me, please."

The brothers looked at one another. Georg had a bitter remark on his lips but kept it to himself.

"Then we won't take up any more of your time." Georg stood up, followed by Robert and Karl. Palm was the last to push back his chair.

"May I ask what your plans are?"

"We will have to sell the villa," Georg replied.

Palm wrinkled his brow. "I'm sincerely sorry. I know what the house meant to your parents."

"To them and to us," Karl said.

"May I be of assistance in finding a buyer?" Palm offered. "It would be the least I could do."

"No need." Georg extended his hand. "We already have an offer. The bank will get its money right on time."

The brothers said their goodbyes and walked to the door.

"I hope we can meet again under more fortuitous circumstances," Palm observed after Georg had opened the door. "For curiosity's sake—and to make sure that the buyer has the funds—who is it?"

"Frederiksen. I'm sure he has the money."

"August Frederiksen?" Palm walked quickly around Georg and shut the door. "Your father's former partner?"

"Quite right."

"Your father hated him!" Palm looked at the brothers, one after the other. "And for good reason!"

"We know. But we have no choice." Robert shrugged.

The banker's expression changed. He pursed his lips. "Out of the question," he declared, and pulled open the door. "Fräulein Handtke, dictation, if you please." He pointed to the conference table. "Please be seated, gentlemen. I will, in your presence, dictate to my secretary that payment of your liabilities be postponed for a full nine months. You will surely have sold the cocoa harvest within that time, right?"

"Certainly!" Robert said enthusiastically.

"Good."

The secretary came in.

"Please take down my words, with copies to Herr Reidel, Herr Müller, and Herr Wirts."

"Yes, sir." Fräulein Handtke sat down and flourished a pencil.

"Heading: approval for postponement of all debts belonging to the firm of Peter Hansen & Sons and for payment of bridging funds," the manager began.

The brothers beamed.

Chapter Five

Cameroon, End of September 1888

It was very early in the morning, the moon still in the sky, and the sun just beginning to announce the coming day. Luise had woken at this same time for the last four days. The first two days, she'd marveled at the sky's varied colors from her window. But on the third, she realized that nobody else was awake and that the plantation—swarming with people by day—looked completely uninhabited. She'd thrown on a bathrobe, made sure that no one saw her, and hurried to the stump next to the cocoa trees where the workers sat to eat their midday meal. There was a wonderful view over the wide landscape all the way to Mount Cameroon. While the scenery was bathed in a delicate pink that grew brighter by the minute, the sky over the mountain was blue gray, seeming to challenge the massif itself. That hour was, for her, the most beautiful one in the day, and it became a ritual. She couldn't quite describe it, but it felt as though the time between night and day belonged to her alone. The colors, the sounds of animals waking, the vastness of the steppe just beyond the plantation and jungle, and even the mountain: everything seemed to exist just for her. Luise felt calm and settled as never before in her life. She had no idea what the future would bring, but she knew it would be in this place.

She'd been trying to help with the harvest, despite her mother forbidding her to. She'd asked Hamza to show her how, but he'd just stared at her and turned away. Maybe he didn't understand her language as well as Meyerdierks had said. So instead she watched the natives work, then found a machete and tried cutting the oval fruits off the tree herself. The harvesters watched her skeptically, but neither helped nor hindered her.

The harvested fruits were gathered together and opened with a single skillful machete blow. Luise watched this over and over, and even tried it herself, but the effortless movements of the natives eluded her. So she limited herself to watching closely and was glad when Meyerdierks appeared beside her one day and explained the various operations. She learned that after the fruit was opened, the seeds, or beans, were removed from the surrounding white flesh in their husk. The fresh, wet cocoa beans were stacked on banana leaves and covered with more leaves to protect them from contamination. She was surprised when Johann explained that the fermentation process was started by heat and the beans were only fermented for a week. In that time, he continued, the flesh still clinging to the beans was liquefied and drained off. The beans were then roasted, sometimes as hot as 120 degrees Fahrenheit, altering the bitter-tart flavor and changing their color from whitish-yellow to a deep brown. Luise was grateful to Johann for educating her and showing her beans in different stages of processing; she'd thought the beans were dark brown straight from the fruit and would simply be packed into sacks and shipped all over the world.

She sensed that Johann was the only person who didn't find her interest in cocoa production peculiar but took sincere delight in it and even encouraged her. Her father was too busy calculating yields for him to learn how cocoa beans were actually processed. Luise understood that her father had to manage the overall operations and the revenue the plantation would generate. But she did think the beauty of processing the precious beans from the fruit deserved more appreciation. The idea of her sister, Martha, let alone her mother, being excited about such things had been banished from Luise's mind the day after they arrived in Cameroon. They had nothing good to say about the wonderful landscape or the inhabitants. And so Luise was glad to be able to keep out of their way on the sprawling plantation.

In the evenings she wrote about the stages of cocoa production and her impressions, before filing the notes in her portfolio. She hoped she would reread it all someday, and she hoped with all her heart it wouldn't be in distant Hamburg that she'd recall her first days in Africa. After being in Cameroon for a few days, the fear of having to leave the colony was her constant companion.

All this whirled in her thoughts as Luise watched the sky change from pink to a bright orange. She looked at the mountain while lingering for one more moment at the tree trunk. Then she walked slowly back to the house with a smile on her face. She crept into her room, slipped off her bathrobe, and crawled under the thin sheet that served as a bedcover. She still saw the pink sky over Cameroon in her mind's eye as she drifted off to sleep.

They were having breakfast on the veranda. It was Sunday, and they were getting ready to leave for church with Johann. The little church was at least an hour away by carriage, although their plantation was one of the closest to the church.

"You don't look well, Luise." Elisabeth held her daughter's chin and examined her face. "Pale and sickly."

"Oh, Elisabeth, *please*," Robert said, rolling his eyes. "We've all got more color from the sun lately than we've gotten in all our Hamburg summers put together."

"That's *not* what I meant," his wife answered, irritated. "Tiredness and lethargy cannot be hidden under even such a dark tan."

"I'm feeling fine, Mother." Luise managed a smile, which wasn't easy, because her mother's carping really got on her nerves.

"I think Mother's right," Martha said. "To be honest, I don't feel well either. Maybe the food here doesn't agree with me or I've picked up something, though I try to keep my distance from those people."

Johann looked at Robert. He clearly wanted to say something, but he refrained.

Luise thought her attitude disgraceful, and it made her furious. "I think they don't want to have anything to do with you either."

"Luise!" her mother shouted, banging her hand on the table. "Don't talk to your sister like that! Robert, would you please handle your daughter?"

"Luise, your tone of voice is inappropriate," Robert began. "But I understand your outrage over what your sister said." He looked at Martha. "Perhaps it would be good for you to work alongside them for a day, to appreciate them the way they deserve."

Martha was wide-eyed. "But, Father!"

"You absolutely do *not* have to do that," Elisabeth interjected.

Robert studied his wife for a moment, placed his napkin next to his plate, and stood up. "Johann, would you excuse my wife and me for a minute?" He turned to Elisabeth. "Come with me, if you please?"

Elisabeth's expression froze; she rose and turned without a word, following her husband into the house.

Martha and Luise looked at each other anxiously. Luise had never seen her father react like that before. He usually simply took her mother's behavior in stride. Luise feared that the discord could turn into a larger argument that would only exacerbate the situation, hardening the separation between Robert and Luise on one side and Elisabeth and Martha on the other. And yet she had to confess she was pleased that her father had reached his limit and was finally declaring her mother's behavior toward the natives unacceptable.

"And are you looking forward to your teacher's arrival in three weeks?" Johann made an attempt to ease the tension.

Luise smiled gratefully. "I'm curious to see how it will go. We've never had a private tutor, Martha, have we?"

"No, never." Her sister answered in a monotone.

"I hope I'll still have enough time for the harvest and helping around the plantation," Luise remarked.

"Certainly. There's always something to do on a plantation, usually more than you can keep up with."

"Why did you come to Africa? Was it business?"

Johann contemplated the ceiling. "Well . . . I think it was for the adventure. When Africa was divided at the Berlin Conference in 1884 and 1885, I wanted to get involved and was one of the first Germans to set foot in Cameroon. But I came to realize the natives were as friendly as they were suspicious. It was a time of awakening for me. I was naively glad to be part of it."

"Do you think that time has passed?" Luise inquired.

"No, I'm afraid a greater push hasn't even begun. But I no longer want any part of it."

"What do you mean?"

"The French, English, Belgians, Portuguese, and we Germans have gone and divided up Africa. The people here weren't asked, weren't involved. There's already unrest in places where the natives are subjugated and abused by Europeans." He studied Martha with a penetrating gaze. "That's why I appeal to you to rethink your attitude toward the people who do the work on the plantation for you."

Martha opened her mouth, then closed it. Tears welled up in her eyes.

"Please forgive me, I didn't mean to offend you." Johann nodded toward Martha, who instantly lowered her eyes.

"Well then, the time has come." Robert and Elisabeth came back onto the veranda. "Are you finished?"

"Yes," Luise replied, and hissed softly at Martha. "Now pull yourself together, or you'll make matters worse!"

Her sister nodded. They got up from their seats. Luise glanced at her mother. Elisabeth was stone-faced. As they went to their carriages, each driven by a native, Luise saw Elisabeth nod and link arms with Robert. She wasn't sure how to interpret that, but one thing was clear: her father had spoken harshly to his wife. Although Luise knew schadenfreude was never good, she had to admit she was secretly glad.

"May I introduce the Hansen family?" Johann Meyerdierks led them to the large awning a bit away from the church, where the Germans gathered to chat, have a drink together, and exchange ideas after service. Luise estimated that about forty people were there.

"Robert Hansen and his wife, Elisabeth." Meyerdierks gestured toward them. "And their charming daughters, Martha and Luise. The Hansens will be taking over my plantation."

"So you're serious about it, then?" A man of about fifty shook hands with Robert. "Admiral Heribert Bischoff, Heribert to you. Honored."

A woman appeared beside him.

"This is my wife, Irmgard. The tall boy back there is our son, Manfred. Welcome to Cameroon!"

Though there weren't all that many, Luise immediately forgot the names of half the people she met.

"Raimund Leffers," a young man, a bit under twenty, introduced himself. "How nice to finally see some younger faces here."

"I'm Luise."

"And I'm Martha, her older sister."

Luise felt a jab in the ribs as Martha pushed her aside.

"Well, Raimund, what do you do here? Are you also in cocoa?"

"No, my father's in the kaiser's service. His commission is to keep Cameroon stable."

"How interesting!" Martha, obviously interested in something, walked over to Raimund and took his arm. "Tell me more. We've seen nothing but beans since we arrived."

She gave a sharp laugh, and Luise rolled her eyes.

"Well, all right," Raimund agreed with a shrug.

Luise smirked. He clearly didn't care to talk about it much but was too polite to say so.

After several hours, they all began to say goodbye and set off across the vast country in every direction. Luise enjoyed meeting her compatriots more than she'd expected. She no longer felt she'd have to choose between her homeland in the German Reich and her new home. She had both right there.

"Did you see how Raimund looked at me?" Martha gushed in the carriage with Elisabeth and Luise.

"I suppose." Luise shrugged.

"I was very pleased with that," Elisabeth said. "He could hardly keep his eyes off you."

"No, he couldn't."

"Have you arranged to see each other again?" Elisabeth asked.

"Unfortunately, no. He's too busy as his father's assistant. I won't see him again until next Sunday."

"More's the pity."

Elisabeth played with Martha's hand.

"Yes. He's extremely attractive, isn't he?" Martha said.

"If you say so." Luise shrugged again. "He looks like any other young man in Hamburg."

"Oh, you're just jealous he spent the whole time with me and not you." Martha arched her eyebrows.

Luise sighed. "I'm definitely *not* jealous."

"Oh no?" Martha snapped back. "Well, *I* would be if I were in your shoes."

Luise had no wish to argue with her sister.

"Yes, you're right. I'm terribly jealous that he didn't pay any attention to me. All right?"

"Don't be so patronizing, Luise Hansen!" Elisabeth rebuked her sharply.

"Yes, Mother."

Luise turned her eyes in the opposite direction and took in the beautiful landscape while Elisabeth and Martha discussed what a good match Raimund would make.

Luise was happy when they arrived at the plantation, and she could finally escape from her mother and sister.

"I'm going over to see the beans."

"You speak as if you were visiting real, live people." Elisabeth shook her head in disapproval. "But you certainly are not going there in that dress—change your clothes first!"

"Yes, Mother."

Luise ran into the house just as Malambuku was leaving it.

"*Jambo*, Malambuku."

"*Jambo, nyango.*"

Luise went to her room, removed her uncomfortable white dress, and put on pants and a blouse. She liked those more than anything she used to wear in Hamburg. She'd sewn two pairs of pants for herself, much to her mother's displeasure. Unlike in respectable clothes, she felt really comfortable in pants and a blouse—much more herself. She tolerated having to wear a dress for show on Sundays, but she was delighted to slip out of it.

She opened her desk drawer, took out the portfolio, and reached for the penholder that was once her grandfather's.

September 23, 1888

Today we went to church for the first time here. The church is white brick with arched windows and an entrance through a pointed arch. The steeple is almost exactly in the center, nothing at all like the Hamburg churches, as if it had been added just before the rest of the building was finished. There's a large wooden lean-to near the church big enough for about sixty people. We met the other Germans there. Everybody was very friendly, and Martha got to know a young man called Raimund Leffers, whose father is in the kaiser's service, and she rhapsodizes about him. I think his enthusiasm for her is rather modest, though Martha and Mother claim otherwise, naturally.

She put down her pen. She didn't want to get worked up about Martha and her mother right now, so she folded up the portfolio. She considered locking the drawer but decided against it. If Martha was going to snoop in her things and come across what she wrote, then she'd learn how Luise felt. And would she ever! She went downstairs.

Her father and Johann were talking with Malambuku a little ways off, so Luise couldn't hear them. She went over where the cocoa beans were piled, but none of the natives were at work. She didn't know whether that was Johann's doing or whether it was the local custom not to work on Sunday. At any rate all the natives were in their huts on the eastern border of the plantation.

Luise went into the shed where the beans were poured into long wooden tubs just over three-by-ten feet and chest high. There they were stirred to sift out even the tiniest stone or wood chip that might have fallen in when the boxes were being filled. Once they had removed all the debris, the beans were packed.

Luise picked up a wooden rake and stirred the beans for a bit. Then she put the tool aside and slipped her hand into the beans. She took some out, rubbed them between her hands, and raised them to her nose to take in the aroma.

"Jambo, nyango."

Luise gasped, startled, and dropped the beans back into the tub.

Hamza, who hadn't before spoken a word to her, had slipped into the shed unnoticed.

"Jambo," she quickly responded.

Hamza laughed.

"What?" Luise asked, a bit displeased. He had never said a word to her, never responded when she asked him a question, and now he was making fun of her after he had startled her.

"Your nose, *nyango*. The cocoa grabbed you."

"The cocoa grabbed me? What does that mean?" Luise was still cross.

Hamza seemed not to notice, but laughed a little louder.

"Stop," Luise said, but the way he was grinning made her smile as well. She wiped her nose with the back of her hand and realized what he meant—her hand was covered with dark-brown cocoa dust.

"This is no laughing matter," Luise said, trying to hold herself together, but then she snorted with a chuckle. They doubled over with laughter, though Luise could only imagine how she looked. Finally she pulled out a handkerchief and wiped her face.

Hamza was still chuckling.

"Better?" Luise asked.

He nodded, and Luise put her handkerchief away.

"What are you doing here?" she asked. "There's no work on Sunday."

"The beans want me to visit them."

Luise giggled. "Do they? Did they ask you to?"

"Beans don't speak, they sing," he replied. "Sing a melody only I can hear."

"You speak our language very well, Hamza."

"You, too, *nyango*."

The quick comeback made Luise laugh again. She wanted to ask him why he hadn't spoken to her before, but refrained.

"Do you like your work?"

"Yes, *nyango*."

She looked at him thoughtfully. She didn't know if it was a good idea, but before she could decide, she had already asked, "Could you call me Luise?"

Hamza formed a *U* with his mouth, trying to pronounce her name correctly.

Luise opened her mouth and placed her tongue behind her front teeth.

"Lllll," she enunciated slowly and clearly. "L-uuuu-iiii-se."

"Luuiise," Hamza repeated.

"Exactly. Luise. Just Luise."

Hamza hesitated. "Just Luise," he said.

"Exactly."

"Luise."

"Very good, Hamza."

"Luise?" She heard her father's voice nearby.

"Yes?"

She went outside.

"Can you please come here?"

"Yes, coming."

She turned to Hamza. "It was nice meeting you. I hope we can talk again sometime."

"We can talk again. Luise." He smiled. She returned his smile.

"Goodbye, Hamza."

"Goodbye, Luise," he said, with a little bow.

Luise smiled, not exactly knowing what to make of their brief encounter. But she sensed how determined Hamza was to perfect his German and was genuinely delighted that the ice between them was broken.

Chapter Six

Cameroon, September 23, 1888

Dear family,
Along with this letter you will receive the first shipment of cocoa beans from our Cameroon plantation, and we can scarcely believe our luck that the crop was a bumper one. In two weeks we'll send you more on the next ship and ask you to give the captain any money you can spare so that we can meet our commitments here.

We hope you, like us, are all enjoying the best of health. Life in Africa is different—quieter but more demanding—from what I would have imagined. People here live in harmony with nature and animals and pay heed to the wind and weather. There's a lot to learn about these things we find strange. I have the impression that the Duala—the natives here who work the plantation—are learning just as much about us as we are about them. Some hold back and are quite reserved, even distrustful. But I think it's only a matter of time before everyone realizes that we don't mean them any harm.

The Germans here are open, forthcoming people, easy to get along with. We met many of them today when we went to church.

Johann Meyerdierks will have left Africa by the time you get this letter. I hope we'll be able to keep running the plantation according to his way of thinking and so maintain what he's built over the last three years. So much for my first impressions.

Elisabeth, Martha, and Luise will add their own letters. Please write and keep us informed. And please give me the address of our new Vienna office as soon as Karl finds a suitable location. Let me know as well how the shipments are to be split. For now I'm sending everything to Hamburg and leaving it all to your sales expertise.

Stay well and write soon!

With heartfelt wishes,

Yours,

Robert

Georg put down the letter and looked at his family, rubbing his eyes.

"Here are the letters for you," he said. "One for you from Elisabeth," he said, handing Vera the envelope. "One for Frederike and Richard from Martha and Luise, and another from Martha to Frederike, and one from Robert to Karl and me. There now."

"How much cocoa has Robert sent?" Vera inquired. "Are you as pleased as he is?" She looked from her husband to Karl.

"Robert took on the heaviest burden of all of us," Karl answered. "And we owe him and his family our gratitude. It's still being weighed, but it might come to two hundred tons."

"And when you take into account that they were only in Cameroon for two weeks before the ship was loaded, it's all the more amazing," Georg added.

"Will it be enough to pay our bills?" Vera asked a little anxiously.

Richard and Frederike looked at their father as expectantly as Vera, who instantly regretted bringing it up before the children.

"Karl and I have been looking for buyers. But around Hamburg the demand is still for coffee. It won't be easy."

"That's why I should go to Vienna straightway," Karl said.

"When can you leave?"

"Tomorrow would be best, as soon as we've put everything in order. We've no time to lose."

"Can I do anything?" Richard asked, to his father's surprise.

"I'm delighted you asked, son." Georg thought for a moment. "You could help me with the paperwork and begin to get an overview of the business."

"Of course."

"I would like to do something, too," Frederike offered, not wanting to be bested by her brother.

"This is *not* woman's work." Vera sounded stern. "The men will take care of it, Frederike."

"Yes, Mother."

Georg stood up. "Karl, would you come with me to the study?"

"Of course." Karl followed him.

As he passed Richard, Georg briefly rested his hand on his son's shoulder. "I'm proud of you," he said.

Richard couldn't recall the last time he'd heard his father say that. He smiled as Georg and Karl left the dining room.

Georg stopped on the stairway before a painting of his parents about the time of their silver wedding anniversary. "I think they would be pleased with us."

"As they should be," Karl responded.

Georg sat behind the massive desk, with its leather pad, and pulled a book from the center drawer. "We have to talk about which payments are the most urgent."

Karl pulled up a chair on the other side of the desk. "You're worried we won't be able to sell the beans fast enough."

"Not many are familiar with the method of processing them into cocoa, at least around here," Georg said.

Karl lit up. "I just thought of something . . . but no, you'll think I'm crazy."

"Let's hear it!"

"We should take some of the beans and make chocolate ourselves. To drink, I mean, with cream and sugar, the way I had it in the cafés in Vienna."

"And sell it?"

Karl hesitated. "Yes, maybe. But more importantly, we must manage to get it on everybody's lips, in the truest sense of the word. We can try it: let's have Anna set up a stand at the market every week and also offer cocoa to all the tearooms around here."

"But we're running an office, Karl. I wouldn't want us to spread ourselves too thin and lose sight of the big picture."

"You might be right, but it's worth a try."

"Vera would think I'm insane."

"Vera can buy a new dress if we're successful." Karl chuckled.

"That will persuade her," Georg said, raising his eyebrows at the joke.

"Then we'll do it?"

Georg stood up. "Yes, let's do it. Get the carriage ready. I'll go tell Vera that we have to go out."

Karl hurried to the stables to inform the coachman, while Georg went to the parlor.

"Karl and I are going to the office."

"Oh?" Vera put her book on her lap. "What for?"

"To fetch some cocoa beans. Tell Anna to get some roasting pans ready in the kitchen."

"Tell me what you're planning, if you don't mind?"

"We're going to roast beans to make hot chocolate."

"You two have gone completely mad."

"Perhaps. But if we're right, you'll soon be able to buy a couple of new dresses."

Vera opened her mouth, then closed it. She rose from the couch. "I'll let Anna know," she announced, with no further word of contradiction.

"Are you sure we're doing it right?" Georg eyed the blackened cocoa beans in the pan skeptically. "They have an acrid smell."

Karl shrugged. "That's how the café owner showed me."

"We've done something wrong."

Georg took the pan off the heat. Vera, Richard, Frederike, and Anna were sitting at the kitchen table, at the brothers' request, waiting to taste the first hot chocolate from the House of Hansen.

"I'm not really familiar with this," Anna said, obviously finding it difficult to be sitting at the table while the men stood at the cast-iron stove. "But it might be that the heat was too high."

Georg looked at her, bewildered, then back at the stove.

"May I?" the housekeeper asked, standing.

"Please do." Georg put the pan down.

Anna took the cloth from Georg's hand, lifted the pan, and sniffed the beans. "These aren't roasted, they're burnt."

Without a moment's hesitation, she tossed the beans into the trash, washed the pan thoroughly, then wiped it dry.

"Sir," she said, turning to Karl. "What did the café owner tell you about the procedure for chocolate making, precisely?"

"That the beans first must be roasted, then shelled and ground. Then you heat the powder in water or milk. Finally, you add sugar and thin it with cream."

Anna nodded. "Good. With the gentlemen's permission, I will try that."

Georg and Karl nodded in encouragement.

"I beg your pardon, but would you please wait at the table? It's difficult having somebody behind me while I'm cooking."

Her great displeasure at having to ask that of her masters was obvious.

Georg and Karl grinned at each other.

"Just like Mother," Georg said with a touch of sarcasm as they sat down at the table.

Anna put the pan on the stove and waited for it to warm up. Then she took it off the heat, reached into the sack, and put a handful of cocoa beans into the pan. She put the pan back on the heat, wrapped a cloth around the handle, and shook the pan continuously. The beans danced around in the cast-iron pan and gradually gave off a sweetish smell. Anna kept shaking the pan, then set it down on the tiles next to the stove. With a small spoon she took out a bean and rubbed it between her fingers. "Feels like a nut." She pressed it a few times, pushing the kernel out of the shell and rubbing it between her fingers. She carefully licked it. "It's a little bitter," she declared, and took another bean out of the pan, pressed it open, and handed it to Karl. "Is this right?"

Karl sniffed it but couldn't tell if it was like the beans he'd tasted after the café owner roasted them. "Well, let's put the water on. We'll soon know."

Frederike helped Anna shell the beans, and even Richard did, too. Georg stood beside Karl, who crushed the beans with the mortar and pestle and dipped a fingertip into the powder and tasted it. The atmosphere that pervaded the kitchen was most unusual, as though everyone wanted to contribute to a successful outcome. Vera alone remained sitting, waiting. When all the beans were shelled and ground, Anna filled a cup with lightly boiling water and added some powder. She stirred, adding a little sugar. The drink seemed thin and translucent.

"It looked stronger in the café," Karl noted.

"We'll have to adjust the amounts to taste," Anna explained, dipping a small spoon into the liquid and tasting it. Her face lit up. "I think we're on the right track."

They all tasted it, one after the other; then they roasted, shelled, and ground more beans. By the time they'd finished, they'd produced several cups of delicious hot chocolate.

"I could drink this forever," Frederike gushed.

"We need a stand in the market," Georg declared. "Anna, you don't have to work on days you're at the market."

"Thank you, sir."

"Who's going to keep things in order here while Anna's away?" Vera spoke up, incensed. "The servants need Anna's supervision. Otherwise there'll be nothing but chaos here."

"We'll find somebody," said Georg calmly.

"I'll say one thing, Georg Hansen: I won't stand for it if the housework is no longer well organized. You cannot expect me and the children to put up with living in disorder."

"Of course you're right, Vera. You could sell our chocolate at the market instead of Anna. What do you think of that?"

Vera gaped. "That's monstrous!"

"I could come back straight after market to do the housework," Anna offered.

"Many thanks, Anna, but we'll think of something. For the time being we need you primarily for the roasting. Frederike, Richard, could you help with the shelling?"

"Yes, Father" came the answer as if from one mouth.

"Thank you. I'm glad you see how crucial this is for our family's survival."

His eyes almost bored through Vera. He shook his head and went out.

Karl left the next day.

"Send me a telegram as soon as you've signed a lease, and let me know where to send the beans." Georg looked up at his younger brother in the carriage with his luggage.

"I will. I've got a good feeling, Georg, that it's going to work!"

"We'll do everything we can to ensure success."

Karl came down, and the brothers hugged and shook hands a second time before Karl retook his seat. He raised a hand in farewell to the children and Vera, who stayed by the front door. She'd said goodbye to her brother-in-law earlier, wishing him bon voyage, so there was no need for her to go to the carriage.

Karl took the train via Hannover and Göttingen to Würzburg, Nuremberg, Regensburg, and Passau, spending the night there in an inn. He planned to cross the Austro-Hungarian border the next day and travel through the cities of Wels, Linz, Amstetten, and Sankt Pölten, arriving in Vienna that afternoon. During the trip he had time to mull things over. He'd miss his family, of course, but he was looking forward to the independence his new life in Vienna would bring. Maybe, he hoped, he'd finally be able to find his place in life. He couldn't describe the feeling, but he'd long sensed that he wasn't interested in the life his brothers led. He'd asked himself time and again what kind of woman he would find truly interesting. He'd had affairs, of course, but none had been rewarding. It had reached the point where the very thought of romance seemed downright absurd. And it wasn't difficult for him to pursue other interests.

When some man about his age, or younger, would recount their amorous experiences, Karl had usually found it repugnant. He was neither looking for an affair nor excited by the thought of settling down with a wife. And he definitely didn't wish to take a wife like Vera or Elisabeth. He was eager to see if women in Vienna were perhaps different, and if he might even develop serious feelings for a woman there. But he had his doubts.

He spent the night in the Passau hotel as planned. The room was simple, to minimize expenses. After all, he had to have rent for an office and warehouse space for three months in advance, still leaving enough for lodging, food, drink, and telegrams. Everything was tightly budgeted, since Georg and he didn't have much leeway.

He asked the inns he'd stopped into on the way if they served chocolate. Not a single one did. And when he remarked that the drink was becoming increasingly popular and that he could provide the beans required, he received nothing but blank stares.

He arrived in Vienna in early evening, rather the worse for wear, but was relieved as he left the train and walked through the Nordbahnhof. During his earlier visit he was amazed by the huge Romantic building that had taken sixty years to complete until it was finished in 1865. The station was designed with playful details and high, generous ceilings. Karl stood on the broad platform and looked around the large five-track hall. He tilted his head back to take in the angled glass skylights letting in the late afternoon sun. His eyes followed with wonder the high iron columns supporting the roof.

He descended the magnificent stairway parallel to the tracks to the arrival hall. He recognized varied stylistic elements, Gothic and Romanesque features, even some Byzantine and Arabian-Moorish ones. Karl thought that people who said the Nordbahnhof was the most beautiful building in Vienna were absolutely right. He exited the station through one of the five arched portals onto Nordbahnstrasse, next to the Nordbahn, which had given the station its name.

Before looking for a room, he went to the café where the owner had showed him the way to make chocolate from cocoa beans.

She recognized him immediately.

"Klaus Hansen, right? The chocolate man." She extended her hand.

"*Karl* Hansen," he corrected her. "Good evening, Fräulein Loising. But 'chocolate man' is truer than ever."

"Really? You've put your plan into action?"

Karl spread out his arms. "Your new cocoa supplier stands before you." He watched her face. "At least I hope so."

"Let's sit down." She waved to the waitress. "Frieda, take over, please."

The waitress nodded and disappeared into the kitchen.

"What would you like to have, Herr Hansen?"

"Chocolate, of course. What else?"

"With pleasure. Please, have a seat. I'll bring it to you."

"Thank you."

Karl went to a table beside the window in the very back corner and sat down. He looked around the room. This café felt special, and not only because of its pretty owner. Therese Loising was about his age, perhaps a year or two younger. Her long dark-blond hair was pinned up loosely and adorned with a silk band. She wore a white blouse and a plain black skirt, which accentuated her petite figure. She'd told Karl on his last visit that she was unmarried and intended to remain so. She was unlike any woman he'd met. Though friendly and obliging, Therese did not seem as though she was aiming to please anyone, not least a man. She was independent and unconventional, with an infectious, bell-like laugh.

The café reflected her character. There were both round and square tables, each with two or four chairs. The chairs were not the same, yet each went well with their respective table. Some were covered in green fabric, others in red. Some were simple dark wooden chairs with high backs. Some had woven inserts on the backs. Karl didn't know whether that was planned or a result of Therese gradually expanding the place. The décor wasn't especially harmonized, and for that very reason it created coherence. The walls were covered with a dark, slightly shimmering red paper. The floorboards were wide and beautifully polished. Nothing matched, yet everything fit. And the customers seemed to like it. All the tables were occupied but two.

Therese came back carrying two cups.

"Chocolate for the chocolate man," she announced with a laugh, putting the cups down and taking a seat.

"Please call me Karl. Although I do like 'chocolate man.'"

"Call me Therese." She raised the cup. "Try it. I've refined our recipe since you were here last."

Karl took a sip. The chocolate was hot, but not enough to burn his tongue, and topped with cool whipped cream. The contrasting sensations were delightful on his palate.

"Delicious," he said, already having drank half his cup.

Therese laughed loudly. "Now you have a second mustache."

Karl pulled out his handkerchief and dabbed around his mouth. If it weren't for the prevailing fashion, he would have shaved off his carefully groomed mustache long ago.

"Better?"

Therese nodded. "I liked it as it was, but it's fine now." She took a sip. "Did you have a good trip from Hamburg?"

"Yes, uneventful. But of course it goes faster when you're by yourself."

"So your brother and nephew didn't make it this time?"

"No," Karl said. "Robert, whom you met, has taken over a cocoa plantation in Cameroon, and my nephew is in Hamburg with his parents."

Therese was animated. "Really? Herr Meyerdierks's plantation, perhaps, the man I introduced you to?"

"That's the one."

"I can't believe it! Oh, how marvelous! Well, you certainly didn't waste any time."

"We thought it was an excellent idea. So why hesitate?"

"At last, a man of action!" She flashed him a smile. "Maybe that's the way people from Hamburg are. Here in Vienna everything gets discussed endlessly, but never decided." She rolled her eyes. "I do believe if I grow tired of being here, I'll go to Hamburg and open a café there."

"Absolutely not!" Karl dictated.

"Why not?"

"Well, for one, I still don't know anything about your Vienna, and I'm hoping you'll educate me."

"Perhaps you're already putting something else into action, Karl Hansen. You could be dangerous for me."

"I hope so."

Their conversation lulled as they sipped their chocolate.

"So what do you think, Therese? Would you be my first client in Vienna?"

"With pleasure. Of course, I'm just about fully stocked, but there's a little space left. How much can you deliver?"

"How much do you need?"

"Fifty pounds? Or is that too much?"

"Twice that wouldn't be too much."

"That's wonderful. And will you give me a better price than the other cafés?"

"I'll give you a very good price," he assured her. "And if you don't tell anyone, I'll see it's a better price than any other café will have." He winked.

She reached out a hand to him. "Then, my dear Karl, you have in me the best guide to Vienna you could wish for."

He took her hand and shook it firmly.

"Have you found a place to stay?" Therese inquired.

"No, I've just arrived."

"And rushed straight over to me—you're doing things the right way," she joked. "I could ask some friends who rent rooms. Or would you rather have more space?"

"No, a room is fine for now. Thank you. I'll also need an office, somewhere I can have the beans sent to."

"How much should it cost?"

Karl shrugged. "I don't need anything special. Just room to store the beans."

"I'm sure we'll find something." She smiled. "Well now, the room. The Viennese are a hospitable people. And I have many friends. Pick me up here at six thirty, and we'll ask around."

"At six thirty."

"Yes. As you can see, I've got more work to do . . ."

Therese waved toward the café, where customers were standing in the doorway, waiting for a table.

"I'll be here." Karl pulled out his wallet.

Therese stood up. "The chocolate's on the house. Welcome to Vienna, chocolate man!"

Chapter Seven

Luise wiped the sweat from her brow. Winter was beginning to arrive in Hamburg, but here it was always around ninety degrees. It didn't cool off until evening. She helped with the harvest every day, earning derision from her mother and Martha. At times she'd have gladly changed places with them or sat with them for a cold drink. But Luise didn't want to give them that satisfaction. She overcame her tired legs, and so she drank some water and kept right on working. The workers' songs often lent her some strength; they sang in unison with a regular rhythm. She could have hummed along with many of the songs, but didn't trust herself, and so only moved to their rhythm, in unison with the others.

Malambuku came often to oversee everything. At first she'd taken him for a kind of foreman, but she'd since learned that he was a real, active overseer who organized and supervised the men, making sure each one performed the work he was assigned. She noticed something else. When Malambuku came out to the cocoa trees, he treated everybody equally, with no special words for Hamza and his brothers. But when Hamza went to the farmhouse to make a report or ask something,

Malambuku treated him with the warmth of a father who loved his son and was exceedingly proud of him.

"Luise can sing along." Hamza was beside her, picking out the little wooden slivers among the beans.

"No, I can't."

"You do when nobody listens." Hamza nodded knowingly.

"Oh, I won't do it," she objected.

Hamza grinned widely. "I heard you."

She tried to think of a retort, but he went to the opposite side of the tub and resumed his work.

At first she'd been annoyed that he always had to have the last word. But eventually she'd realized that he was just one of those people who stopped talking when everything had been said.

"Do you want to be an overseer someday like your father?" she said to continue the conversation.

"Yes, someday when my father is dead."

Luise gave a start. "But surely Malambuku won't work his whole life. I mean when he retires."

Hamza furrowed his brow, not recognizing the word.

"I mean when he's old and has worked enough and then can just"—she groped for an example—"herd cattle."

"That is work for boys. My father is a strong man."

"Yes, of course. You're right."

The language barrier between them troubled her at times. Hamza spoke German extremely well, but some things just didn't translate. It wasn't always clear if it was because of the language or the culture.

"And you? Will you do your father's work some day?"

Luise reflected for a moment. She'd felt from the beginning that her home was here and nowhere else. But would she ever be in a position to take over the plantation? That Martha wasn't interested was obvious. If anyone, it would be her cousin Richard. But she? A woman in Africa? It sounded too absurd.

"At home the men earn the money, you see, and women don't work. I mean, those who have enough money not to have to."

"But you are a woman?"

"Yes."

"And you work here." He mused for a minute. "Your mother and sister have money enough and you do not?"

"Good point," she said, laughing. "They don't like to work. I do."

Hamza shook his head, and Luise realized that she couldn't explain what she was thinking. No wonder. Not even the other German colonists understood why she was helping with the harvest. Luise had seen quickly that she didn't fit in with their world of high-ranking people whose goals were so different from her own.

"If not run the plantation, what will you do?"

"I'll probably have to go back to Hamburg eventually." She added silently to herself, *And get married.*

"What is in Hamburg?"

"It's where I'm from, and the rest of my family lives there: my uncle, aunt, and two cousins."

Hamza nodded.

"I would like to go there."

"To Hamburg?"

Another nod.

"Whatever for?"

"My father says there you can learn to write and read. And buy your own beans and take care of your family and whole tribe."

"You want to learn to read and write German? I had no idea."

"My brothers don't. But I do. When Father was young, there were hardly any white men here. But now there are many. I like to learn their language, learn their customs."

"Well, Hamza." She cocked her head. "You *already* speak my language, but I don't speak yours. You're much cleverer than me."

"I speak, but not good enough."

"If you like, I could help you with it."

"Help?"

"We can talk together, and I'll help you to speak better and better. Just like a German."

Hamza beamed. "It would be very beautiful," he responded, making a kind of bow. "What do you like in exchange?"

"What would you like in exchange—that's the correct way."

Hamza, recognizing that the lessons had begun, repeated, "What would you like in exchange?"

"Very good." She smiled at him. "We are friends, Hamza. I just want to help you."

"Friends?"

Luise nodded. "That's how I feel. Strictly speaking, you're the only friend I have."

Hamza didn't quite know what to say. "Thank you," he managed, adding, "my friend Luise."

She almost corrected him, giving him the German word for a woman friend, but she liked his use of the masculine word.

Over the next few days, Luise and Hamza had fun with their daily language learning. At first the Duala seemed suspicious, but they quickly adjusted to the fact that Luise and Hamza were now friends. Hamza was very able, repeating every sentence she spoke. And his German improved faster than Luise imagined possible. His sentences grew longer, and he used subject, object, and verb in the correct order. Sometimes Luise heard something of her own teacher in her voice when talking with Hamza. On the other hand, when her private tutor was teaching her, she barely listened.

Some days earlier, letters had arrived from home. Luise never thought she'd be so excited about a few lines from her relatives. Uncle Georg had enclosed a packet of newspapers so that the émigrés would have some news from the homeland. Luise was startled by her mother's reaction: she burst into tears and ran sobbing up to her room.

Luise and Martha had never seen such an outburst from their mother. She hadn't even cried when she heard her father had died. Elisabeth's mother had died when Elisabeth was Luise's age. Her daughters had asked about it once, but discovered it was a subject she wouldn't discuss. So they never wasted any more words on it.

Robert rushed after Elisabeth, leaving the sisters to wait apprehensively. When their parents returned, it appeared they had talked it out. At least, Elisabeth made an obvious effort to put herself in a better mood—but that was precisely what made Luise anxious. Her mother had never taken pains to hide the mood she happened to be in.

For a while Luise feared her mother might have extracted a promise from her father to abandon the plantation and return to Hamburg once the largest debts were paid off. She paid close attention at the dinner table for any sign that their time in Cameroon might be ending, but fortunately nothing indicated it.

Luise habitually got out of bed at dawn and walked over to the tree to savor the silence and the landscape. Now she took her portfolio with her, committing her thoughts to paper, sometimes even drawing what she saw or from memory; she'd sketched several very good pictures of the church.

She usually stayed for an hour before stealing back into the house and crawling back into bed until it was time to go to work.

That morning Malambuku was not at his usual place on the veranda, so Luise went again into the house, having nothing to do. The sun was already well up, and there was no apparent reason for the change. When she went to the dining room, she needed a moment to understand why her family was there, waiting for her: a cake in the center of the table adorned with several candles.

Her mother approached her with arms outstretched, and her father followed.

"All the best on your birthday, my child!" she said.

Luise couldn't have been more stunned. Was it the third of December already?

"Happy birthday, my little one!" Robert said, giving her a big hug.

"Thank you," Luise managed to say, utterly surprised and a little moved.

"Here, Luise." Elisabeth handed her a small box.

Luise untied the little bow and lifted the lid.

"Grandmother's brooch!" She looked from her mother to Martha.

"You were always so fond of it, and I think your grandfather just forgot to mention it in his will. Georg, Vera, and your cousins all agreed that you should have it."

"Thank you so much! This means a lot to me." Tears welled up in her eyes.

"We've something else," Robert announced, and Martha handed her sister another present wrapped in newspaper. A book, Luise guessed from the shape. She undid the bow and folded the paper back. A leather-bound book appeared, and she opened it to find the pages blank.

"Martha told us you've been writing your thoughts for some time. Now you can write them in there."

Luise was wide-eyed, opened the book again, and gasped. "I don't believe it." She hugged Martha enthusiastically, then her father and, with a little more reserve, her mother. "You've made me so very happy! Thank you!"

"But we're not quite finished," Robert said with a broad smile. "Malambuku!" he called, and a few seconds later Malambuku came in bearing a large cage.

"Present for *nyango* Luise."

Luise was overcome with delight when she saw what Malambuku had with him.

"Caesar!" she exclaimed, unable to hold back her tears. "It can't be!"

"We know how hard it was for you to say goodbye to Caesar. And so that he won't be lonely, Martha and Frederike's rabbits came with him, naturally." Robert smiled at his daughter. "Once again, all our love for your fifteenth birthday, Luise."

Luise threw her arms around her father's neck and ran to the cage Malambuku had put down on the floor. She carefully took Caesar out and tenderly pressed him to her. "I've missed you so very much!"

Martha cleared her throat. She held a letter in her hand. "Will you listen, though you only have eyes for the rabbit?"

Luise nodded and took Caesar in her arms over to a chair. She didn't give a fig whether her mother liked it or not. She was far too happy to care about anything. Martha began to read aloud.

Dear Luise,

All of us send best wishes for health, good fortune, and happiness on your fifteenth birthday!

We hope you'll be wholeheartedly delighted with your presents and wish we could see your face when you take Caesar and his comrades into your arms. It is Frederike's personal gift to you, to let you have her bunny so that the three of them won't be separated. We know they are in the best of hands.

We send many warm hugs and will think of you lovingly on the third of December! And on every day, too, that we wish we could spend with you and your family here in Hamburg.

All our love,

Uncle Georg, Aunt Vera, Richard, and Frederike

Luise felt tears drip onto Caesar's fur. Martha folded the letter and laid it on the table in front of Luise.

"I thank all of you so very, very much," Luise said, deeply moved. "This is the most beautiful birthday I've ever had!"

"But, but," Robert said, "the day's just beginning. We thought we wouldn't work today, but take you to Victoria instead. Would you like that?"

"But that would be lovely." Luise hid the fact that she'd much rather stay on the plantation. Her relatives in Hamburg and her family here had taken great pains to make her happy. Luise would have felt ungrateful to turn down the offer.

"Then you should go and change, and we'll leave right after breakfast," Elisabeth said, delighted. "Victoria has a proper main street and shops we can look at. Oh, it will be marvelous!"

"Yes, Mother, it will be." Luise smiled at her, rose from the chair, and tucked Caesar back in the cage, giving a quick pat to the other two, still unnamed. "Wherever did they hide that cage?"

"Hamza took care of the animals," Robert said. "He took the cage to the village and guarded it with his life."

Luise smiled. "I'll be dressed in two minutes."

At that moment Malambuku came back into the room.

"Oh, good. Could you please remove these rabbits from the dining room?" Elisabeth asked, with a hint of disgust in her voice.

"Yes, *nyango*." Malambuku picked up the cage.

"Take them to the place we agreed upon," Robert said.

"Yes, *sango*, I will take them there."

"Thank you, Malambuku."

Luise's eyes followed him with some longing. She'd have liked to run after him to see the rabbits' new home, and to pet and hold them once more. Instead she took her new book and the box with the brooch to her room and changed her clothes. They had all made such an effort. She did not want to disappoint them.

Chapter Eight

Vienna, December 20, 1888

Karl had spent every day with Therese since arriving in Vienna at the end of October. She'd helped him with everything he'd needed to accomplish there. He took a room in the house of a widow Therese had known for many years, whom she often looked in on. The room wasn't large, but was cozy and well kept, and the widow fussed over him like a mother. And the storehouse he'd leased was only a few minutes away from his lodgings. Of course, he knew that he'd have to look for something more imposing if he was going to launch a serious business in Vienna. But for the moment he liked things as they were.

He had in the meantime signed up six cafés as clients—in addition to Therese, who regularly ordered their beans; more deals had to be made, and he had to telegraph Georg more and more frequently for yet another shipment. The demand from the Viennese for the sweet delicacy seemed enormous.

Karl was happy with how things were progressing. Even apart from his excellent business deals, he felt better here in Vienna than he ever had in Hamburg. People were different here, more open and sociable. They wanted to enjoy life. Therese regularly invited friends and acquaintances to the café after closing time, and interested customers were welcome as well. Sometimes a visiting author would read from his work or a young painter would hang some paintings, hoping to find a rich patron, and sometimes there were just informal gatherings, everyone laughing and drinking. Therese's circle was altogether a merry group.

Friedhelm, a twenty-three-year-old who worked in his father's bank during the day, often brought his guitar, and they would sing, drink, and have a wonderful time. Karl felt a freedom he'd never known before. And right then—it hadn't even been two months—he couldn't imagine returning to stuffy old Hamburg.

"What are you doing for Christmas?" Therese asked after the last customer had left and she was closing up. "Going back to Hamburg?"

"No." Karl shook his head and picked up the basket of unsold pastries she was taking home. "I've already telegraphed my brother that I'd be spending Christmas here."

"Is it difficult?"

"To be away from home for Christmas?" Karl thought while they strolled along Rotenturmstrasse. "Honestly, no," he concluded. "Christmas with the family is nice, but it's not the same with Mother and Father gone."

"Oh, I didn't realize."

"Mother died a few years ago, and Father earlier this year." He hesitated. "A heart attack," he added, though he felt uncomfortable lying. But he had to keep the family's story and couldn't make an exception for Therese. "Are your parents living?"

"Yes, in Korneuburg. About an hour from here."

"And you'll be there for Christmas?"

"For one day, yes. Though I'd prefer to get out of it. We don't have much to do with one another."

"Why not?"

"They don't like how I live."

"What's not to like? Your café's successful, you've good friends, and you're independent."

Therese gave a loud laugh. "That's exactly it: those are the three things they disapprove of." She shook her head. "I'm going to trust you with something." She stopped in her tracks. "My family is wealthy, extremely. And it's a smirch on their reputation that I run a café and am still unmarried in my late twenties."

They started walking again.

"What do they expect from you?"

"Oh, who knows. I think they'd like me to do something more important than serving chocolate and cakes. But that's what makes me happy. And that's just what my parents can't understand. Now, my brother is the opposite—my parents' pride and joy. One of these days all Austria-Hungary will be his."

"You sound bitter."

"Oh no, perhaps a little sad. I wish they'd understand that I like my life. I saved every penny until I had enough for the café."

"Your parents didn't support you financially?"

Another shake of the head. "No. And I wouldn't have wanted it, anyway. My father always reminded me how hard my great-grandfather worked to build our family fortune and that he'd started with nothing. My grandfather carried on the business and passed it to my father. Florentinus will be next, and he will surely do my parents proud, which I've never managed to do."

Karl moved the basket to the other hand and put his arm around Therese's shoulders. "I know what it's like to grow up amid high expectations."

"And so here we are, at the bottom of the barrel," Therese said in jest. "Though you're doing something useful, dealing in grand style. But"—she raised her forefinger and grinned—"you're older than me and haven't found a wife. That's awful, really horrible!"

"Well, I hadn't met anybody like you until now."

Therese stopped again and looked at him searchingly. "I didn't mean it like that, Karl. I wasn't trying to . . ."

"I know." He stroked her cheek. "That isn't like you." He leaned down and kissed her on the mouth. "I have never before met a person like you, Therese Loising."

"You mustn't do that out of pity." She eyed him with a pinched look on her face.

He put down the basket, took her in his arms, and kissed her again, this time not tenderly but with some urgency. Therese responded to his kiss. Ignoring people's stares, she threw her arms around his waist and pressed against him. They stayed like that for a long moment.

When they finally pulled apart, Therese's cheeks were aglow. She looked at Karl, smiling.

"What would you think about coming to my parents' for Christmas?"

They walked on.

"I don't know." Karl shook his head back and forth.

"They would definitely be kinder if they were presented with one of my friends."

"Now then, Therese Loising, you're exploiting me."

"Why, naturally. You mean you didn't know?" She produced that bright, bell-like laugh of hers, so familiar to Karl by then.

"Oh, women always try to use me to serve their own purposes."

He rolled his eyes. Therese punched him on the arm and laughed more loudly.

"Well, why the devil not?" Karl said. "After all, I'm a respectable man from a good family." He brushed an imaginary speck of dust off his shoulder. "We can show your parents that someone can be absolutely taken with you. But not because they say so."

"And are you taken with me?" Therese looked at the ground intently.

"You're different when you talk about your parents, did you know that?"

"Really?"

"Yes."

They strolled without speaking for a while.

"What am I like?" Therese broke the silence.

"Not yourself anymore, not happy, full of self-doubt."

"I know. I always feel I can't do anything right in their eyes."

"I know that feeling all too well. I've always thought I had to keep up with my brothers. To be honest, that didn't change until a few months ago."

"How'd that happen?"

"Like you I grew up in a well-to-do family. My father was Peter Hansen, *the* Peter Hansen, a successful merchant and very well known in Hamburg. They were big shoes that my brothers and I had to fill. Georg, the eldest, was always the smartest one. Everything came naturally to him, whether in school or with the accounts. One look was all he needed to understand anything. Exactly like my father. Robert, on the other hand, was always the bravest. He used to get—and give— more beatings than we two together."

"Sounds painful," Therese observed with a smile.

"My mother always said that Robert had an untamed character. I worshipped him for it."

"And you? How would you describe yourself? We've got one smart brother and one wild one—so what's the third?"

"Not worth much so far."

Therese halted abruptly. "Don't say that! You're worth far more than most people I've known." She started walking again.

"Can I tell you something in confidence?"

"Sure."

"I've always felt worthless for as long as I can remember. That didn't change until recently."

"How?"

"Don't be alarmed when I say this, but it was because my father died. Not that I didn't love and admire him. But he ran into problems with the business, and we had no idea how big they really were. We had to band together after he died, and suddenly each of us became indispensable to our success. That's when I saw that my work and help were significant." He turned to her. "I hope you don't think ill of me because it took my father's death for me to recognize my own worth."

"Of course not. That coming together, is that why you're here?"

"Yes."

"And now everything's moving along the way you and your brothers want?"

"Even better."

"If this works out, will you go back to Hamburg?" A trace of anxiety appeared in her voice.

"I've been thinking about that a lot lately. My family's in Hamburg—that's where our main office is. But in the short time I've been here, I've felt that Vienna has become my home. I'd prefer not to go back."

She raised her head and laughed. "I must say, that appeals to me."

"Oh really?"

She was beaming as she nodded. "Oh, you know that."

They'd come to Therese's place. She pulled out her key but didn't go in.

"So—are you coming for Christmas or not?"

"Yes," he decided. "I'd be pleased to join you."

The twenty-fifth of December arrived, and Karl dressed in his best suit and vest with a high collar and an ascot with a pearl stickpin. He examined himself before leaving for Therese's. His hair was parted precisely in the middle and slicked down with an apple-scented pomade. His beard was neatly trimmed, and he was very pleased with what he saw in the mirror.

"Chic" was Therese's verdict upon opening the door.

"May I return the compliment?"

He took her hand and spun her around. Therese was wearing a white dress with a lace bodice, tight-fighting sleeves, and a wide skirt with layers of flounces. Hanging from a silk band around her neck was a stone amulet painted with a gentian. Her long dark-blond hair was artfully pinned up.

"What a marvelous dress! You should wear it more often."

"This? I'd knock into every table." She swung her wide skirt in one direction, then the other. "But I do like to put it on occasionally. And I would prefer my hair more loosely pinned . . ."

"It does look very pretty loose."

"Believe me, my mother would stare with disapproval throughout dinner and never stop shaking her head. Or she'd take me aside as soon as we arrived and whisper that there'd been a mishap and I must get to the bathroom right away and fix my hair." She gave a hearty laugh. "Shall we?" She handed him the cake she'd just baked.

Karl took it and said, "Yes, let's be off."

They went to the street where a coach was waiting. Karl hadn't noticed it when he arrived.

"My parents sent their carriage," Therese explained.

At that moment the footman dismounted and opened the door.

"At your service, Miss Therese, and Merry Christmas!"

"Good morning, Thomas. And a Merry Christmas to you, too." She smiled at the elderly man, who'd been in her parents' service for as long as she could remember. "I haven't seen you in a long time. Are things well?"

"My sciatica hurts. But I can't complain, Miss Therese."

She touched his arm for a second. "It's nice to see you, Thomas."

Karl helped her up, then followed, and Thomas closed the door.

The trip took about an hour. Karl noticed that as they got closer, Therese began to knead her hands anxiously. He laid his hand on hers reassuringly.

"It'll be all right."

"I hope so. Why do I do this to myself? I could easily have said I had too much work to come."

"You worry too much. It's only a few hours, and you're not alone."

She smiled at him. "Yes, that's right. I'm happy to have you beside me."

He leaned over and kissed her cheek. When the coach stopped, he looked into her eyes. "Ready?"

She nodded. "Ready!"

"Mother, Father, I wish you a Merry Christmas. May I introduce Karl Hansen? Karl, my parents, Margarete and Friedrich Loising."

Karl made a flawless formal bow and breathed a kiss on the hand of Margarete Loising, who appeared to be a somewhat older, more corpulent version of Therese.

"It is my pleasure, madame. The question of how Therese received her beauty has been answered by our meeting today. I wish you a Merry Christmas."

"Herr Hansen, you are a flatterer."

"An honest flatterer." Karl smiled and firmly shook Friedrich Loising's hand. In his dark-blue suit and vest, he reminded Karl a little of his own father. "Herr Loising."

"I am honored, Herr Hansen."

"Where is Florentinus?" Therese asked.

"Here," a voice boomed from the stairway, and they turned toward a slim, tall young man with hair parted to the side, descending with a bounce in his step. Beaming, he went to Therese, took her in his arms, and whirled her around.

"My dear little sister, you look gorgeous."

Therese gave a cheerful laugh.

Florentinus set her down and gave her a kiss on the cheek. Then he turned to Karl. "And who is the lucky man who can call himself your escort?"

Therese took her brother's arm. "Florentinus, may I introduce you to Karl Hansen?"

"Pleased to meet you, Herr Hansen."

"Herr Loising."

They shook hands.

"Oh, Herr Loising is standing next to me, call me Florentinus—or better, we'll drink too much absinthe and you can call me Tino like my friends."

"Delighted. Call me Karl."

"Please, do come in." Margarete Loising turned, saying somewhat reproachfully, "You haven't been home for so long, Therese."

"I've so much work, Mother."

"Nonsense." Margarete made a dismissive gesture and took her husband's arm. "Ladies in society don't work; they enjoy activities."

Therese stifled the reply on her lips.

Karl offered her his arm. "I'm delighted to be here with you today. My sincere thanks for the invitation."

Thomas, who was still at the door, cleared his throat. Therese slipped her arm out of Karl's and retrieved the pastry from the old man's hands. "Thank you, Thomas." She gave her mother the cake. "I hope you like it."

Margarete received it and looked around uncertainly. A domestic hurried over.

"Take this to the kitchen."

"Yes, madame." The girl curtsied.

"Shall we go into the parlor?" Friedrich Loising invited his wife to precede him, followed by the others.

They had an aperitif and spoke until a servant appeared and announced that soup was ready to be served. Friedrich shepherded them into the dining room, where he took his seat at the head of the table. His wife sat to his right, Florentinus beside her and Karl opposite him with Therese to her father's left. Two servants brought the soup.

"Herr Hansen," Friedrich began, "might I ask what your occupation is?"

"Would the name Peter Hansen & Sons, Coffee Merchants, mean anything to you?"

"Hmm . . ." Friedrich seemed surprised and thought about it for a moment. "I have heard the name before. Maybe from one of my colleagues. Is that your father?"

"Quite right. Unfortunately, my late father."

"Oh, I *am* sorry. The firm is in the northern part of the German Reich, isn't it?"

"Indeed. Our main office is in Hamburg."

Margarete Loising studied him with interest. "So you have a business, how nice!"

"Along with my brothers, yes. We used to just sell coffee, but we've recently discovered that cocoa is also a profitable commodity."

"Karl is the supplier for my café," Therese interjected.

Her mother arched her eyebrows. "That place can hardly be called a true café, surely."

Therese swallowed.

"You find that surprising?" Karl asked, turning to Margarete.

"What do you mean?"

"Therese's café. It's the smallest café I know in Vienna. And yet that's where the most chocolate and coffee are sold. We merchants call that a lucrative source."

Margarete looked at him wide-eyed.

Karl turned to Therese. "You should be proud of what you've built."

"And all without any financial support," Florentinus added. "My little sister really showed what she can do."

"Now let's not exaggerate," his father urged.

"I'm not, by any means. Think about it. You got the factory and your wealth from Grandfather, just like your father before you. And unless I do something particularly idiotic, I don't have to worry about earning a living for the rest of my life. Karl inherited the business from his father, too. But our Therese, she's done it all by herself. Without any support." He raised his glass. "We're very proud of you, my little sister."

He paused, throwing an admonishing glance at his parents. Friedrich and Margarete reluctantly picked up their glasses. Karl smiled and followed suit.

"To Therese, who showed us men up properly. May your success last forever!"

"To Therese!" Karl repeated, as the Loisings took a quick sip from their glasses and nodded in the direction of their daughter.

Florentinus and Karl exchanged glances. Karl struggled to contain a smile.

Chapter Nine

Hamburg, December 25, 1888

The mood at the table was dreary. As far back as Georg could recall, the Hansen family Christmas gatherings had been special. A joyful time, when everybody sat together at the table, talking and enjoying one another's company. But now they were down to four, and Georg, who was never at a loss for words, couldn't find anything to leaven the mood.

"So, Richard," he said gamely, "are you pleased with your scholastic achievement this year?"

Richard shrugged and shoved a piece of meat into his mouth.

"Richard, when your father asks you something, give him a decent answer!" Vera admonished.

"I did what I could," Richard answered with his mouth full.

"I wish the family were here," Frederike blurted out.

"We *are* a family," Vera said, irritated.

"I mean Uncle Robert and Aunt Elisabeth. Especially Martha and Luise. And Uncle Karl, too. I miss them. We've always had Christmas together." The sixteen-year-old had tears in her eyes.

"We all miss them, Frederike."

"Everybody was here last year, even Grandfather. But now it seems so sad."

"We can have just as nice a Christmas, just the four of us," Vera said. "We just have to make an effort."

"That's not true," Richard said, contradicting her.

"Richard, watch your tone of voice!" Vera looked at her son angrily.

"Leave him be," Georg pleaded. "Frederike, we'd love to have them here as much as you. But times have changed."

"Does that mean we'll never celebrate Christmas the way we used to?" Frederike put down her knife and fork.

"No, of course not. This villa is our home, the true home of the whole Hansen family. We'll all come together again, here—I'm sure of it," Georg said, trying to cheer up his children.

"But when? I don't want to spend another Christmas here if it's going to be like this," Frederike protested.

Vera burst into tears.

Georg handed her a linen handkerchief. "Please try to compose yourself, Vera."

"We try to keep up appearances," Vera sobbed. "You are so ungrateful."

"I'm so sorry, Mother, I didn't mean it that way."

Vera sobbed a bit more before looking up, red eyed. "If you'll excuse me. I'm tired and would like to go to bed."

"But we haven't sung yet," Frederike managed to get out, stunned.

Vera rose from her seat. "Whether you have four voices or three, it won't make a bit of difference. Excuse me."

With that, she left the room.

A short while later, Richard and Frederike also asked to be excused. Georg didn't object. He wouldn't have admitted it to himself, but he was relieved to be left alone. He picked up his glass of wine and went to the parlor, where he poured himself a cognac and brought the half-full decanter to the leather armchair that had been his father's. Georg finished his wine, then lifted the other glass and downed it in one gulp. Then he poured himself a second. He sank farther into the chair, leaned his head back, and closed his eyes.

What a miserable time it was just now! Four days ago his spirits could scarcely have been higher, having paid off the final third of their debt to the bank. Now their regular payments were on schedule, and the warehouse was well stocked. If his personal circumstances had been different, Georg would have been quite happy. Robert shipped cocoa beans every two weeks. They followed their original plan to ship beans from Hamburg on to Vienna because Karl hadn't yet found storage for larger quantities. The expense was a bit greater, but Georg firmly felt that they were on their way to rebuilding the business.

Still, as good as sales in Vienna were, they were lagging in Hamburg. People there didn't ask for any sweetened chocolate; they wanted coffee. Yes, there were other uses for the beans, but Georg hadn't been able to interest a confectionary or pastry shop in trying any. And the experiment of selling hot chocolate at the market was a failure. If the good people of Hamburg wanted a hot drink on a cold day, they went for mulled wine or grog. Anna and her chocolate stand received sneers instead.

Nor were the chocolate tastings in cafés successful. So Georg made the decision to revive the coffee side of the business that had received short shrift in recent months. Negotiations with potential customers, however, continued to be tough. And honestly, he was annoyed when he got one glowing report after another from Robert and Karl, whereas the head office was merely treading water under his control. Still, his brothers' achievements averted the looming threat of bankruptcy, so Georg was granted a little breathing room on that front at least.

At the bank four days ago, he had let Herr Palm know that the final payment had been made and thanked him for his vote of confidence in the brothers and, consequently, in their firm. Palm was delighted, congratulating Georg on the rapid success of their business plan. Palm's enthusiasm was sincere, and Georg had the impression that he was more than a little relieved because of the risk he'd taken on their behalf by postponing the payments.

Palm truly cared that the firm of Peter Hansen & Sons was stable again. And Georg suspected that his dislike of August Frederiksen played its part. He didn't fully understand, but he tried to find out more about it. But Palm merely congratulated Georg again on his success and excused himself on account of urgent work that had to be finished before the holidays.

Georg thought of his brothers, and especially the plantation in distant Cameroon that had become the basis of the whole family's survival. It was with a feeling of yearning that he slipped off to sleep that night, to dream of a country he'd never seen.

◆　◆　◆

Cameroon, December 25, 1888

Luise felt strange singing "Come, Ye Shepherds" with the congregation while sweat ran down the back of her neck. It was the first time in Cameroon she'd felt a pang of homesickness. It seemed wrong not to be celebrating Christmas in the grand Hamburg villa. Not to mention the fact that here it was so hot and humid that the Christmas carol felt like a rehearsal for a much later performance.

Malambuku wanted to prepare a celebratory feast that day out of respect for the Germans' religion. Luise had no idea what it would be, but she suspected it wouldn't please her mother. The last time she'd been happy was on Luise's birthday—until they reached Victoria and her mother discovered that the main street was nothing but a broad dirt road without any proper shops. Victoria turned out to be nothing but a chaotic arena for aggressive vendors with poor-quality wares.

Elisabeth's last, tiny hope for a society environment like the one she was used to was crushed, and from then on, she'd shut herself away all day and barely uttered a word. Luise and Martha could see the worry in their father's eyes, but he had no solution for his wife's distress. Still, that day, Christmas Day, Elisabeth had braced herself and gone to church. Luise could see how miserable her mother felt. In spite of the bit of color her skin had gotten from the sun, she seemed pale and wan. She could barely follow the conversation; she seemed absentminded and extremely tired. Luise looked at her as the pastor delivered his sermon of hope and thanksgiving. They sang "Jesus, Great and Wondrous Star" and closed the service with "Silent Night."

After, some people stayed for a drink, but Robert said goodbye, wishing everyone a Merry Christmas and steering his family toward the carriages—much to the annoyance of Martha, who had just spotted Raimund Leffers.

"You can talk to him next time. Now come along, Martha," Robert urged.

Martha sighed and pressed her lips together in anger. She glared at Elisabeth, who let her husband help her into the carriage as though in a trance. Robert climbed in beside her and Luise and Martha got into the carriage behind theirs.

"It's so unfair!" Martha complained as quietly as she could. "Sometimes I just *hate* Mother."

"Stop that! You can see she's not well."

"She hasn't been well since we've been here. But that's no reason to destroy our lives, too!"

"Let it go," Luise said; this was getting on her nerves. "She's not destroying our lives just because you can't talk to Raimund."

"Oh no? And how am I going to get ahead here? I'll be seventeen in two months. Other girls my age in Hamburg already know the man they're going to marry."

Luise didn't know what to say to that.

"And wasn't it Mother who always told us to keep a stiff upper lip and maintain our composure? And what's she doing? Letting herself go, bit by bit, every day. People are talking."

"Martha, could you do me a favor because it's Christmastime?"

Martha looked at her in surprise. "What's that?"

"Could you simply be quiet until we get home?"

Martha looked at her, fuming.

"Yes, that's it. Thank you." Luise turned and looked the other way.

And Martha didn't say another word, but her silent curses now included her sister.

"I have an announcement to make," Robert said at dinner. He put his hand on his wife's. "And it will be of special interest to you, my love, of very special interest."

She looked at him but didn't attempt a smile.

"When the harvest is in, we're going to Hamburg."

Elisabeth's reaction was remarkable, as if something had roused her from a deep sleep.

"Hamburg?" She stared at Robert.

"Yes, my dear. Hamburg. Our home."

◆　◆　◆

Vienna, December 26, 1888

They spent the night at the Loisings' villa. Therese slept in her old room, and Karl in a guest room. Nobody had expected the evening to go on so late. Margarete and Friedrich had retired early, but Florentinus, Karl, and Therese talked half the night away. The siblings regaled Karl with stories from their childhood and the tricks they used to play, about which their parents still knew very little. They tried to outdo each other, and it became a tipsy, rollicking good evening. When they finally went to bed, it was going on two and they were all joyful.

Therese was glad she'd invited Karl to share their Christmas dinner. She lay awake for a while thinking about that Karl Hansen. He was a dashing fellow with a very fine bearing, good looks, and excellent manners. He knew when he should speak up or keep quiet. And he made her laugh when many men hardly wrung a smile from her. He'd become a good friend, the best she'd ever had. But did she love him? She couldn't come up with an answer, and sleep soon overcame her.

The next morning they said goodbye to all three Loisings and took off in the carriage for the journey home. Florentinus had promised to come by the café before long and to visit her in Vienna more often; they were agreed that the friendship they'd let go dormant should be revived permanently.

As the carriage departed, Therese leaned out and waved to her family. Then she sat down and reached for Karl's hand.

"Thank you."

"What for?"

"It was so wonderful, and all because of you."

"Nonsense, it would have been the same without me."

Therese leaned her head on his shoulder. "No, it wouldn't. And the way you took my side with my parents! I mean, when you said how amazing it was that my little café turns a serious profit, I think that really impressed them."

"Well, it's only the truth."

"Yes, but nobody's ever given me such support."

"Florentinus praised you to the skies."

"That's true. He's really sweet."

"Frankly, the way you were with each other surprised me. From what you'd said, I expected you two couldn't stand each other."

"Really?"

"Yes. You said that he always does everything right, but whatever you do is never good enough."

"And that's how it is. But that's not Tino's fault. He does his job well and deserves any praise he gets. I could never keep up with him. But as a big brother, he's divine."

"I like him very much, too."

"I hope he keeps his promise and comes to Vienna more often. I'm only now recognizing how much I've missed him."

"I hope so as well."

They said nothing for a while as they pursued their separate thoughts.

"What are you going to do for the rest of the day?" Therese broke the silence.

Karl shrugged. "Selling cocoa beans the day after Christmas probably wouldn't be appropriate. I've nothing planned."

"Shall we spend the day together?"

"I'd be delighted."

"You can come with me now, and we can stay at my place," she offered.

Karl shook his head. "I'd like a change of clothes first. But I'd be glad to come after, if you'd like."

"Yes, that would be nice."

"Good."

They talked until Thomas let Therese off at her place before driving Karl to the widow's home.

Karl took great pains to go to his room as quietly as possible. He wished to avoid making conversation and was pleased when he eased shut the door behind him and locked it. Carefully hanging up his suit and vest, he peeled off his shirt and stripped down to his underwear. He dropped onto the bed facedown and closed his eyes, exhausted.

Scenes from the night before danced through his mind. He could understand why Therese didn't want to have much to do with her parents. A free spirit like hers wasn't compatible with the Loisings' narrow-mindedness. He couldn't help thinking of his niece Luise. Unlike Frederike and Martha, she was a nonconformist and didn't know how to live up to the ideal image her mother had in mind.

Karl turned onto his back and folded his hands behind his head. He looked up at the ceiling, where the paint had yellowed in many places. Otherwise the room was flawless. His room in the Hansen villa was larger and substantially more luxuriously decorated. But the size of his present room didn't bother him.

And anyway, he'd never felt more at ease than he did right then in Vienna. He looked forward to that evening, when Therese would open the café and invite her friends to meet. He so liked the informal ambiance and the sound of Friedhelm's guitar. And the Christmas he'd just celebrated was his best ever: no coercion, no communal family singing. He finally felt liberated. Free in a way he'd never experienced before.

He'd always felt a bit as if he were performing on a stage. Not in a leading role but a minor one, not the focus of the audience's attention. Here in Vienna, in the simplicity of a modest existence, he finally sensed what he himself was. He felt he was learning a little more about Karl Hansen every day, the one he'd seen in the mirror for all those twenty-nine years. He knew that there was more to discover in the eyes of this man than he had already seen. He was like a mystery to himself, and he wanted to know the personality hidden behind the facade of KH. He was confident he'd find the answer in Vienna.

He closed his eyes and sighed deeply. When he got out of bed, he'd been asleep for two hours.

Chapter Ten

Cameroon, March 1889

The last beans had been loaded on the ship, and Luise felt more miserable than she ever had in her life. She should have been happy to be returning to Hamburg after the eventful months in this faraway land. She consoled herself with the thought that they would only be in Hamburg a week; but when the journey was considered, she wouldn't be in Cameroon again for two months. Moreover, anxiety whispered to her that something could go wrong, being away from the plantation so long. She didn't even want to think about it.

She'd even gone so far as to ask her father to let her stay in Cameroon. She'd offered to supervise the plantation during his absence. But Robert had laughed and promised that they would definitely return and not stay in Hamburg more than a week. In the end Luise accepted this—she had no choice. She looked toward the beach as the *Carl Woermann* weighed anchor and slowly moved out of the bay. About twenty Duala people had come to say goodbye. Malambuku stood at the front; he'd promised that he and Hamza would ensure the plantation ran smoothly during their time away.

Luise raised her hand but was immediately scolded by her mother. "Luise, you will *not* wave to Negroes! What would people think?"

Luise put her hand back down. She was ashamed to admit it, but she'd rather have her mother lying lethargically in bed than having returned to possessing the strength to point out her daughter's mistakes and inadequacies almost hourly. Luise left the rail, unsure how long she could hold back her tears. She went to the other side of the ship; Martha followed.

"If Raimund flirts with another girl while I'm away, I'll go crazy!"

"So what." Luise rolled her eyes. "He's not the least bit interested in you."

"What do you mean?"

"He's polite, that's all. And everybody sees it but you."

Luise expected Martha to fly into a rage and turn on her heel, but her sister just folded her arms across her chest.

"That shows how immature you still are. Not even close to understanding what love between adults is like."

"Well, I suppose that's true," Luise responded with equanimity.

"You haven't a clue what's already gone on between us."

Now Luise was curious. "Between you and Raimund?"

Martha put on a triumphant smile. "Yes. Between me and Raimund." She looked at the ocean and raised her chin.

Luise looked at her briefly before turning back to gaze at the water.

"Would you like to know?" Martha kept looking straight ahead.

"If you want to tell me."

Luise pretended to be more indifferent than she was. If something had happened between her sister and the son of the Leffers family, then yes, she was keen to learn more about it.

"It was New Year's Eve." Martha leaned over to her in a conspiratorial way. "I noticed that Raimund was staying close to me all evening."

Luise resisted remarking that it was actually the opposite.

"Everybody was saying Happy New Year when he drew me to him and kissed me."

"No!" Luise stared at her sister, dumbstruck. She hadn't seen it coming. "Really?"

Martha nodded sharply. "And then he whispered, 'Happy New Year,' into my ear and put his fingertips on my neck. I had gooseflesh all over."

Luise was impressed even though she remained a little skeptical: Would Raimund have told the same story from his point of view?

"Does that mean you're a couple now?"

"Why certainly! You don't think he'd do that with any girl."

"No, of course not."

Martha seemed satisfied; then her expression changed. "But that dreadful Maria Lehmbach's always slinking around Raimund. I'm sure she's out to grab him."

"Maria's a year younger than I am," Luise replied, baffled.

"So what. I've seen how she looks at Raimund. And not everybody is such a late bloomer as you are."

"But I've only just turned fifteen."

"When I was your age, I was looking for potential matches in school. But you only have eyes for those awful beans."

Luise didn't have a reply. So they stood together in silence.

"Oh, don't worry. If you make a bit of an effort, you'll succeed at some point in getting a man to notice you. You're not ugly. You'd have to learn to act more like a lady. If Mother hadn't forbidden it, you'd have come on board wearing those dreadful pants you always have on around the plantation."

Luise reflected for a minute. "I don't know if I want a man at all."

Martha looked aghast. "What do you mean by *that*? Every woman wants a man!"

"I don't think I do." Luise shrugged.

"Who's going to provide for you?"

"I will, myself." It sounded possible. "I could start a plantation and go into trading."

"As a woman?"

"I'd hardly be able to pretend I'm a man."

"You're crazy! Something's really not quite right with you."

Luise didn't answer, mainly because she was afraid there might be some truth to what Martha said. How often had her mother scolded her and told her to change her behavior if she didn't want to become an old maid? And she never failed to mention how embarrassing her tomboyish antics were and that there surely wasn't a man in the world who would waste time with a woman like Luise. She hardly listened during these rants anymore. But deep down inside she wondered what her future life would look like and whether it wouldn't be better to listen to her mother's admonitions after all.

They anchored a few hours later in Calabar and then in Lagos, ports in British-colonized West Africa, where the crew unloaded some cargo and took on new wares. From there they traveled via Cotonou, a French-controlled port within the Dahomey Kingdom, itself a Portuguese protectorate; to Lomé in the German colony of Togoland. The next ports of call were Accra, the capital of the Gold Coast, a British colony; Takoradi; Abidjan; and Monrovia in Liberia. Each stop took a long time. Since steamers like the *Carl Woermann* had too great a draft and often couldn't anchor in the harbor directly, so-called Kru boys, named for their ethnic group, would ferry people and cargo from ship to land in their small boats, which was very time consuming. Leaving Monrovia, the *Carl Woermann* proceeded to Freetown and to Dakar, in Senegal.

At some point Luise became bored watching the cargo being loaded and unloaded. Eventually despite the monotony of everyday life on board, she realized that they'd left Africa and the Portuguese and Spanish coasts and that Bordeaux was their next port of call. After leaving the Bay of Biscay, passing through the English Channel, and stopping in Amsterdam, they at last approached the North Sea coast of Germany and, ultimately, the port of Hamburg—twenty-seven days after leaving Cameroon.

A young boy—he might have been eight or nine—ran up to one of the men helping to unload.

"Is this ship from Cameroon?"

"Why do you want to know?"

"I have to report it. Is this the ship?"

"Yes."

The boy didn't thank him but raced off as if the devil himself were at his heels. He ran all the way to a looming office building.

"I want to see Herr Georg Hansen," he said to the woman at the front desk.

"Herr Hansen is a very busy man. What do you want from him, boy?"

"I'm to report, told me so himself."

"Report what?"

"When the ship from Cameroon comes in."

"And now it's arrived?"

"Yes, but you mustn't tell him. *I* have to tell him or I won't get the money."

"Wait a minute."

The little boy watched her go down the corridor toward the back. He wanted to follow to make sure Georg Hansen wouldn't get the news from her and then deny him payment. But soon he saw the man who'd commissioned him approaching. Apparently she had told him, because he was smiling with delight.

"You did a very good job," he said, reaching into his pocket. "Here's your money, my boy."

"Thank you, Herr Hansen." The boy turned serious. "I can always tell you when ships come in. I'd like that very much. Really."

"I was only interested in this particular ship. But if I need you again, I'll look for you in the port."

"Thank you, Herr Hansen."

The boy left the building, followed by Georg. They walked together for a while on the way to the harbor; then when he saw his friends waiting for him, he dashed away. Georg walked rapidly to the quay, waving a hand when he spotted Robert. When Robert saw his brother, he tried not to push past his fellow passengers. He'd barely found his feet on firm ground when Georg rushed up and embraced him.

"Robert! It's so good to see you!"

They laughed as they held each other by the arm and clapped each other on the back again and again. Elisabeth, Martha, and Luise were greeted just as heartily and almost moved to tears.

"You're back home at last! Thank God."

Georg waved two carriages over. Robert and he took the first one, the women the second.

"You've gotten so dark I almost didn't recognize you," Georg joked as he studied his brother more closely.

"I see that better, now that I'm beside you. When you're surrounded by black people, you always feel a little pale. But here . . ." He compared his arm to Georg's. "Good heavens, it's quite a difference!"

"How have you been faring?" Georg asked. "Everything going well?"

"You've seen it for yourself—the plantation's bringing in more than I'd have imagined in my wildest dreams."

"Yes, that's true. But that's not what I meant. I mean how are *you*, the four of you? Have you gotten used to living there?"

"Luise and I love it. Martha only has eyes for the son of the imperial envoy and finds she can put up with it. Elisabeth . . ." He hesitated. "Elisabeth hates it and is quite depressed."

"Really?"

Robert nodded. "She often doesn't get out of bed all day."

"For heaven's sake! How do you cope?"

Robert shrugged. "What can I do? There's no alternative to the plantation. But it's no life for my wife. She hasn't even tried to settle in

Cameroon. Her attitude was better at first, on Sundays at church with the other Germans. She'd complain to the other women there about her life of deprivation . . . But none of them seemed as concerned about it as she was." He sighed. "I think she hates me for making her live that way."

"But, but maybe she just needs more time."

"No. She'll never adapt. I hope our time here in Hamburg will do her some good and make it a little more bearable for her. I'm hoping that from here, from this distance away, she might learn to appreciate more about Cameroon."

"Everything will be all right."

Georg put a friendly arm around his brother's shoulders. Then he became serious. "You've taken on a lot, more than Karl, to say nothing of me."

"How's the office going? And what happened when you paid the money back on schedule?"

"I admit I celebrated a little. A good feeling, no question about it. I only wish I could have contributed more to our success myself than just storing the cocoa and sending most of it on to Vienna."

"So sales in Hamburg are still not making headway?"

Georg shook his head. "No, unfortunately. People here want coffee or tea, not chocolate."

"Have you bought back into coffee a little?"

"Yes, some of it is supposed to be on your ship. But I didn't want to risk too much. Revenue is steady, but we're still on thin ice. We have to pay careful attention so as not to fall through it again."

"We'll manage, Georg, have faith!"

"I wish I could be as confident as you and Karl."

"What do you mean?"

Georg slowly shook his head. "I've done a lot of thinking over the last few months. You two went to Vienna and came back with a complete, well-thought-out plan that you immediately implemented.

I was a mere spectator. Nonetheless we all took the same share of the profits, although you took on and achieved far more than Karl or I did."

"You think too much, as always," Robert said. "I like what I'm doing." He grinned at his brother. "I'm just the best of us. You two simply have to adjust to that fact." He laughed heartily and punched Georg's arm. "Now wipe that expression off your face."

After some hesitation Georg chuckled. "Nice to have you here."

"Yes," Robert said. "It's good to be home."

As the carriages drew up to the villa, Elisabeth burst into tears of joy. Before they had even stopped, the front door was flung open, and Vera, Richard, and Frederike came running out with Anna behind them. The drivers stopped the carriages, and the others ran out to greet them.

"Vera!" Elisabeth exclaimed through tears, dismounting without even waiting for a hand to assist her. She lifted her skirts and ran to her sister-in-law. The women embraced as if they would never let go. Martha and Luise jumped down as well and hugged Frederike, and even Richard, who was otherwise not inclined to outbursts of emotion, gave the cousins a hearty hug.

It seemed to Luise as if an eternity had passed since she'd been in the villa. A peculiar feeling. The family gathered in the dining room as they always had was something to celebrate or to discuss. In this case, it was both.

"You must tell us everything," Vera insisted. "Really *everything*. How did you get along?"

"Cameroon is unbelievable," Robert enthused, though he sensed his wife making a face. "The plantation is enormous, about thirty times the size of our property here."

"Thirty times! Including the park here?"

"That's right. The plantation stretches from the house across a huge distance filled with cocoa trees, all the way to the slopes of the steppe. Everything's green and lush."

"I thought that steppe climates were dry," Richard said, puzzled.

"When you look out over the plain"—now Luise spoke—"everything's a dark green. The odd thing is when you get closer and let the earth run through your fingers, the ground is quite dry. It's amazing that the growth is so lush."

"And the people? What are they like?" Georg inquired.

"The Duala?" Robert took a sip from the beer Anna had brought. "You have to learn how to understand their way of life. At first they were wary of us, just watching and waiting. When they understood we meant them no harm, they opened up and were very friendly. They're extremely hardworking. You wouldn't find better workers anywhere."

"And the local Germans?" Vera wanted to know.

"Very diverse. One can get along fine with any of them. We have no complaints."

"Martha has gotten to know a young man there," Elisabeth announced with some pride. "His father is in the kaiser's service, if you must know."

"Really?" Vera appeared most interested.

Martha nodded happily and blushed. "His name's Raimund." She said nothing more, but the look she gave Frederike foreshadowed a more detailed report later.

"And you, Luise? How are things with you?" Vera asked, turning to her other niece.

"Luise is only interested in cocoa beans," said Martha disparagingly.

Luise was annoyed but held back a sharp retort. Though Martha and she had actually gotten along well in Cameroon, at home she was transformed into the same old Martha. A disappointment for Luise.

"Luise was terrific in getting used to life in Cameroon," Robert said. "She even helps out with the work and knows every single step in extracting the beans."

"All of it is most unbecoming for a young girl from a good family," Elisabeth interjected.

"Well, if Luise has helped so much with the work and understands cocoa beans so well, then we owe her a debt of gratitude," Georg declared. "We've earned enough in the last few months to put the Hansen family back on its feet. If it keeps up like this, our financial worries will be a thing of the past. And will be for a long time."

Eyes lowered, Luise said, "The work is fun." It sounded defensive.

"Joy in your work is the key to success," Georg said, "as our father used to say, right, Robert?"

"I'll drink to that." Robert raised a glass, and everyone else followed. "To joy and success!"

"To joy and success!"

Georg cast a smile all around. Then he stood up. "A letter from Karl came yesterday. We correspond frequently. I informed him that you were coming home on the next ship and would stay for several days. I'll fetch the letter." Georg returned, letter in hand, and passed it on to Robert.

"Would you like to read it to us?"

"Glad to." Robert unfolded the letter.

Dear family,

I hope that Robert, Elisabeth, and family have arrived home safely by the time this letter reaches you. Welcome back to the homeland, dear ones! I so wanted to be in Hamburg for a few days, too, to see you again. But my work prevents me at this time, unfortunately.

Word of mouth seems to have spread about the excellence of our cocoa beans around all Vienna. As

I have already telegraphed Georg, I will need a new shipment to be able to meet the high demand. There is an office available to lease, though I'm a little taken aback by the size of the building. It was used to store textiles, and there's plenty of space, but it's not in the best condition. On the other hand, the rent is low, and I've made some friends here who will help with the improvements. So we're creating storage space and also a salesroom at the front of the building to sell beans in small quantities. The front windows make everything very bright and friendly. I think it will be a jewel, and I'll do everything I can to make it one of the best businesses in the area. When we are ready I'll write in the hope that you'll be able to come to Vienna some day and see it for yourselves. I can hardly wait for that day.

And something else has happened that you absolutely must know. Therese, the café owner we met on our first visit, has been an indispensable help to me and become a vital part of my life. And for that reason—you will have seen this coming—I have asked her to be my wife. I am the happiest man in the world because Therese said yes.

The wedding will be a modest one until our whole family manages to come and share the real celebration of that day. Therese is looking forward to getting to know all of you. Maybe we can celebrate the event in a few months, before the next harvest time? If that won't be possible, sometime next year is good, too.

Please work this out among yourselves and suggest some dates.

I send you warm greetings.

Karl

Robert put down the letter. "I don't believe it. Karl's getting married?" "We're all so happy for him," Georg said. "Who would have thought he'd have such good luck in Vienna so soon? Perhaps it was fate that he had to get away from here to meet the woman of his heart."

"*You* talking about fate? I don't know you anymore!" Vera stared at her husband in amazement.

"Ah, I can still surprise you after all these years." He clasped her hand.

And so they ate together, sharing their laughter, and it seemed as if everyone in the family was enjoying the reunion. But Luise kept looking around the room. She couldn't describe her feelings and found it extremely confusing. Somehow she felt out of place, as if she weren't part of this anymore. Her old home had become strange to her.

Chapter Eleven

Hamburg, March 1889

Georg and Robert enjoyed their time together. The brothers felt closer than they had in a long time, perhaps more than ever before. It was a joy for Robert to be in the office daily, to go through the inventory with Georg, to review the books, and to forge plans for the future. He became conscious of how much he'd missed interacting with a partner. He did, to be sure, discuss with Malambuku the state of the harvest, how much the different sections of the plantation would yield, and how much could be sent to Germany on the next ship. But that was different. In Cameroon he was the *sango*, the master, and Malambuku was the go-between for the Hansen family and the Duala people. And even though he appreciated and respected Malambuku, they couldn't be equal partners, considering not the least their quintessential differences in cultures and mentalities. Being with Georg in the office created a very different sense of partnership for Robert.

One day they looked in on Herr Palm at the bank. Palm was sincerely delighted the brothers had come, despite the workload on his desk, and asked Robert how he liked life in Cameroon. Afterward, Georg and Robert went for a stroll along Hamburg's streets, looking at newly opened stores and enjoying their time together.

"I'd really prefer to have you stay," Georg mused as they meandered along.

"Right now I feel the same way. Why did we never take time to do this before? Or can you recall spending time like this when we both lived in Hamburg?"

Georg shook his head. "No, not a single occasion. We probably didn't appreciate each other enough."

Robert nodded thoughtfully. "Please tell me honestly: Are things going well?"

"How do you mean?"

"Well, it's understandable that since Father died, and we were faced with all those problems, you'd be tense, on edge. Happened to me, too. But since then the financial pressure has let up and selling the villa isn't a threat, I feel more relaxed, less tense. But I wonder if things aren't actually getting any better for you."

Georg thought about that. "Have you ever wondered about the meaning?"

"What meaning?"

"The meaning of our life, the meaning that Mother had to die such a painful death, Father's death, business worries. Our own existence and actions."

Robert thought for a few seconds. "You always were too serious, you know. You think too much."

"I wish I could change. But there are days when I ask myself if that's really all there is. Father worked hard his whole life and gave his all so we could grow up respectably and be safe. And in the end . . ." He didn't finish the sentence, but Robert had a good idea of what it would have been.

"Do you know what the Duala think?"

"No."

"They don't think about the future the way we do. Malambuku has great difficulty in answering my questions about, say, planning. He doesn't understand why we give it so much thought. The Duala live in the here and now. Their people don't quarrel over yesterday the way we do. After all, that's done and gone. And they don't spend so much time worrying about the future either. They have an almost unshakable belief in the good and are puzzled if other people don't. Do you know why they even accept us in their country at all and help us with the harvest?"

"I suppose because of the treaties of protection."

"No." Robert shook his head. "I don't believe Malambuku would obey what a tribal chief signed years ago without exactly knowing what it meant. No, they don't regard us as conquerors; they don't think we've taken something from them. That's a big advantage."

"But now the land belongs to us, the land that used to be theirs."

"Not in the Duala's way of thinking. Land belongs to nobody. We Germans came—and so did the English, French, and Belgians—and took the fruits growing there. That's exactly what they themselves had always done—nothing to object to there. But we trade and exchange goods with them. Which is exactly what the wages we pay mean to them. They barter. They exchange money for things they need. They regard us as men who—exactly like them—cultivate the land. And we must see to it that they get something for it. That's basically how the Duala see it. An interesting way of thinking, isn't it?"

"Sounds enticing. Sometimes I'd like to let go of everything, too."

"That's the very thing I've learned during my months in Cameroon," Robert continued earnestly. "I'm seeing the world through different eyes. Do you know what fascinates me the most?"

"What?"

"There's no envy. At least not on our plantation. When we go to church on Sunday and meet with other Germans afterward, I notice women comparing clothes or jewelry. Or men who show off their medals and flaunt diamonds in their tiepins. But when I go back to the plantation, all that melts away. Malambuku reports on what's been happening and whether the fencing has to be repaired to keep the chickens in. That's it. No entitlement, no jealousy, no striving to get ahead, or trying to be better or richer—or at the very least to appear to be so. Simply existing, living, and working."

"If you keep talking like that, I'll pack my bags and go with you."

"You're most welcome to join us."

"I think it's the feeling of inadequacy that I can't stand. I always believe I've never done enough, not sold enough, not provided enough to do right by everybody."

"And will anything ever be enough?"

Georg raised his shoulders and lowered them slowly.

"No, I'm serious," Robert kept at it. "Think about it. When is enough enough? Our two goals were not to have to sell the villa and to pay off the loan. And we got there. After that the goal was to stabilize our finances and revive the business. And we did it again. And now?"

"Well, let's stay the course until we've paid Meyerdierks fully for the plantation, and then secure our incomes."

"Yes, Georg, we'll stay the course. We'll pay Meyerdierks, buy our ladies beautiful clothes, guarantee our children a secure future. And let's suppose we've achieved all that. We're back at the point I was asking you: When is enough enough?"

Georg shrugged. "I'm afraid I can't answer your question."

"Well, I can. Because I really don't want to have more and more, and some more after that. I'd like to be happy instead, to enjoy a sunset with a good glass of wine, and to be able to be happy with all my heart. I'd like to laugh, Georg, just laugh on impulse. I'd like good conversation, like to see that other people are happy and that I played a part in it."

"Father would say you're a dreamer."

"He was a realist, of course, but I wonder if he was happy with what he had."

They walked on for a while without saying anything. Then Georg spoke up. "Even as a little boy, I envied you, did you know that?"

"You—me?"

Georg nodded. "Can you remember the fight we had with the Schulze brothers?"

"Dieter and Kurt, yes, I remember. How old were we?"

"I must have been about nine and you seven, I think. They were bullies, and Father always said we should simply ignore them and stay out of their way."

Robert chuckled. "I remember."

"I did what he said. Even when they took my ball away, I caved in. But you didn't."

Robert laughed heartily. "I got into a bit of trouble with Father because of it." He patted his rear end. "I think I can still feel that caning even today."

"I admired you for getting my ball back and going after them. Good heavens, how Dieter looked afterward! He had that black eye for a long time."

"I think he never looked better." Robert laughed. "But if it was so hard for you, why didn't you defend yourself?"

Georg shrugged. "Because Mother and Father said it wouldn't be proper. They expected that I, their eldest son, should rise above such things and maintain my composure."

"They told me something along those lines, too. They said, 'A Hansen does not do such things.'" Robert wagged a forefinger and laughed again. "Worked beautifully in my case."

"But that's exactly my point. You just *did not* listen to them. I was never that brave."

"It wasn't bravery, it was defiance," Robert summed it up. "I fought tooth and nail not to be like you."

"Really?"

"Yes. Because I knew I could never meet your level, let alone be better than you. Everything you did was perfect. Your pants were less wrinkled, you stood up straighter, your whole appearance when you were a child shouted out that you'd be head of the family someday. I could never be like you, and didn't want to, anyway. It was the easy way out for me to be the little brother who'd have his wild ideas knocked out of him at some point."

"The head of the family," Georg repeated Robert's words dreamily. "I've the feeling that I've completely botched it."

"But why?"

"You packed your bags and were decisive and confident when you took your family to Cameroon, fearlessly took over a plantation, though you didn't have the foggiest idea about cocoa beans. And revenues from them are higher than they ever were in the coffee business—Karl's having great success selling them in Vienna. Now he's building up his own business, and I'm certain he'll make it work." He sighed. "Don't get me wrong—I don't begrudge you two your accomplishments. I've gained considerably from them, after all. But I feel consigned to the role of spectator, like a parasite enjoying a good life at your expense."

Robert stopped in his tracks. "What on earth are you talking about? You're running the business here in Hamburg."

Georg also stopped, but then walked slowly on, so Robert had to catch up to him. "Yes, I run the office. But I'm not able to close the big deals."

Robert put his hand on his brother's shoulder. "Just for now, my dear brother. The good citizens of Hamburg are stolid, you know that. They aren't frivolous or eager about trying something new. Give it time. Chocolate will become just as popular as coffee is now, you'll see."

"I hope you'll be proven right."

"I will be."

They'd found their way back to the office.

"Do you know what? Let's tell Fräulein Denker we're finished for the day and go find a tavern and celebrate my last day in Hamburg together!"

"In the middle of the day?" Georg looked at him skeptically.

"Yes, Georg, in the middle of the day. Now push yourself!"

Georg dithered for a moment before opening the door and going up to the secretary's desk.

"Fräulein Denker, my brother and I won't be coming back to the office today," he announced.

"Have you an appointment somewhere else?" she asked in surprise, immediately leafing through her calendar. "There's nothing written in."

Robert came up to the desk and stood beside his brother. "You're right, Fräulein Denker, there's nothing on the calendar. Hold the fort and enjoy a very fine day."

He grabbed Georg by the arm and took him outside. "You wanted to backtrack—I was watching!"

"This damn conscience, I can't get rid of it!" he shook his head.

"We'll drown it in beer, one hundred percent of it," Robert stated.

They both doffed their hats with a friendly hello as a man passed them.

"We wish you a good day's work," Robert said with a half bow.

Then the two smiled as they went to the entertainment section of town—the main square in Sankt Pauli.

The day they were to leave finally arrived, and Luise crept out of bed before five to get ready. She tiptoed out so as not to wake Martha. She recalled with longing her rising at the crack of dawn in Cameroon and sneaking outside to watch the sunrise. She didn't even have to look out the window to know it wouldn't be worth it in the Hamburg fog. She wondered where she could go at that hour without disturbing anybody. Then she scurried across the hallway and went into Uncle Georg's study, silently closing the door behind her.

She thought she could still smell her grandfather's scent in the room, though it was really the leather furniture that had been there all her life. She walked over to her grandfather's beloved armchair and curled up in it like a cat. Just the way she had when she'd ask to stay there with him, if she promised not to bother him while he was working. She closed her eyes and imagined it was again the way it used to be.

She breathed deeply in and out and thought she heard the fountain pen in her grandfather's hand, scratching on paper. Luise smiled. He was there, very near; she mustn't open her eyes, so that everything would stay as it was. She saw him before her, large and imposing, in a dark-blue suit, matching vest, and a white shirt and wearing a cravat fastened with a pearl stickpin. As always when working, he furrowed his brow, scrutinizing the documents in front of him. Then he would make a note of something and place the paper on a pile to his right, open the next envelope, and read more of his correspondence.

He once told Luise that whatever she did in life she was to hold on to one thing: do not put off a day's work until the next day. Under no circumstances, no matter how long the work was. "Postponitis" he called it and said far too many people had made it a habit. Luise lay still for a while, meditating on her grandfather and dreaming about the years of her childhood. When she heard the first sounds from the kitchen, she sighed deeply. Anna was starting to work, and gradually everyone in the house would begin their day. She'd have preferred to stay there a bit longer exploring her feelings. She reluctantly opened her eyes, stretched, and stood up. She walked to the door, leaned her forehead against the wood. "Goodbye, Grandfather," she whispered, and pressed down on the latch.

She turned around once more, glancing at the empty desk chair. Then she withdrew with a heavy heart and softly shut the door.

It was almost half past six when everybody arrived for breakfast. Georg and Robert showed the effects of indulging in alcohol, and their wives' displeasure was clear.

"I have carefully considered what I shall now say to you," Elisabeth suddenly spoke, raising her head up high. She paused dramatically. "I shall not return to Cameroon."

Robert almost spat his coffee back into his cup. He coughed, and the liquid caught in his throat. When he had recomposed himself, he glared at his wife. "What did you say?"

"You heard me correctly. I shall not go back to Cameroon. At least not today," she replied, qualifying her original statement.

Robert stood up and threw his napkin down beside his plate. "Would you please come with me for a minute?"

"No," Elisabeth stated firmly. "There is nothing to discuss which other people may not hear."

Robert threw his wife a withering look. "We need to talk."

"No. I have too often let myself be controlled by you. My decision is firm."

Vera looked nervously at Georg, then from Elisabeth to Robert. "Shall we perhaps go to the next room so that the children can have their breakfast in peace?"

Elisabeth sipped some coffee before turning to her daughters. "You two are old enough to decide if you want to go back to Cameroon or stay here with me in Hamburg. As for you, Luise, I know what you will say. And so, Martha, think about it."

Robert was boiling with rage. "We will *all* go back to Cameroon, as a family!"

"No. We shall not."

Robert came around the table and grabbed his wife's arm. Elisabeth screamed.

"You can lay hands on me as you wish, but it won't change anything. No one will force me on that ship today, Robert Hansen. No one!"

"Please, Robert, let go of her," Vera pleaded.

Robert loosened his grip. "I've never hurt you, and I will certainly not do so now," he spat out.

Elisabeth shrugged as if she didn't care. "Georg, I must ask you as head of the family if you will permit me to continue to live in this house, though my husband is not here."

Georg looked at Robert.

"Georg won't deny you anything," Robert said as he regained his composure. "You are part of the family. Therefore, if you wish to live in this house, you may do so."

Georg's relief was obvious. Robert walked around the table again and sat down at his place. "Martha, you heard what your mother said. I know it's difficult, but we don't have much time. The ship will be sailing in a little over two hours. Think hard about what you would like, and disregard what your mother or I say. You're free to decide, but you must decide for yourself."

Luise looked at her sister anxiously. She was happy her mother's words had anticipated her decision. On the other hand, she was truly sorry for Martha. She reached for her sister's hand under the table.

Martha's eyes filled with tears. "I don't know what to do. Please, Mother, let's all go back together?"

Her daughter's "please" left Elisabeth unmoved. She coldly shook her head.

"Father, couldn't we go on the next ship and stay here a little longer? Then we'd have time to figure things out." Martha swallowed hard.

Robert hesitated, but he'd made up his mind. "I will leave today for Cameroon," he declared. "If you wish to come with me, you are welcome. If Luise, or you, or the two of you would like to stay here, I will not be angry with you. But you've got to make up your mind yourselves."

Martha broke into tears, shoved her chair back, and fled the room. She ran up the stairs and slammed the door behind her.

"I'll go to her," Frederike offered.

"No, *I* will," Vera said, leaving the room.

"Please excuse me." Robert got to his feet. "I must get my things."

"Me, too," Luise hastened to say, and stood up as well.

Georg, Elisabeth, Richard, and Frederike stayed seated. Not one of them touched their breakfast again.

About an hour later Luise gave her suitcase to a boatswain, who carried it on board. She hugged her uncle and aunt, her cousins, and last of all her sister. She could hardly hold back her tears.

"Come anytime later, when you're ready," she whispered in her sister's ear as they embraced.

Martha nodded amid sobs; she couldn't get a word out.

Robert said goodbye as he took Luise by the arm and boarded the ship. They waved from the rail to the family who had come to see them off. Elisabeth was not among them. Luise was relieved when the ship began to move. She felt that everything would be different from that day on. And she wondered if she would ever return to Hamburg.

Chapter Twelve

Karl was on pins and needles. They had decided on a private ceremony, but their friends somehow found out, and Karl suspected that some additional surprise or another was inevitable.

Georg's telegram two days ago had shaken him. He'd never held Elisabeth in particularly high esteem, but he struggled to believe she'd turn against her husband like that. He resolved to write to Robert, offering help and support if the need arose.

For a moment Robert's circumstances made Karl wonder if marrying Therese was a good idea. He had qualms about getting married at all. What was troubling him the most was whether his feeling for Therese was the kind of romantic love that unites two people in marriage or if it was just close friendship. Therese was a woman the likes of whom he'd never met. She was honest, straightforward, said what she thought, and had a laugh more beautiful than any he'd ever heard. Karl enjoyed every moment they were together, and as a matter of fact, he couldn't imagine being without Therese for a day in his life. She made him laugh, and he felt at ease in her presence more than with anybody else. But their relationship was completely different from his brothers' marriages, and given the recent events in Robert's life, it was to Karl and Therese's advantage.

He adjusted the bowtie Florentinus had lent him for the occasion. Florentinus was Therese's witness; Friedhelm, the guitar player, was Karl's. They went in two carriages to the little chapel where Therese's parents were waiting. Karl and Friedhelm arrived first, followed a few minutes later by Florentinus and Therese. Karl smiled at his bride. She looked beautiful. Her dress resembled the one she wore to Christmas at her parents' villa. But this one was set off by contrasting pink ribbons and a pearl necklace he guessed was rather expensive. Karl smiled again, noticing that she'd pinned her hair up loosely, the way he thought was the most beautiful.

Therese and Karl looked at the little chapel where they were about to be married. It wasn't grand or ostentatious, but Karl thought it possessed a certain charm. Karl offered Therese his arm, and they walked in together.

Margarete came up to Therese. "You could freshen up quickly," she whispered to her. "Your hair is a little untidy."

Therese laughed casually. "My hair is perfect, Mother. But thank you for your kindness and concern."

Margarete arched an eyebrow arrogantly, waiting for Friedrich to take her arm.

"Good day, ladies and gentlemen." A priest of about sixty approached them. "The Loising bridal couple, I presume?"

"Yes."

He nodded his welcome to them. "My name is Josef Edlmayr, and I will be officiating."

"Karl Hansen, and this is my bride, Therese Loising. Good day, Father."

"If you would follow me, please?"

The priest waited in the chapel entrance until they'd caught up to him. As they entered, the organ started playing.

"This is your last chance to change your mind," Karl whispered in Therese's ear.

She looked at him, smiled, and shook her head vigorously.

"As you wish. You'll have to live with me from now on."

He kissed her on the cheek. They followed the priest leisurely down the red-carpeted aisle to the altar. As the priest reached the altar and turned to them, the few people in attendance took their seats, and the music died away.

Karl listened to the priest's words as if in a trance. He wasn't really listening to what the priest said; most of it went over his head. He hadn't known what to expect for the ceremony, and it could have been a little more solemn, he thought, but Therese had wanted it that way. So he was more startled than sorry when the priest finished and pronounced Karl and Therese Hansen a lawfully married couple.

Therese's parents were the first to congratulate them, followed by Florentinus and Friedhelm. They thanked the priest and left the chapel. All in all, the whole thing had lasted less than an hour.

"Strange," Karl remarked as he went out with Therese on his arm. "I remembered my brothers' weddings differently."

"How so?"

"More grandiose, I'd say."

"Presumably your brothers had a *proper* wedding, that is to say, with friends and relatives and a full church," Margarete interrupted, having overheard Karl's words.

"We had a *proper* wedding, Mother. And we'll have a larger ceremony when all of Karl's family can be with us."

Therese had swung around to speak to her mother and then looked ahead, rolling her eyes. Karl noticed and smiled. They'd discussed planning a celebration for that day but decided against it. Not because they didn't want to celebrate, but it seemed wrong to do so without Karl's family. It could wait until later.

"What does the young couple intend to do now?" Florentinus asked.

"Therese would like to drop by the café to see that everything is in order. And then we'll go to our newly renovated office. But I'm taking my bride out to dinner tonight."

"You're going to revert to your daily routine? Are you serious?" Florentinus asked, flabbergasted.

"We just wanted to say, 'I do,' for today and celebrate later, as we've said," Karl explained.

At the doorway, Therese suddenly took a step back, seeing a crowd outside that had obviously come for her. They immediately surrounded them, congratulating and hugging her. All her friends were there. Therese hadn't expected or wanted this, but she was genuinely happy. She was shocked to see her staff among the friends.

"Frieda! If you're here, who's minding the café?"

"Nobody."

Therese's father came up and faced his daughter. "Forget about a small gathering. A wedding is a matter of immense importance and must be appropriately savored. I've taken the liberty of closing your café for the day and leaving a day's earnings in your register. By the way, that's an impressive machine, I must say."

Therese was about to object, but Florentinus shook his head. "Father is absolutely right. You've gotten married, and that must be celebrated."

"And since I assumed you didn't want a public celebration, I engaged two chefs who've prepared delicacies now awaiting you in your café, to be accompanied by a good glass of champagne," Herr Loising ended his speech.

Was Therese hallucinating, or had a smile just flashed across her father's face?

Karl shook his father-in-law's hand. "This is a wonderful surprise! Thank you so very much!" Turning to their friends, he said in a louder voice, "Many thanks to you all! And now let's celebrate!"

Boisterous cheers resounded, and as if on command the four-passenger carriages Friedrich Loising had ordered pulled up. Thomas drove the first one; it was reserved for Karl and Therese, the only twosome.

They were hardly seated when Karl saw Therese's teary eyes.

"What's the matter?" he asked affectionately.

"Oh, nothing. It's just that my father has never done anything this nice for me. And there are our friends, who ought to be at work, and yet they all came to congratulate us." She leaned against Karl's arm. "I'm happy, Karl, happy with all my heart!"

"Me, too."

Therese looked up at him, and Karl bent his head to kiss her long and tenderly. She snuggled against his arm once more, and they enjoyed their closeness until they reached Therese's café.

Thomas stepped down from his seat with a groan and opened the door.

"We've arrived, Fräulein Therese." The driver reflected for a second. "But no. You're no longer Fräulein." He shook his head. "I don't know if I can get used to it. I must beg your pardon if I continue to call you Fräulein Therese."

She took his hand and descended. They had barely reached the door—framed in wood and inlaid with glass in the upper half—when it opened from inside.

"Frau Hansen, Herr Hansen, our best wishes on your wedding day." Two men in chef's hats stood on either side of the entrance.

"Thank you very much." Therese entered her café and was overwhelmed. The tables had been arranged into one long table covered with closely spaced floral arrangements. "It looks splendid!"

Her parents, brother, and Friedhelm had followed her in, and Therese was so overcome that she threw her arms around her father's neck. "Father, it's gorgeous. Thank you!"

Her father was surprised. Emotional outbursts and affectionate behavior were not his areas of strength. Yet he enjoyed his daughter's warm embrace and shared her happiness over his successfully arranged surprise party. Margarete seemed to be about to admonish her daughter, but kept herself in check.

One by one carriages with their friends arrived, and the café filled up. When everyone was seated, four waitresses Friedrich Loising had hired brought in full plates of food. Karl looked around at the people who'd come to celebrate him and his new wife. He thought of his family, whom he missed terribly in that joyous moment. They'd been wrong to not plan a proper celebration, and he already regretted their decision. Karl was all the happier that his father-in-law had taken charge, though he was sure that Florentinus had a hand in it. He was grateful to be able to celebrate with such dear friends.

At first the conversation was cheerful, though somewhat decorous. After the tables were cleared, Friedhelm picked up his guitar and began to play. Margarete's face displayed equal parts horror and disgust, but her husband applauded and smiled. And so the small celebration that the newlyweds had planned was transformed into a lively party, which Karl and Therese were the first to leave as midnight approached.

Friedrich Loising insisted that they not help to put the café back in order and assured his daughter that in the morning there'd be no trace of the previous night's event. For the second time in two hours, Therese gave her father a warm hug, this time adding a kiss on his cheek. "Thank you, Papa. You made today one of the happiest of my life."

Friedrich Loising gulped noticeably. "And now it's high time you were home! It's your wedding night after all, and I'm sure your husband doesn't want to share it with us any longer." He gave her a quick wink.

Therese raised herself up on her toes and gave him a kiss on the other cheek. "Thank you!"

"You've already said that. Now be off!"

He accompanied them to their carriage, opened the door, and instructed Thomas to take the couple back home and return at once. When they reached Therese's place, where they would be living from now on, the bride was still beaming.

"What a magnificent day!" she gushed.

Thomas opened the door and helped her down. She raised herself up on her toes and kissed the cheek of her old driver, who couldn't have been more surprised.

"I'm probably a bit tipsy," she said with a laugh. "And I do like to kiss too much."

Karl chuckled when he saw the shock on the driver's face. "Many thanks, Thomas. I'll look after my wife from here."

Karl took Therese by the waist and brought her into the house. They laughed as he helped her up the stairs to her second-floor apartment.

"Frau Therese Hansen." Therese looked around on the stairway. "I've never come here as Frau Therese Hansen."

"Don't make it harder, Therese Hansen." Karl steered her around the corner. "Where's the key?"

"I've got it."

"Wonderful. Where?"

Therese lifted up her handbag. "In there. It's in there somewhere." She laughed.

Karl leaned her against the wall, making sure she didn't lose her footing, and took the key from her bag. "Keep standing," he admonished her.

"I'll stand here like a good girl." She closed her eyes and yawned.

Karl unlocked the door, swooped Therese up in his arms, and carried her across the threshold, to her great delight. She laughed joyfully, but covered her mouth immediately, afraid of disturbing the neighbors.

Karl put her down and led his new wife into the bedroom.

"I bought a new nightgown especially for tonight."

"Wonderful. Do you think you can get it on all by yourself?"

"Of course. I *am* a lady!" She fell backward on the bed, and Karl laughed as she struggled to sit up again.

He knelt down before her, slipped off her shoes, and raised her arm so he could reach the clasp on the back of her dress. He carefully loosened it, peeling it off her shoulders. He'd hardly let go of her when she sank back onto the bed. Karl gave a little sigh, then chuckled as he took off her dress, leaving her in her underwear. He turned down the cover, picked up Therese, laid her down with her head on the pillow, and tucked her in.

"Frau Therese Hansen," she murmured.

Karl neatly hung his clothes up on hangers and climbed into bed beside her. "Good night, Therese," he said, but she was already in a deep, deep sleep. He rolled onto his side and was likewise soon asleep.

"Are you mad at me?"

Karl had just opened his eyes and needed a moment to orient himself. Therese had brought him a cup of coffee. Karl sat up. "Thank you." He took a sip. "Why would I be mad at you?"

"Because I was tipsy."

"Tipsy, eh? That you were—hours before we went home. By the end you were hopelessly drunk." Karl grinned broadly.

"Don't tease me. I'm ashamed enough as it is. I don't understand how it happened. Everything seemed fine in the café, but the moment we left . . ." She rolled her eyes. "I'm not even sure how I got here."

"Well, with me. With your loving husband, who even managed to carry you across the threshold."

"And I didn't even properly celebrate our wedding night with you." She shook her head as if she couldn't believe it herself.

"What?" He looked at her in horror. "You don't remember?"

Therese was wide-eyed. "But did we . . . I mean, I . . . of course . . . uh, it's gradually coming back."

Karl laughed loudly, almost spilling his coffee. "No, we didn't," he made it clear. "It was a little joke."

"You are a bad man." She gave him a playful slap on the arm. "Don't ever tease me like that, Karl Hansen!"

"Oh, Therese." He put his coffee aside. "Don't give it a thought. Everything's wonderful. I think we had a perfect wedding, and our marriage certainly won't suffer if we consummate it a bit later." He took her in his arms. "We're the same today as we were yesterday at this time. Let's laugh together and have fun and not take anything so terribly seriously. That's not for us."

"I'm so happy." She pulled out of his embrace and looked at him intently. "And I love you."

"I love you, too, Therese."

They shared a tender kiss, which became more passionate, urgent. But suddenly Karl broke it off.

"Still, my dear wife, we have to get up so we can get to work on time."

"Oh?" she asked, disappointed. "I thought we could . . ." She left the sentence unfinished.

He looked at his watch and shook his head. "I've got to be at our new office in half an hour."

"I should have taken the opportunity last night," she said, getting to her feet.

"We have many, many nights," Karl responded, getting up and giving her another kiss. "At least I hope you won't be drunk every night."

"Karl Hansen! Go clean yourself up right now!" She acted angry, but was smiling. "And then get to the kitchen—I've made breakfast. If time is short, then take something with you." She tossed her hair and left the room.

Karl gazed after her. No doubt about it: he loved that woman!

"Will these windows ever get clean?" Karl took a step back to study the facade of his new office building.

"Sure, but we haven't gotten to it yet," Martin explained; he was a friend helping out with the renovations. "We've just done the rough work and wanted to finish the painting next."

"I'll take care of it myself, then."

"May I help?" Therese had come up behind him unnoticed. "Hello, Martin."

"Nice to see you, Therese."

Karl brightened up at once. "Therese." He gave her a kiss. "What brings you here? Have you closed the café already?"

"No, not yet. I just wanted to look in. Frieda can manage for a while by herself. How are things going?"

"There are a thousand little things. The rough work is almost finished. So we can see that we're making progress. But there's always something and then something else, and I think we'll never really be done."

"That's how it was at the café. And I'm still not finished. But it doesn't matter, because nobody other than me knows what still has to be done."

"You're a ray of sunshine, did you know that?" He gave her another kiss.

"Are you hungry? I brought some pastries," she said, pointing to the basket she carried.

"Your husband is absolutely right, you *are* a ray of sunshine, Therese. I'm starved."

Therese held out the basket. "Help yourself."

"Thanks." Martin dug in with delight.

"That's sweet of you. But I don't want you to overexert yourself with all this extra work."

"Do I look fragile to you?" she said incredulously. "I may not be tall or robust, but I can do the work of five men, believe me."

"Oh, I believe you."

Therese hugged her husband, said goodbye to Martin, and had them both promise to share the pastries with the workers inside the building. She stepped lightly out the door.

As promised, she returned two hours later when Karl was up a ladder, busily cleaning windows.

"You're doing it wrong," she called up to him. "You'll never get them clean like that."

"What am I not doing right?"

"You're rubbing in circles and making streaks."

"And you can do it better?"

"Absolutely! Come down, and I'll show you."

Karl came down off the ladder and handed her the rag.

She shook her head. "How can you expect to clean glass with a dirty cloth?"

He gawked at her.

"Exactly. Let me show you."

She went inside to the large sink with a pump, where a few months ago fabrics were cleaned. She took a piece of soap and rubbed it into the rag until it foamed. She rinsed the cloth again and again until the soap was gone, then poured a little vinegar on it. She filled a pail half full with water, added a dash of vinegar, picked up some dry cloths and went back outside.

"Now I'll show you how to do it." She handed Karl the pail and climbed the ladder. After cleaning the first three upper windows, she climbed down to rinse out the rag. "Well? What do you say?"

"How did you do it? I scrubbed and scrubbed and didn't see any difference."

"I work magic," she said with a peal of her bell-like laughter.

Shortly after Therese's arrival, the three men working inside had called it a day, but only one of them could come back over the next few days. Karl didn't anticipate finishing the renovation quickly; he hoped more of his friends would have time for it over the weekend.

Therese and Karl worked for another five hours. On the way home, exhausted, they could barely lift their feet; they made it home, but were too tired to eat. So they quickly washed the dirt off and fell into bed, dog-tired. Neither had the slightest thought of anything more.

They did nothing but work on the renovations for the next two weeks. Therese became worried that her husband really didn't want to take her in his arms; she only hoped that it would change once the office was open. After all, they *were* married. But for now, it felt as though they were merely living in a shared apartment and were still the good friends they'd always been. Therese tried to curb her impatience, but she couldn't help but wonder if maybe she wasn't pretty enough for her husband.

Chapter Thirteen

Finally! Luise could hardly wait for the ship to drop anchor and the little boats to take her and her father to land. The voyage had seemed longer than their previous trips. Maybe it was because she felt the need to divert her father from his worries during the journey. Apparently he felt the same way; they'd never talked so much as during those few weeks on board the ship. At the same time, they prudently left the subject of Elisabeth off limits.

That she would miss Martha, she knew already, although her sister hadn't been particularly kind to her in Hamburg. It was something about home that made her different, more petulant. Luise was sure that Martha would tire of it soon and ask Uncle Georg for passage to Cameroon—he and her father had arranged for that possibility. Georg would also ensure that an adult accompany Martha and keep an eye on her during the voyage.

When they sailed into Victoria Bay, Luise immediately recognized Hamza, who, along with some other Duala, was watching for them. Her heart skipped a beat. She was home at last; everything would be good again. Luise had wondered many times, just before falling asleep, what it was going to be like to live without her mother. She'd listened to her inner self intently to find the least hint of sadness about it. But try as she might, she just didn't feel that way.

Luise waved at Hamza as they caught sight of each other. He waved back, and she even thought she saw his broad grin at that distance. He was paddling one of the bright boats and helped Luise into it.

"Hamza!" Robert clapped him on the shoulder. "How nice you've come to meet us."

"I'm so glad to see you, Hamza," Luise said. "How did you know we'd be arriving today?"

"I came here often and waited." He beamed at her.

Luise didn't ask how many days he'd done this. She was just glad to see him again. "I'm happy to be home at last," she said.

"And home is happy that Luise is here again," Hamza responded. Then he craned his neck and looked around. "Your mother and sister not with you?"

"No, they'll be coming later," she said tersely.

"Did anything special happen at the plantation? Was there any trouble while we were away?" Robert inquired.

"There was a big rain. A lot of water."

"Was there any damage to the cocoa trees?"

Hamza shook his head. "The beans were very happy about the water. Only the bad ones are gone. The good ones still as strong as ever."

Robert wasn't quite sure how to interpret his words and felt a little uneasy.

When they reached the beach, Hamza helped Luise out of the boat.

"I'd rather walk than be carried, Father. Is that all right?"

"Well, yes." Robert hesitated. "If Hamza's escorting you back, I may ride on ahead . . ."

Luise noticed he was worried. "Of course. Do go on ahead."

"Fine." Robert walked up to the horses. He had learned enough Duala to make himself understood, which in this case wasn't necessary, because one of the men had selected a horse for him as soon as he'd arrived.

Hamza made sure the bearers would take Robert's and Luise's luggage to the plantation. Then Hamza and Luise started out together.

"Your German has improved," Luise said as they walked together.

"Thank you, Luise," Hamza said with a broad grin. "I keep hearing your voice in my head and speak the words after you."

"Really improved."

"Was it nice in your homeland?"

Luise sighed. "It was nice, but it's not my homeland anymore," she said pensively.

Hamza gave her a quizzical look.

"You know," she continued, "everything in Hamburg's foreign to me now. It's all so dark and heavy. I don't know how to describe it."

"Heavy? Did you have to work hard?"

"No, I don't mean it that way." She thought for a few seconds. "I've shown you my room at the farmhouse, haven't I?"

"Yes. Like the room."

"It would be better if you say, '*I* find something nice,' and not, 'Finds something nice.'"

"I understand. I"—he pointed to his chest—"like the room."

"Exactly." She smiled at him. "You remember my little desk?"

"Yes."

"It's white and has one drawer. I could easily pick it up."

He nodded.

"Now I have another desk in Hamburg. It's made of dark wood with three heavy drawers on each side. I couldn't move it a bit even if I wanted to. And that's exactly the way it is with all the things in my homeland. Everything looks dark and heavy, while here it's light and bright. It's warm here, cold there." She rubbed her arms. "I froze there all day long. And do you know what strikes me just now about Hamburg?"

"No, what?"

"Nobody sings." Luise started to hum. "We do that here all the time, if we're working or relaxing. We sing and hum and move to a rhythm. Almost nobody sings there, and they all make a face like this." She put on a scowl and looked at Hamza.

Hamza laughed. "You are not so . . ."—he searched for the right word—"pretty when you do that."

"And otherwise I am?"

Hamza looked astonished. "You are the prettiest woman I ever see."

"*I have* ever *seen*," she corrected him.

"I have ever seen," Hamza repeated.

"Thank you." She smiled at him again. "Hamza?"

"Yes, Luise?"

"Would you sing something for me?"

He looked at her sideways and started humming. Luise modified her pace. Still walking steadily, she moved to the rhythm of his humming, and then she started skipping. She spun around, spread her arms, and turned in a circle a few more times. She reverted to walking straight ahead but continued to follow his beat.

"I feel so free here, Hamza."

He stopped humming. "What do you mean by *free*, Luise?"

"It's hard to describe. You know the way you feel when you run too fast and can hardly breathe?"

Hamza nodded.

"It's tight here." She laid her hand on her chest. "That's how I felt in Hamburg. There was this pressure, like I couldn't get enough air."

"Then it is good you are here again," Hamza said. "There is air all around here. You can breathe, Luise. I will look out for you."

"Yes, I know that. Thank you, Hamza."

He hummed some more, then sang a song Luise had heard during harvest time. She hummed and sang along and was sorry when they came to where the road branched off to the plantation. She would have liked to go on humming and singing and dancing with him all day. She looked at the house that welcomed her, bright and friendly in the sunlight. She was back home. Finally!

She was mostly at her father's side during the following days. On Sunday they had to face questions from the German churchgoers about Elisabeth's and Martha's whereabouts. The official version was that they would stay in Hamburg for a while because of important matters regarding Martha's schooling, but they would come after it was sorted out. That Elisabeth would never again set foot in Cameroon could always be explained later. The rest was no one else's concern.

Another thing had caught the interest of the local Germans a great deal more, anyway: there had been raids that were attributed to the Bantu. Until then, it had just been the theft of goods, but many Germans were worried it might not stop there. Felicitas Leffers, Raimund's mother, feared that people who once thought relations with the natives were quite simple would soon suffer the consequences of their mistake. There was a general consensus among the Germans that an end must be put to these raids at once.

After church, Robert was monosyllabic on the way back to the plantation.

Luise couldn't tell if he was concerned or angered at the derogatory way the other Germans spoke about the natives.

It was after the second harvest, so everybody had less to do. Hamza helped Luise construct a pen for the rabbits, where they could run around, find some shade, and cool off in a little watering hole.

"What do you know about the Bantu?" Luise asked as they pounded a post into the ground.

"We are Bantu," Hamza answered.

Luise straightened up. "But I thought you were Duala?"

Hamza thought for a moment. "You are German."

"Yes."

"And where your homeland is, you are Hamburg."

"I am from Hamburg, yes."

"I am Duala. And I am Bantu."

Luise couldn't quite follow.

Hamza picked up a stick and drew a small face in the sand. "That is Hamza." He drew a circle around it. "Hamza is Duala together with the others here." Then he made a circle around it all before scratching a few more faces in the sand. "That is the Bakoko tribe." He circled it again and drew more heads inside it. "That is Mabea tribe." He dragged the stick around all the heads in a large circle. "Duala, Bakoko, Mabea, all are Bantu."

"I understand," Luise said. "I am from Hamburg. But there are people from Berlin, Frankfurt, Munich . . . and we all are Germans."

Hamza's face lit up. "Yes, exactly."

Luise went back to the posts. "Then the Germans are absolutely wrong. They made it sound like the Bantu were a separate tribe. They are said to have carried out raids."

Hamza shook his head. "The men who did steal do not belong to a tribe anymore. They were Oroko until the tribe chief throw them out."

"Until the tribe's chief *threw* them out."

Hamza repeated her words.

"I understand. I'll talk to my father about this. I think the Germans have a totally wrong idea."

"I do not like the men who did that," Hamza said. "My father says they are bad for the Duala, and everybody. They have not . . . I do not know the word . . . they do not help the tribe."

"You mean they don't feel associated with it?"

Hamza thought about whether her words could express what he was trying to say. "Associated," he repeated. "Every one of them only takes things he needs himself. Not for others."

"Sounds like us Germans," Luise remarked with a shake of her head.

Hamza didn't know what she meant, so continued, "Your father must tell the other Germans that the Duala do not like these men, too."

"I will, Hamza, I promise."

It was already dusk by the time they'd finished their work. Luise was satisfied and looking forward to putting Caesar and his still-unnamed companions into the pen. She wanted to help Hamza carry the cage, but he said no and went to get it himself. When they'd moved the rabbits into the pen, the animals quickly crept into their shelter, sizing up their new home. Luise and Hamza waited a little before deciding to leave the rabbits in peace and return to the farmhouse.

Luise was surprised to see that Sigmund Leffers, Raimund's father and the kaiser's envoy, was paying them a visit. They'd never had a visitor during all that time in Cameroon. They only met other people during the get-togethers after church.

"Good evening."

Luise approached, and Leffers stood up and extended a hand of welcome.

"Fräulein Luise."

"Sigmund has come to discuss the current situation. Come join us, Luise. This concerns you, too."

Hamza waited off the veranda.

"I'll go and quickly freshen up and be right back," Luise said. "Hamza, I'll see you tomorrow."

Hamza raised his hand. "Good night, Luise," he said. "Good night, *sango*."

"Good night, Hamza," Robert replied, waving to Malambuku's son.

"He calls your daughter by her given name?" Luise heard Leffers ask. She paused behind the door to hear her father's answer.

"Yes. Hamza and Luise have become friends. She doesn't like him to address her formally."

"If you ask me, a friendship between a German and a native is out of the question. It may concur with our desire to treat them humanely, but ultimately we must see them for what they are: animals who do our bidding."

Luise blinked.

"Really? Is that how you see people here?" her father responded.

"We all do. Otherwise we wouldn't be here, making our fortunes by enslaving the natives, but most aren't honest enough to admit it. Our kaiser conquered this country, and it is our duty to tame and civilize the savages."

Luise brushed back her hair and stood up straight. She pushed aside the idea of washing up; she was enraged by what she'd just heard. She took a resolute step out from behind the door and sat down at the table.

"So, Sigmund"—Robert eyed the man opposite him—"would you please tell Luise what you just told me?"

"Of course. You mustn't worry, Luise. The kaiser is sending men to guarantee our security. But there have been some incidents we cannot ignore. As you probably heard after church, there are some men from the Bantu tribe who are acting rebelliously."

"The Bantu are not a tribe," Luise replied, unfazed.

"What do you mean?" Leffers wondered.

"Bantu is a collective term for all the tribes around here," Luise said, correcting him. "It's as if you said that there are no Berliners, just Germans."

Robert grinned. He suspected she'd heard Leffers's disparaging words about the natives.

"It has been reported to me otherwise," Leffers said.

"Well, I know it from the people here. And they surely know which tribe they belong to."

"Luise," her father cautioned.

"I beg your pardon. But in my opinion there is much that we Germans do not understand, yet we presume to judge the situation. I admit this disturbs me."

"Without wishing to offend you, Luise, I wonder if you might identify too much with the natives."

"Identify? In what way?" She cocked her head and gave him a friendly look. But anyone who knew her would know that she was seething.

"Well, in the sense that you harbor too much sympathy for them."

"But who *wouldn't* find these warmhearted, honest people sympathetic? Who wouldn't be grateful that they ensure us a good income and make our accomplishments possible?"

"They are the workers and we are their masters, Luise. Is that not clear? We are superior to them in every way. And with that superiority comes the responsibility to lead the simpleminded."

The corners of Luise's mouth twitched. "Perhaps I haven't the time to fully comprehend what you've said. But the people absolutely do not seem stupid at all, let alone inferior in any way. In fact, we learn a lot from them. They just don't show it plainly because they don't want to embarrass us."

Leffers shook his head. "Robert, who taught your daughter such nonsense?"

Luise watched her father carefully, afraid of his answer.

"Me, of course," he said, and Luise breathed a sigh of relief. "In any case, I think we won't arrive at any consensus here."

"You wish, then, to withdraw from the coalition of the Germans?"

"Not at all. We'll stay in the community and do everything to ensure its success. And if it comes to fighting those responsible for the attacks, we will happily be at your side. Along with our Duala."

Leffers rose to his feet. "That is not quite what I hoped for, but we at least agree in this respect."

"Essentially, yes." Robert stood up also and offered Leffers his hand in goodbye.

"Luise," Leffers said, and made a slight bow and walked back to his horse. He whipped the horse's flank without waiting for his servant.

"Sorry if I spoke rashly," Luise said.

"Our behavior wasn't particularly astute," Robert said, and went over to Luise and stood behind her in her chair, putting his hands on her shoulders. "But I can't stomach that inhumane blather." He kissed her head.

"Do you think things could become dangerous?"

"Maybe. But I'll never discuss it with a person like Leffers. I'll ask Malambuku about it in the morning. His counsel is more valuable."

"I'm glad you don't think like the rest of the Germans."

"And unfortunately, with one exception, we Germans aren't even the worst. Take the English, the French—they all think they can enslave the natives and abuse them for their purposes."

"One exception?"

"Carl Peters." Robert sat back down facing his daughter.

She shrugged. "I don't know him."

"He's the founder of the colony of German East Africa. That's his official title. Truth is, he's a butcher planning to completely subjugate the natives and slaughter everybody who won't submit. Wherever Peters goes, he leaves many bodies behind."

Luise covered her mouth in horror.

Robert rubbed his tired eyes. "I don't want to scare you. It's been a hard day. I'll talk to Malambuku tomorrow. Then we'll decide where we'll go from there."

"Where is he now?"

"With his people in the village. Some of them caught the fever, and he's trying to help."

"Good. I'll go and tidy myself up and be right back." She rose.

"Didn't you do that already?"

Luise felt caught and blurted out, "No, I heard what Leffers was saying and wanted to be with you."

"I thought so." Robert chuckled. "Now get a move on. I'm hungry."

"I will," she replied. "Me, too."

Chapter Fourteen

Hamburg, End of April 1889

"You *can't* do that!"

A furious Elisabeth paced back and forth in Georg's office.

"I'm only doing what your husband asked me to do," Georg explained. "And he's right. He's providing you with an income. You can't ask more of him than that."

"With an income?" She stopped to glare at him in anger. "Feeding me can hardly be called an income."

"What do you expect, Elisabeth, after what you did to him? A bed of roses?"

"*I* did to *him*? You are mad. How is it that nobody sees what *he's* done to *me*? He dragged me off to Africa and kept me like an animal."

"Elisabeth, please. I know my brother well enough to know that's not true."

"Oh really? Ask Martha, she'll tell you. Everything there is dirty, and there are savages all over, waiting to kill you."

"Robert says he has very reliable natives working for him."

"They are *Negroes*, Georg! They run with naked torsos and a flimsy cloth below that is lifted by the slightest gust of wind. Georg, now I ask *you*, is that a life for a Hamburg society woman?"

"Robert is doing it for *us*, Elisabeth," Georg said pointedly. "Have you really not grasped that? He's not in Cameroon because he wants to be there. He's there to make money for the family." He paused to consider whether he should tell her what he was thinking. "Do you know how badly off we were before your husband made that courageous decision?"

Elisabeth sat in front of Georg's desk. "No. How was I to know? You never spoke a word to us about finances."

"Because you only want to be taken care of. You and Vera don't care where the money's coming from," Georg remonstrated.

"That's *not* fair, Georg. You keep us out of everything, don't share any information, and then accuse us of not understanding anything."

Georg swallowed his annoyance. His sister-in-law wasn't entirely wrong, though he'd never seen her or his wife show even a passing interest in the family's business.

"If you want to know the details, we were a hair's breadth away from having to sell the villa."

Elisabeth opened her eyes wide in shock. "The *villa*?"

"Yes, the villa. We couldn't service our debt anymore, and we owe it to Robert alone that our banker, Palm, gave us one final postponement. It's only because of Robert's plantation scheme and the profit he made that Palm could be persuaded."

Georg didn't say that the deciding factor had been the mention of August Frederiksen as the potential new owner of the villa.

Elisabeth kneaded her fingers nervously. "I had no idea," she admitted in a small voice.

"If Robert hadn't gotten up his courage and gone to Cameroon, you wouldn't be in the villa right now but in some apartment somewhere, happy just to have enough to eat."

Elisabeth covered her face with her hands. "I am ashamed of myself, Georg," she said, bursting into tears.

Georg took out his handkerchief and handed it to her. "You and your husband ought to have discussed it more thoroughly," he said. "Then maybe you would be with him where you belong."

Elisabeth dabbed her tears away. "I suppose I would be with him. But that's not where I belong." She looked at him, red eyed. "I think that Robert and I simply don't belong together. I should never have married him."

"The very idea! You've enjoyed many happy years together."

She shook her head. "No, we have not. Robert was never the man I wanted." She took a deep breath.

"No." She lifted her head. "I only chose him so I could be near you."

Georg looked at her, stunned. "That's absurd, Elisabeth."

"No. It is time I told you. I will start to be honest now, after more than eighteen years."

"I really don't follow."

"Do you remember when we met, Georg?"

"I don't recall." He thought hard. "It was at some function, right?"

"Quite right. It was at the Rudolfs'. My father introduced us, and yes, Georg, I fell in love with you right then and there."

Georg looked at her incredulously. "Honestly, I can't believe it."

"Why not?"

"You've never given the slightest hint."

"You were already engaged to Vera, and I had no right to come between you two. Besides, the feelings were unrequited."

Georg looked at her in a way she couldn't interpret. "I'll grant one thing. I've never thought you two were a good fit."

"Neither are you and Vera."

"You think not?"

"Of course. We both know she hasn't made you happy."

"You really think that?"

146

Elisabeth stopped him with a wave of her hand. "Well, that has nothing to do with me."

Georg looked at her, thinking for a minute before clearing his throat. "I'm sorry, Elisabeth, but I can't give you more than Robert has allowed for," he declared, returning to the initial topic of their conversation.

Elisabeth got to her feet. "No matter. One thing has become clear to me."

"Which is?"

"I ought to move out of the villa."

"But, Elisabeth, where will you go? Into an apartment with Martha?"

"It is a nightmare, I know. But I have been fooling myself for too long."

"You would be ostracized from society, and that's so important to you."

"I am aware of that. But how can I go on like this?"

"The important thing is not to be hasty. The situation is difficult. But I'm convinced that you and Robert will get it under control."

"But I do not love him . . ."

"There'll be nobody in your apartment who you love either. So why give up your position? At some point, I'm sure Robert will leave Cameroon behind."

Elisabeth went to Georg and stood beside him, looking down at him. "I'll think more about it. Many thanks for your advice."

She brushed his cheek tenderly and left without another word.

As she rode back to the villa, she mulled everything over. Clever, well-considered tactics were crucial. Needless to say, she hadn't intended for a moment to move out of the villa into an apartment. Never! She had needs, after all, primarily for social standing. She had to manage to paint Robert as a bad husband while saying only good things about him and building up some understanding for future ploys. No easy task. But she would not be Elisabeth Hansen if she caved at this point.

Her little scene with Georg had been improvised. She'd wanted to get him to guarantee her a monthly sum that would cover her passion for the finer things in life. It was not in her nature to be spontaneous, but she saw the look on his face and recognized the doubt she'd kindled in him. Or was it lust?

By the time she arrived at the villa, she'd designed a plan. She smiled as she left the carriage and glanced up at the villa's facade. A genuinely beautiful building, one that was worthy of her. She was determined not to let a day go by where she didn't do everything within her power to satisfy her desires. Hers and Martha's, whose future lay in her hands alone. She climbed up the front stairs with a firm tread.

Upon entering the house, she heard voices in the parlor.

"I'm back," she said, opening the door.

"Oh, Elisabeth." Vera appeared distraught, talking with her son.

"What happened?" Elisabeth asked.

"Come in and close the door," her sister-in-law said in a conspiratorial tone of voice.

Elisabeth sat down beside Vera on the couch; Richard was in the armchair opposite.

"Here." Vera handed her a letter. "When Georg sees this, I don't know what will happen."

Elisabeth skimmed the contents. "So you might have to leave the school without graduating?"

Richard made a fist. "It's not my fault. Well, not only. The teachers have it in for me. Maybe because I'm a Hansen, I don't know."

"Why should they have something against the Hansen family?" Elisabeth asked, puzzled.

"Stop it!" Vera answered. "Don't pay any attention to his excuses, Elisabeth. My son is just looking for a scapegoat to hide his own failures."

"What have you been up to?" Elisabeth asked her nephew. "One does not receive a letter such as this just because of poor grades."

"There was something going on. But I just went along with it. It wasn't my idea."

"What did you do?" Vera gave him a harsh look. "You tell me the whole truth now, or God help you!"

"There's a stand near the school where apple farmers sell cider. We gradually bought up all the cider and never returned the empties. Well, anyway . . . Eberhard and Matthias lured the farmer away, and we switched out the bottles."

"What do you mean?"

"We took the bottles we'd collected over the last few weeks, and when the farmer was away with Eberhard and Matthias, we switched the cider and beer bottles, and when the farmer came back, he sold beer to everybody and didn't realize it." He couldn't resist a grin. "The bottles sold like never before once the other students discovered what was in them. Almost everybody got blind drunk."

"If you laugh, Richard, you'll get a beating, I swear it!" Vera said, raising her hand.

"Who else was in on it? Who are Eberhard and Matthias?"

"Eberhard Breitenbaum and Matthias Wittbold. They got the same letter."

"Who else?" Vera kept pushing.

Richard shook his head. "He only helped us with the switch because I asked him to. I won't say who."

"You tell me right now who else was involved!" Vera demanded.

Richard looked her squarely in the eye. "Nobody knows he helped, and I won't betray him."

"Your father will punish you if you don't tell us his name, you can count on it!"

"Bah! Father punish me?" He raised his eyebrows. "If you say so. But I won't tell you his name no matter what."

Vera turned to Elisabeth for help. "What am I to do?"

Elisabeth thought for a minute. "Nothing at all." She stood up. "Is the principal still there?" she asked Richard.

"I think so. They gave me the letter this morning and said I had to leave school right away. I didn't come home directly. I just walked around for a while. But classes are still on. I don't know if Big Cheeks Hajo is still there."

"Big Cheeks Hajo?" Elisabeth looked at him, mystified.

"Hajo Feldkamp, the principal. He looks like a hamster, so somebody came up with the nickname."

Elisabeth sighed. "Stand up and come with me."

"What are you going to do?" Vera got up, too.

"I'll go with Richard to the school and try to clear up this matter. Your father will find out about it nevertheless and will certainly not be happy. It would be better if we make an agreement with the principal and present your father with that."

"You'll take him there?" Vera hugged her sister-in-law. "Thank you so much! I'm no good at these things and would likely just start to cry." She paused. "Or should we wait for Georg?"

"Georg has plenty to do at the office. And I've caused you distress and worry by not returning to Cameroon. If I can begin to make up for it in this way, I wish to try."

"You two go, and I'll keep my fingers crossed that all this can be laid to rest somehow." Vera hugged Elisabeth again, looked angrily at Richard, and called for a carriage.

"Let's be off." Elisabeth pointed to the door. "And you will do what I tell you and not make any insolent remarks!"

"Yes, Aunt Elisabeth," Richard responded sullenly.

"Good. Now come. And straighten your jacket and pants. Even if you can't see it, the next few hours will determine your whole future."

Richard nodded, looking intimidated. They didn't exchange a word during the whole ride. Richard became more and more nervous and was visibly uncomfortable, but Elisabeth was completely lost in thought.

She could not grasp her good luck at how this played into her hands. She'd already formed a plan but didn't know how to convert it into action. But that had changed thanks to her nephew's misconduct. She would fight for him as she never would have done under normal circumstances; she'd do anything she could to fend off the ominous punishment—presumably expulsion. She hadn't figured out how exactly she was going to sort everything out, but she would make a go of it. Not for Richard, God forbid, but for her own sake.

When the carriage stopped at the school, Elisabeth coached her nephew carefully on what to say. Richard promised he would follow it to the letter.

"Principal Feldkamp will see you now," the secretary said after Elisabeth had introduced themselves and urgently requested a meeting with the principal.

"Good day, Principal Feldkamp. My name is Elisabeth Hansen, and I am this young man's aunt. Thank you very much for seeing us."

Elisabeth saw how apt the nickname Big Cheeks was. The short, squat gentleman did indeed have the face of a hamster.

"Frau Hansen, it is a pleasure to meet you, though the circumstances are most problematic."

"They certainly are." She held out her hand for him to kiss.

"Please, sit down."

Elisabeth thanked him and chose one of the chairs, Richard the other. She unfolded Richard's letter and addressed her nephew.

"What do you wish to say to Principal Feldkamp?"

"I want to apologize for my childish and inappropriate behavior and accept the punishment for my misconduct. It was my idea, and I request that my friends not be punished for it. I have neglected to show the school proper respect, which is a serious transgression and must have consequences."

Elisabeth was pleased. Richard had said word for word what she had told him beforehand. Whatever the scholastic failings of her nephew, memorization wasn't among them.

Principal Feldkamp studied Richard carefully.

"Well-chosen words, Hansen. It was indeed a grave offense."

"And that is exactly the reason my nephew will accept any punishment, no matter how severe."

"We asked your nephew for the name of the fourth accomplice, but he has refused to divulge it."

"Now in that regard, I support my nephew, even if it may appear disconcerting. We Hansens protect those to whom we feel honor bound."

"But, Frau Hansen, he is a delinquent and deserves to be punished."

"Well now, I would not call this young man a delinquent," Elisabeth contended. "He probably did not realize the full consequences of his actions until the moment the others were caught. He made a mistake. But now he not only realizes he has done something seriously wrong, he has also learned what genuine friendship, honor, and loyalty mean. A precious possession, don't you think? If I understand Richard correctly, these are the very values your institution has dedicated itself to. Unless I am mistaken?"

"He told you that?"

"Yes, and not only today. For that reason my nephew is ashamed of himself—and for another: the feeling, Principal Feldkamp, that he has disappointed you personally. And that is why he wishes to take punishment upon himself alone, though I told him you will find out no matter what that it was not his idea at all. But a wrong is a wrong and always will be, and Richard recognizes that. We will accept whatever punishment you deem appropriate without argument, even if it should mean that Richard will be denied the privilege of being further instructed at this school."

"It wasn't his idea?" the principal followed up.

"That is not important. Richard understands that only by dealing impeccably with the present situation can he show that he has internalized the values imparted here and thus show himself worthy of the education that he has received."

"His punishment would be substantially more lenient if he says who thought up this wretched prank."

Elisabeth looked at Richard. "Would you be so kind as to go outside for a minute so I may speak to Principal Feldkamp in private?"

"Yes, Aunt," Richard said, standing up straightway.

"Thank you."

She waited until he'd closed the door before turning back to the principal.

"I should like to tell you something in confidence, Principal Feldkamp, and I ask you urgently that my words not leave this room."

"I give you my word on it, Frau Hansen."

"One only has to look into your eyes to know that you are the kind of man one can trust." She took a deep breath as though speaking her next words would be difficult. "Richard is going through a difficult time. I presume word has spread about it already . . . Richard's mother is, how shall I put it, not particularly stable at the moment."

"What's the matter with her?"

"A nervous disorder, presumably. She has had problems for years, the poor woman, and her husband, Georg, my brother-in-law, suffers with her. The burden on the family is enormous. It weighs so heavily that I have decided not to live with my husband in Cameroon—where he runs a very successful plantation—but to support my sister-in-law and protect my nephew and my niece as much as possible. They are helpless, of course, as far as their mother's conduct is concerned."

"How terrible! I had no idea. I did hear that your husband runs a plantation in Africa and you live in Hamburg, but the rest was unknown to me."

"It is hard on all of us. And I sympathize with my sister-in-law, who often is unable to help herself, as . . ." She broke off. "No, I cannot discuss the details."

"No need to, my dear Frau Hansen. I understand fully, most fully."

"Thank you, Principal Feldkamp." Elisabeth brushed a tear aside with her finger. "I must say it is a relief to be able to speak openly here."

"If I had known the family's situation, I would, of course, have assessed Richard's lapse completely differently."

"You are most kind."

She leaned forward, laid her hand on his, and squeezed it quickly before sitting back upright.

"But Richard doesn't want special treatment. He made a mistake, and he knows it. I would like you to understand his emotional state and that he only allowed himself to be talked into this stupid prank because his friends offered him a degree of support. Which I likewise try to provide. Of course, it's not easy to be there for everyone—my daughter, my brother-in-law, his children—and protect Vera, Richard's mother, from herself, if you understand my meaning."

The principal shook his head. "I have seen your sister-in-law on several occasions. It would never have crossed my mind that she suffered so behind her flawless comportment."

"You cannot tell by looking, it is true. Do you know, I sometimes think if people knew how she really is, it might be easier on her. Of course, I am aware that you must tell Richard's teachers about his mother's condition. But I implore you to ask your staff to swear never to speak to Vera or Georg about this directly—they would be humiliated."

"I give you my word."

"As it is, I suppose many of them will guess what afflicts Vera. But please understand me: I wish to protect my family."

"You are sacrificing yourself, Frau Hansen. That must require a great deal of strength. Do please look after yourself."

"Of course, it has become more difficult since my husband has been in Cameroon. Now here I am, a wife without a husband and no longer a welcome guest. But I can endure it if I can help Vera in this way." She wiped the corner of her eye again.

"If there is anything at all I can do to make your life any easier, I will gladly do it. Please do not hesitate to turn to me in complete confidence."

"I thank you. I should like to know how you intend to punish my nephew." She forced a smile.

"It was just a prank, and nobody was harmed," he summarized. "I will issue a recommendation to caution him in hopes that he will not be led to behave so mischievously ever again."

"And what consequences might this caution bring with it?"

"None. This was not the first time your nephew has attracted attention. But in view of what you have just told me, I am impressed at his mostly irreproachable behavior. He needs strong people around him now who will help him find his way. We at the school will do our best to support him."

"I can scarcely believe it. You are a most understanding man, Principal Feldkamp."

"Well, well, it's the least . . ."

Elisabeth stood up, as did the principal.

"I shall place no further claim on your time. I hope that we will have the chance for another conversation under pleasanter circumstances."

"It was an honor for me, Frau Hansen." He made a gesture of kissing her hand.

"Goodbye, Herr Feldkamp."

Elisabeth walked to the door, paused for a moment to brush away a few tears, and left the office.

"Come, Richard," she said simply, and after saying goodbye to the secretary, she and Richard left the school.

"Well?" Richard asked after they were on the way home.

"I think I shall have to stand by you more often in the future. And I expect a radical change in your behavior."

"Yes, Aunt Elisabeth."

"Do not just say, 'Yes, Aunt Elisabeth,' but comport yourself accordingly. You'll refrain from any nonsense in the future and will work harder. Yes, your father will find out about this, but I will see to it that you receive no further punishment."

"And what's my punishment from the school?"

She looked at him, and a smile played around her lips. "You will receive a caution."

"And what else?"

"Nothing else. That is everything. Your behavior will have no further consequences."

Richard's eyes grew large. "How did you do it?"

"I can be very convincing when I need to be. Keep close to me in the future."

"Thank you," Richard gasped, relieved. "Honestly, thank you very much!"

She nodded.

"Aunt Elisabeth, may I ask you something?"

"Certainly."

"Why are you helping me?"

"Because you are my nephew, and I see that your mother doesn't support you sufficiently. Excuse my frankness. Best if that stays between us."

"Of course."

"Good. I will offer you the future support that she can't or won't give. Just rely on me. Things will sort themselves out."

Richard was impressed. He'd never heard his aunt talk like that, and he couldn't recall her ever taking any special interest in him. But that she cleared up this matter so efficiently drew a measure of admiration from him—most of all because there were no consequences for him. Maybe she wasn't as cold as he'd thought after all and it was just not in her nature to show particularly warm feelings for him and Frederike. His aunt had fought for him and intended to stand by him in the future. He made a decision not to disappoint her.

When they arrived at the villa and stepped down from the carriage, he offered Elisabeth his arm.

"About time I began to act like a man," he declared.

She smiled at him. "That, my dear Richard, would be very much to my liking."

Chapter Fifteen

Vienna, Mid-August 1889

Dear Georg,

We are finally ready; the office is now open. Who would have thought it would drag out for so long? Therese and I are relieved because there were times when we doubted this would end well. The water damage from the defective pump was considerable, and after we'd fixed the pump, we had to wait a month for everything to dry before we could go back to work. That was stressful not just for both of us, but also for the friends helping us renovate. I feared that someone wouldn't show up the next day or that I might lose friends if a sharp word happened to escape my lips out of impatience. But they are all still there and celebrated joyfully with us at the opening ceremony. Now that most of the work is complete, and we can finally do business properly here, Therese and I hope to get a little rest.

Do you know when Robert will be in Germany so we can all celebrate our wedding together? How are things at home and with the company? Is the warehouse still well stocked? I can now store more beans if you'd like to send a shipment. The supply I've got left will hardly last until Robert brings in the next harvest.

We hope you are all in the best of health and that we may soon expect a letter from you. We haven't seen one another for far too long, and as soon as the business and the café permit, we'd love to come to Hamburg for a couple of days. I miss you all very much.

With all my heart,
Your loving brother Karl

Karl sighed as he read the letter through and placed it in the envelope. What he'd written was an understatement. Recent months had demoralized him and Therese. They were exhausted, not just from the heavy work but more from the setbacks caused by the water damage and the ensuing delays. At times they'd forgotten how to laugh, in the truest sense of the word, so that the joyfulness that prevailed between them had given way to tension. Karl firmly made up his mind that this must change. He intended to do everything possible to return to the easy cheerfulness that had brought them together at the beginning.

It wasn't only the heavy workload that strained the couple's relationship. There was another reason, presumably more critical, though Karl hated to bring it up to his wife. Clearly, she exaggerated when she said they had enjoyed only a few cuddles and caresses. Yes, they had made love fewer than a dozen times in the months they'd shared a bed. But wasn't that reasonable, given all the work they had to get done? As much as he loved his wife, he hated that she brought up the subject time and again. She was almost obsessed, as if nothing were more important in the life of any married couple. That was absurd. It bothered him most of all that Therese's questions made him feel guilty, though she always said she didn't mean to. And just as often, when they did make love, he couldn't achieve the necessary stiffness. Therese had been understanding, and they both faulted the workload. But in his mind, Karl was anxious about it; he was tortured by the feeling he wasn't a real man.

Therese had asked him once if he would go to a doctor to see if there was a potential cause. He dismissed her harshly, saying it was ridiculous and that any further questions on the subject would not be tolerated. Therese had stormed out in anger and hadn't returned until some hours later. Karl lay on his side and feigned sleep. But he heard her creep into bed and cry softly.

What could he do? He'd known for some time that something wasn't right. And he didn't want a doctor to confirm it under any circumstances. The few times he'd made love with Therese had been a strenuous effort. He'd had to summon images in his mind's eye to excite himself and give himself some rigidity for a while, images that did not include his wife. Karl felt bad about it because it seemed like cheating on Therese, although it was only in his head. He couldn't understand it. Therese was attractive, beautiful, in fact; had a kind disposition; and loved him. And he loved her in return and felt devoted to her. But he didn't have the least interest in sleeping with her.

How long could he keep Therese close before she rejected him completely and their marriage would become like so many others that lasted only because of exchanged rings and a piece of paper? He asked himself bitterly if it made any sense at all to stage a second church ceremony to celebrate their wedding again when their marriage almost looked as if it had failed already. But he didn't want to give up just yet. He *had* to make it work, to banish those images from his mind that made him hate himself so much. They brought him nothing but grief and prevented him from having the life with Therese that they wished to have. He must put an end to it!

He brought the letter to the post office. On the way home, he went over everything in his mind thoroughly one more time. He did not want to lose Therese. Everything had to change from that day on. His wife deserved to be happy. And he, too. He would see to it. Therese was the most important person in his life. He did not want to lose her; he *must* not.

When he opened the apartment door, he heard voices in the kitchen: Therese's bell-like laughter and a man talking. She gave another merry laugh.

"Good evening," Karl said as he entered.

"Ah, my dear brother-in-law, you're back!" Florentinus got up, hugged him, and clapped him on the shoulder.

"I had some business in Vienna and didn't want to miss an opportunity to see you two."

Karl was genuinely happy. Florentinus had kept his Christmastime promise and visited them often. He'd become a welcome guest at their apartment the past few months.

Karl gave Therese a tender kiss on the mouth. "Good evening, my little sunshine." He nearly always called her that and was just as reliably rewarded with a smile.

"Good evening. I'm afraid I haven't started dinner. Florentinus and I lost track of the time talking."

"There's sure to be something edible," Karl said, giving her another kiss, this time on the forehead.

"Since I'm the cause, I'd like to make amends by taking us all out to a restaurant," Florentinus said. "Come on, you two. It will appease my guilty conscience."

Therese and Karl looked at each other, and Therese nodded. "I hope you've enough money on you. I'm hungry as a horse."

Karl quickly washed up. Therese used the time to pin up her hair again and put on some eau de toilette Karl had given her for her birthday. The three of them then went to Piaristenkeller, a fine, old, traditional Viennese restaurant. Therese ordered the day's special, while Karl and Florentinus both chose veal schnitzel with sides. They drank a bottle of wine and ordered a second before the first was finished. The pressure of recent days seemed to vanish into thin air; they were carefree and exuberant. Therese and Karl kept touching one another lovingly during the meal, exchanging glances and tender caresses.

"If you turtledoves would excuse me for a minute," Florentinus said, standing. "Nature calls."

"Therese," Karl started to say the moment Florentinus was out of earshot, "I've been thinking a lot about us and want to tell you something."

"Sure."

"The thing we've talked about a lot recently . . . you know?"

"Yes?"

"I'd like us to pay more attention to each other. I'm going to make a serious effort. You are the most important person in the world to me. My life would be pointless without you."

She squeezed his hand and looked deep into his eyes. "I'm so glad you said that."

"Who cares about work? All the money in the world isn't worth it if we don't have each other."

"That's right. You've made me very happy."

They gazed lovingly at each other as Florentinus returned to the table.

"I've ordered another bottle," he announced, and sat down.

"Another?" Therese looked at him wide-eyed. "Tino, it's the middle of the week, and we have an early morning. Well, Karl and I at least."

"Oh, my dear little sister, don't always be so reasonable. There's something to celebrate."

"Well. What?"

"Well, today's Wednesday."

"And?"

"Wednesday, August 14, 1889."

"And?"

"Well, it's a holiday. A major holiday." He raised his glass. "Everybody knows that, and I'll drink to it."

The trio clinked glasses.

"Florentinus Loising, you're completely insane!" Therese gave a hearty laugh, hiccupped, and closed her eyes briefly. "Oh dear. Hiccups. I think I'm a little tipsy."

"Just a little? That's not enough," Florentinus said, and laughed when the waiter appeared and refilled their glasses.

When they left half an hour later, Florentinus paid and took the half-full bottle along.

"You haven't seen our new office yet," Karl said with a bit of a thick tongue. "Come on. Let's go to the office, and I'll boast about it properly."

"No," Therese replied. "I want to go to my bed."

"Come on, Therese, for my sake," Karl implored her. "I desperately want to show off to my brother-in-law, just for a bit."

Therese couldn't stop yawning. She pointed a finger straight ahead. "I will go straight down this street and home. The two of you will turn left, and you, my dear love, can show Tino the office. But I'm going to bed."

Karl protested, but she was already on her way.

"I'll leave a blanket and pillow on the chaise longue," she promised her brother. "And you two be very quiet when you come home, understand?"

"Yes, madame." Karl bowed, almost losing his balance. Florentinus grabbed him before he fell over.

"Fervent thanks, dear brother-in-law, my fervent thanks," Karl said, and Florentinus laughed.

Arm in arm and singing loudly, the two of them headed for Karl's office and stopped in front of the facade.

"All this is mine," Karl declared, and made a wide, sweeping gesture that almost cost him his balance again.

"The Hansen Company," Florentinus read on the sign over the entrance.

"The Viennese Hansen, that's me." Karl thumped his chest, fumbled for the key, and opened the door on the fourth try. "Be you pleased to enter, Herr Loising."

"I thank you so very, very much, Herr Hansen. After you. I insist." Florentinus bowed as deeply as he could without staggering.

Karl entered. "Let there be light." He flipped the switch beside the door, and the room was illuminated by electric light.

Florentinus exclaimed excitedly. "So bright!" He went around the room, taking in the scent of cocoa beans. Dark wooden shelves stood behind the waist-high counter stacked with large china containers standing neatly next to one another. The goods were ready and waiting for customers to make their selection.

"The previous owner was one of the first here to install electricity." Karl made another sweeping gesture. "Impressive, isn't it?"

Florentinus slid a hand over the counter as he took in the space. "Herr Hansen, I must say, you've made a real jewel out of this old ruin."

"Thank you, Herr Loising, a thousand thanks. I'll drink to that."

Karl grabbed the bottle out of Florentinus's hand and took a good swig before handing it back.

"Come this way. I'll show you the storage area."

They went through a door in the back, where Karl switched on another light. Here, too, racks were hung on the walls, but in a lighter color than those in the salesroom; they held sacks with various labels and identifying marks.

"It's all coffee and cocoa, anywhere you look."

"I'll drink to your success, Karl!" Florentinus lifted the bottle and drank deeply.

"To success!" Karl took the bottle and drank the last drop before putting it down on the floor and looking around. "This used to be stuffed with textiles, did you know that? Filled to the brim. But you can make more money with beans," he went on.

"You and Therese have done so much." Florentinus walked to the nearest rack, ran his hand over the rough sacking, and leaned against the wall. "I wish I had your courage."

"Courage? It's nothing to try to stand on your own two feet. *You* are the one with courage. You've had to measure yourself against your father's success every day."

Florentinus smiled. "No, I'll never be able to hold a candle to him. They don't say it, but I'm a failure in their opinion."

"You? The firm is better off than ever, isn't it?"

"Money . . . It's just money. But what's here, you can see it and touch it. Passion and sweat are in these walls. You have built something. I'll never manage to do that my whole life."

"And here I had thought you never doubted yourself," Karl said, taking a step closer. "My wife's successful big brother, always in a good mood, while success just falls into his lap."

Florentinus snorted. "Nonsense. Quite the opposite."

Karl looked at his brother-in-law. Something strange and exciting in an improper way radiated from Florentinus in that moment. Their eyes met; neither said a word.

Then Florentinus turned his head to the side. "Don't look at me like that. I can't bear it." He made eye contact again.

"What can't you bear?" Karl asked, his throat now feeling dry and rough.

Florentinus paused before pushing off from the rack and taking a step toward Karl so that they were very close. Florentinus raised a hand, stroked Karl's cheek, trailing down past his chin. "I love my sister, but I desire her husband."

Karl's heart was in his throat. He knew he ought to turn on his heel and leave as quickly as possible. That would be the right thing to do. Leave Florentinus there and forget what he'd just said forever. Instead he closed his eyes and drew nearer to his brother-in-law, until their lips met. A shiver ran through his whole body. He gingerly lifted his hand, put it on Florentinus's neck, and drew him closer. They embraced, holding on to each other like people drowning, their kisses growing more urgent, more demanding. Then they tore off their clothes and yielded absolutely to their desire. Nothing existed at that moment but the two of them and their longing for each other.

Afterward, breathless, they looked into each other's eyes and kissed once more. Neither said a word. When some time had passed, they dressed, picked up the empty wine bottle, and left.

Before Karl turned out the lights, he looked around the room again. Everything was the same as before. And yet what had just occurred would transform their lives forever. They left the building together, and Karl locked up.

"Therese must never know of this," he said without looking up.

"No," Florentinus answered. "Never."

They walked to the apartment in silence. Florentinus lay on the chaise longue, and Karl crept into bed with Therese. Neither slept a wink before the gray of dawn.

Chapter Sixteen

Cameroon, September 1889

Entry in Luise Hansen's diary:

September 2, 1889

I'm looking forward to harvest time, it's almost here. Hamza and I have been together every day for the last several weeks. I know him so well now, better than anybody else. We talk a lot, share our thoughts. He's learned to speak German fluently, almost perfectly. He told me in confidence that it was his greatest wish to go to Germany for some education so he could go into business for himself, despite his love for his people. Because of him, I realize how lucky I am to have been born in Germany and for the opportunities it's given me that I'd never have if I'd been born here. Yes, I'm a woman, but I have choices. And I've come to the conclusion that I don't want a life like my mother's or my aunt's. I want to stay here in Cameroon and take over Father's plantation one day.

I've had the same dream the last several nights in a row, and it is confusing and wonderful. I'm standing in front of the farmhouse and looking out over the plantation. There's no one else around, and I marvel at the stillness. I can't see anybody working on the plantation, so I go out to look. On the way, I hear children's bright laughter, and I'm reminded of the Duala in their village. As I get closer I see a young boy and a little girl, and then I recognize Hamza playing with them. He waves, and the children run to me, hug me, and call me Mother. Then Hamza kisses me, intimately and tenderly. Everything feels right, everything good. Neither of us says a word.

When I wake up, I need a moment to remember it was only a dream and Hamza is not my husband, but Malambuku's son. He's more to me than that, though I know that dream can never come true. We are on the same continent, in the same place, on the same plantation. Nevertheless, we live in different worlds. I wish he could actually go and live in Germany, though I would miss him with all my heart.

Father and I have talked a lot without Mother and Martha here. And we see a lot of things more clearly now. I don't think either one of us will ever return to Germany except for the occasional visit. And not only because of the plantation or the revenue but because Father and I realize that we don't belong there. It's odd. Hamza is burning with desire to go to Germany, and I'm longing just as much to stay here.

We went to church yesterday and talked to the other Germans as usual. I think there's a looming divide among us, with different opinions that will affect the life of everyone in the colony. To my surprise I've been getting along well with Raimund Leffers— Martha used to fancy him. He's just as different from his father as I am from my mother. I cannot stand Sigmund Leffers and the way he talks about the Africans, and what he says about conquering them and being their masters is absolutely sickening. Raimund sees it the same way, but it's impossible for him to avoid his father's ideas. Sometimes when Sigmund rants about the natives and says how stupid they are, I see Raimund lower his eyes in shame so as not to look at his father. I cherish the hope that he'll take over his father's position as the imperial envoy in a few years and show the natives the respect and esteem his father doesn't.

We keep hearing stories about real atrocities in East Africa that Carl Peters is said to have committed. Some Germans believe them; others don't. For my part I don't know what to make of them. Is it conceivable that a German man, whose father was a missionary with connections to the highest circles of society, can behave like that? Is it thinkable that any man could do what Peters is accused of doing? I can scarcely imagine it. And yet I hear his name again and again, and there have already been meetings with some tribal chiefs here in Cameroon who have heard these allegations and fear for their safety.

Sigmund Leffers has a strong opinion about it, of course. He said the natives are afraid for no reason because no German is stupid enough to kill them when they are more useful than pigs. Then he laughed, and Raimund and I looked at each other. I tried to console him by smiling sadly, but his despair over his father's words was unmistakable.

A letter arrived from Martha a few days ago. She said things were going well in Hamburg and Mother was much better. I don't know if I believe it, but I must admit I don't really care one way or the other. I feel so separated from Hamburg and life there that it would take more than one trip for me to return to my old life.

As I write this, I wonder what was really so important about Hamburg. And no matter how hard I try, I can't think of a single thing. On the other hand, everything that happens here touches our lives. Everything feels real: the colors in the sky; the animals on the steppe; the Duala and their rhythmic, melodic songs. No wasted words about morality and civility, solidarity and love. And yet these words are truly lived out, and with an intensity unlike anything I saw in Hamburg. It saddens me that I frittered away the first fifteen years of my life on superficial and mindless things. Here I can pick up a handful of soil and let the earth run through my fingers, feel the sun's rays on my skin, sweat from the hard work, and smile when I see a Duala mother holding her child protectively in her arms. Here nature is raw and yet beautiful—it bestows the beans on us.

I'm putting my pen down and will sleep until the sun turns the sky pink. I'm looking forward to that moment already.

Luise snapped her diary shut and put it back in her desk. Then she crawled under the sheets and closed her eyes. Several hours must have passed, but day hadn't broken when she was awakened by loud voices. She needed a few seconds to get oriented. Then she quickly put on her bathrobe and ran into the hallway. A babble of voices came from in front of the house. She couldn't figure out what was happening, so she raced down the stairs and outside.

Luise looked around—and her heart was in her throat. The smell of smoke nearly suffocated her. What had happened? Where was her father? She looked toward the forest and put a hand to her mouth in horror. Flames reached high into the night sky. Close to the plantation, but the flames hadn't reached it yet.

Luise ran back up to her room to put on pants and a blouse. She hastily tied her hair back and rushed out of the house, following some Duala running toward the fire. She saw her father helping pass pails of water from the reservoir above the plantation to a chain of natives attempting to fight the fire. She joined the line, handing the pails along.

The flames devoured the jungle piece by piece, moving toward the plantation. Luise saw Hamza shouting directions to his people. He looked wild-eyed at the flames, then at the reservoir. Luise ran to her father.

"We won't be able to do it like this, Father!" she shouted at him.

Robert didn't answer, just glanced up at her. Desperation was etched on his face. If the flames managed to get to the plantation, the harvest, the trees, and their whole future were lost.

Hamza shouted something Luise didn't understand. At this the Duala dropped their pails and followed him.

"Hey, where are you going? Come back!" Robert shouted after them, but nobody listened.

Under Hamza's direction the men began pounding the stones on the reinforced east bank of the reservoir, then pulling them out to allow the water to flow into the forest.

Luise stared up at the reservoir, transfixed. The water ran along a narrow pathway on the border between the plantation and the jungle, broadened out, then transformed into a torrent. The plantation's border was drenched as the water wet the trees and spread into the forest. The ground hissed as the fire was extinguished, but flames continued burning in the upper reaches of the trees. Hamza yelled again, and the Duala followed him, grabbed their machetes, and ran back to the forest, where they cut down wet branches that fell hissing into the flames. Luise got her machete and slashed wildly at the branches, working alongside the Duala as they moved ahead little by little.

The fire was pushed back farther and farther from the plantation so that it was contained. It took hours, but by the end only a small area of the forest was still burning, and she finally dropped her machete, completely exhausted.

Robert came to his daughter while Hamza rushed to the plantation to check on damage to the trees and fruit.

"We did it," Robert said, exhausted and sighing.

"Yes," said Luise, whose face was black with soot and whose unruly hair stuck out in every direction.

Hamza returned from the plantation with Malambuku.

"How bad is it?" Robert asked immediately.

Malambuku, whose expression betrayed nothing, grinned. "The fruits protected the beans," he reported.

Hamza nodded in confirmation. "The fruits were not hurt. The harvest will be good."

Luise and her father looked at each other and embraced. They wouldn't suffer much loss. Tears of relief welled up in Luise's eyes.

When they inspected everything later that day, they saw the fire had indeed been devastating, though the plantation had been spared. Smoke still rose from the forest and hung heavy in the air. Everything smelled of burnt wood, and Luise was alarmed to discover a layer of soot blanketing the rabbit pen. The animals had crept into their shelter and looked terrified when Luise pulled them out one by one. But apart from some ash on their coats, they were unhurt.

Malambuku, Hamza, Robert, and Luise went to the forest on the edge of the plantation.

"What do you think, Malambuku? What caused it?"

"The fire came from there," he said, pointing to where he meant. "Sometimes, when very warm for a long time, the fire comes."

"So you don't think it was set on purpose?"

Malambuku shook his head. "Why should anyone do that?"

Robert shrugged.

"I do not think it was set intentionally," Hamza stated. "If somebody wants to cause damage, he sets fire to the plantation."

"Maybe he tried to make it look less obvious," Robert said.

"I do not know." Hamza shook his head. "But I do not think that is how it was."

"From now on I'd like us to be on the lookout for any person who doesn't belong on the plantation. Keep a sharp eye out!" he ordered.

"Yes, *sango*." Malambuku nodded.

"Do you really think it was arson?" Luise asked.

"I don't know. But we should be alert. If the harvest had been destroyed, we might have gone bankrupt."

"Have you any suspicions?"

"No, that would be saying too much. But I know that some of the other plantation owners will have worse harvests this year."

"Who?"

Robert shook his head. "We don't need a witch hunt. We escaped a big scare, and that's a good thing. But it's a warning, too."

Luise was satisfied with his answer, though she sensed her father hadn't told her everything. But she let it drop. From that moment on, she had the feeling that the worry-free existence she'd had on the plantation was a thing of the past.

The plantation returned to its daily routine. A burnt smell still hung in the air, but Luise adjusted to it. She was happy that nothing extraordinary had happened since then, and even the rumors about emerging unrest among neighboring tribes had gradually evaporated. But she heard the Germans talking every Sunday about skirmishes between the colonial European powers and Africans that not infrequently led to death.

Luise was worried about this. She'd been completely uninterested four years ago when Germany signed the Treaty of Berlin dividing up African territory. She was barely eleven at the time, and anything taking place outside Hamburg's city limits belonged to another universe. But now that she was living in Africa and intending to stay there, she listened intently whenever the conversation turned to political conflict, especially the rumors. She wanted to understand what was going on.

It was early morning, and Luise was sitting on her favorite tree and watching the pink of the sky grow stronger. All of a sudden she heard a noise. Just a soft crackle, but she was sure she heard something, so she turned around. Her concern eased at once when she saw Hamza, who smiled. He sat down beside her.

"You're up early," Luise noted.

"You, too. I thought I would find you here."

"Really?" Luise was surprised. "Why?"

"Because I watched you a few times when you first came to Cameroon."

"You watched me?" She smiled. "I didn't even notice."

"At the start, because I did not know what you were going to do and I was afraid you might walk into the forest. But I was sure after a few days that you only wanted to be here, alone. So I left you."

"I never saw you."

"Then I did everything right."

Neither of them spoke for a long time. Then Luise asked, "Are you worried?"

"Worried? Why?"

"I don't know. It's how it seemed to me lately."

He nodded slowly. "You are a good observer."

"Do you want to tell me what's bothering you?"

"It is hard for me. I want to tell you in confidence, but you must not tell your father."

"Why not?"

"He owns the plantation, and the Duala work for him."

Luise bit her lip and thought for a moment. "I won't tell him a thing. You can trust me."

"The Duala have received an offer from another *sango* to bring in his harvest and would have to move there."

"What are you saying?"

"Some in the village are for it, others against. I do not know what the decision will be in the end."

"But why? We pay the workers fairly and do everything we can to get along with you."

"It has nothing to do with you. Promises were made to some men in the tribe. I think they are being deceived."

"Can I do something?"

"No, it is tribe's matter."

"What does your father think?"

"He is against leaving the plantation, but he is not the chief."

"Would you go, too?"

Hamza shrugged. "I would have no choice."

Luise gulped hard. "If you go, we couldn't work the plantation."

"I know."

"We'd be ruined."

"What does that word mean?"

"Ruin?" She thought for a few seconds. "It's a word that means we would have no more money and would have no idea how we were going to live."

"I understand. I will do what I can to see we stay."

"Thank you."

Luise wondered if it was wise to tell him her next thought. "I wouldn't want to lose you," she heard herself say.

Hamza was silent.

Luise was immediately filled with regret. "I'm sorry, I shouldn't have said that."

"Won't you leave here someday?"

She looked at him. "No. Why should we?"

"*Sango* Meyerdierks has gone."

"He wanted to take care of his mother. She's sick and needs him."

"And your mother?"

Luise grimaced. "She doesn't need me, believe me. Besides, she has my sister." Luise sighed. "We don't get along particularly well, you know?"

"Yes, I know."

"Oh really?"

"I could see it when she was here."

"It was that obvious?"

"Yes."

"My father and I are not planning to go back to Hamburg. We're staying here. That's why I hope you won't be leaving us."

"There are other workers he can get if we go."

"But you won't be among them."

Hamza reflected briefly. "The man who often came to visit . . . ," he started to say.

"Do you mean Raimund, Raimund Leffers?"

"Yes, him."

"What about him?"

"Will you marry him?"

"What? Me and Raimund Leffers?" Luise laughed out loud. "No, most definitely not."

"Why not? You must choose a husband eventually."

Luise had no reply.

"I have to take a wife soon."

Luise looked at him in surprise. "Oh" was all she could get out. Then she looked straight ahead again.

"But I do not want to," Hamza declared.

"No?"

"No."

"Why not?" Luise swallowed hard in anticipation of his answer.

Hamza said nothing. Hesitating for a moment, he took her hand and held it firmly. And so they sat until the workday began.

Chapter Seventeen

Hamburg, Beginning of September 1889

She was pleased. It was all playing out in an eminently gratifying way. Richard's grades had improved, and nobody could complain about Frederike or Martha once Elisabeth took the reins. Only the day before, Georg had praised her dedication to the family. Georg and she were becoming closer, anyway—not in the physical sense, but it was noticeable how her assistance helped him concentrate on his office work. By contrast Georg and Vera's relationship had worsened considerably. The couple only stated what was necessary after Georg had said during an argument that he wished from her the same commitment Elisabeth had demonstrated. It was easy to feel sorry for Vera.

Vera had told Elisabeth a few weeks ago that she felt increasingly uneasy at social engagements. She was convinced people were watching her and whispering behind her back. Elisabeth said she was just imagining it and ought to relax, but Vera grew more and more tense and insecure. Vera had taken Elisabeth's suggestion and seen her doctor. He attributed Vera's complaints to overstimulation, because of the ever-increasing pace of life. He had a long list of patients—many of them women—who suffered from the same symptoms, felt depressed and insecure and whose lives were out of balance. He'd prescribed her the latest medication to improve her sleep and calm her nerves as well. Vera was grateful to him and convinced she'd soon improve. She did notice the medication led to a certain lethargy, but she was prepared to live with that temporarily. She had no idea that Elisabeth had been to another doctor, who had prescribed the same medication for her, and soon Vera was being administered double the prescribed dose with her meals every day.

Elisabeth would console Vera when Georg reproached her for lack of motivation if Vera felt too weak to get up in the morning. But even these reproaches became less frequent since Georg began to see that helping his wife was love's labor lost. But Elisabeth was always present, saw to it that the children did their chores and the staff carried out their duties. Everything was so perfectly organized that Georg only had to deal with business matters.

Vera seemed to be bowing out of the family more and more, and her children reacted very differently to their mother's withdrawal from everyday life. Richard showed no concern that she was, for all intents and purposes, living among them invisibly, and he concentrated entirely on his upcoming final exams. Frederike, on the other hand, made a considerable effort to address the situation. She tried to coax her mother into coming to the family meals, or she'd sit and read to her or attempt to have a conversation. But since Vera barely reacted to her daughter's devotion, Frederike grew frustrated and gradually stopped trying to get her attention.

Georg had recently invited Elisabeth to his study to inform her that he would be putting a monthly sum at her disposal as soon as Robert's next shipment came in and new money came into the business. Elisabeth had thanked him, knowing he'd soon be paying her more than he imagined.

"Would you be so kind as to accompany me to the Palms' reception tomorrow night?" he asked at dinner one night.

Elisabeth looked up in surprise, and Richard, Frederike, and Martha did the same.

"Me?" Elisabeth raised her eyebrows.

"Of course. You're invited as well. And it's obvious that Vera"—he pointed to her vacant seat—"cannot go in her present condition."

"Won't people talk?"

"About what?" Georg sipped his wine. "Your husband's in Africa, and my wife is ill. Everybody there knows that. It would be more noteworthy if we arrived in separate carriages and gave the impression that we were avoiding each other."

"I hadn't considered that," Elisabeth said, turning to the children. "What do you think?"

Richard shrugged. "And even if people do talk . . . when you appear together the next time, nobody will care anymore."

Frederike and Martha nodded in agreement.

"I'd like to ask Vera if it's all right with her," said Elisabeth, withholding her acceptance. "If she's not opposed, I'll gladly accompany you to the Palms', Georg."

"Good."

For him the matter had been laid to rest.

It had been easy for Elisabeth to obtain Vera's consent, and she even made her feel she herself had asked Elisabeth to go with Georg. Now Elisabeth sat before the mirror over her dressing table. Everything was turning out precisely according to plan. She brushed back her hair, smoothed her eyebrows, and dotted on some lip cream. She turned her head, studying her hair from each side. Her hair was artfully swept up, everything about her was impeccable. She sprayed some eau de toilette on her neck and stood up. The dark-red dress suited her beautifully. She rarely wore it, but it seemed perfect for that day. She felt a pang of nervousness. If everything went well, she would remake her life from the bottom up. She had orchestrated everything and been patient. Now it was just a matter of harvesting the fruits of her scheme.

"You look enchanting, Elisabeth." Georg watched as she descended the stairs step by step.

"Thank you, my dear brother-in-law." She smiled at him. "I must say I am looking forward to this evening."

They exchanged pleasantries in the carriage on the way. Elisabeth made an effort to show her admiration for Georg through small gestures, praising him for his business acumen. Then she withdrew a little, expressing her concern for his wife's health and her hope that medication would bring a clear improvement. Georg's answers revealed that he neither shared this hope nor expected Vera to rally.

"I think it is also a social problem," Elisabeth said casually. "Did you know that writers like Heyse, Mann, Fontane, and Hauptmann discuss the illness neurasthenia in their works?"

"Really? No, I didn't."

Elisabeth didn't tell him it had been her doctor who told her that, while criticizing the influence of literary works on popular opinion.

"Yes, it is a fact. Vera's condition prompted me to research the subject thoroughly. Everybody is talking about it so much it's almost a cliché, this neurasthenia. If you ask me, people are only making themselves crazy."

"You are a clever and practical woman, Elisabeth. I think I've misjudged you all these years."

"I shall be frank with you, Georg. My worry about Vera's condition is greater than I would care to admit. Do you know that there are some good clinics for patients like Vera?"

"I hope you don't mean the kind of place where people are tied to their beds."

"Oh, for heaven's sake, Georg! This is my sister-in-law we're talking about. Of course I don't mean anything of the kind, but rather facilities that specialize in treating and healing mentally ill people, not torturing them." She waved off his attempt to speak. "Oh, let's drop the subject. I'm sure I don't know enough about it."

Georg grew pensive and silent until the carriage came up to the Palms' house. Elisabeth looked at him from the corner of her eye. The seed of doubt had been sown. Now it just needed to sprout.

"Here we are," Georg said, happy to break the silence as the carriage stopped. Without waiting for the driver, he opened the door, climbed down, and offered his sister-in-law his hand.

"The Hansens!" Georg heard his host exclaim even before he'd turned around. Ernst Palm and his wife were in front of their house, smiling at them.

Elisabeth gathered up her dress and took Georg's arm. They stopped before their hosts, and she held out her hand to be kissed. "Herr Palm, Frau Palm, how lovely of you to invite us!"

As the women said their hellos, Ernst Palm shook Georg's hand. "I am sincerely happy you and your sister-in-law accepted our invitation. I know it's not easy . . ."

"We're delighted."

"Please go in and have a glass of champagne. Many of the guests are here already."

"How kind. Many thanks."

Elisabeth nodded to Georg, and they walked into the villa. All eyes were on them. Many guests merely registered their arrival; others let their gaze linger a moment too long. Principal Hajo Feldkamp and his wife were the first to leave a small group of people and come over to them. "Frau Hansen, Herr Hansen. When we heard you were coming tonight, my wife and I were most pleased."

"Herr Feldkamp." Elisabeth smiled broadly. "Georg, may I introduce you to Richard's savior."

"Oh, Frau Hansen, you give me too much credit."

"My sister-in-law told me about your actions on my son's behalf. I am delighted to be able to thank you in person."

"Brunhilde." Feldkamp turned to his wife. "You know the Hansens."

"Why, yes," his wife said. "Elisabeth and I have met many times."

"And it was always delightful," Elisabeth added.

"Indeed," Frau Feldkamp agreed. "Please allow me to introduce you to some people, and we'll have a glass of champagne."

Elisabeth traded Georg's arm for Brunhilde's.

"I am so looking forward to this evening, my dear."

"Are you happy with the course of the evening?" Elisabeth asked her brother-in-law as the carriage took them back to the villa.

"You were wonderful, Elisabeth, you know?" His speech sounded a little slurred. "You've done me a great service tonight."

"Really?"

"I made a couple of new business contacts—thanks to my lovely sister-in-law."

"Nonsense, you deserve the credit. I did nothing."

"But you did. You were exceedingly charming and captivating. I'm serious, and I thank you for it." He took her hand and kissed it.

Elisabeth smiled. "Glad to do it, my dear." She put a hand on her chest. "I am afraid I drank too much wine and am a little tipsy."

"I know for certain that I did drink too much," Georg responded. "But that's all right. It can even do you some good." He sank down farther into the seat.

"I am sorry I cannot be of more help to you day-to-day. You should have it."

"You're doing what you can, I know. Vera is the one who should support me, not you."

Elisabeth sighed. "I'm trying to make up for what I failed to do at my husband's side. It is my contribution to the success of the business, so to speak."

Georg didn't answer, having nodded off.

The carriage stopped in front of the villa, and the driver opened the door and helped Elisabeth out first, then Georg, who stumbled.

"'S'all right," he said, pushing the driver away.

"I'll do it," Elisabeth said, and took him by the arm. Even before they made it up the stairs, the door opened.

"Wait, I'll help you!" Anna hurried to them and supported Georg on the other side. The women brought him inside together.

"Into the parlor," Elisabeth gasped.

"Shouldn't we try to get him upstairs?"

"No! The parlor. Are the children asleep?"

"The children went to their rooms hours ago, and I've not seen them since," the housekeeper reported.

"And Vera?"

"Madame is also in bed."

"I c'n make it m'self," Georg slurred.

The women ignored his words and laid him on the couch in the parlor.

"Thank you, Anna," Elisabeth said. "I'll manage from here."

"Good night, madame."

"Good night, Anna."

Elisabeth quickly went upstairs, took off her clothes, slipped into her nightgown, and put her bathrobe on top. She took a flask from the dressing table and sprayed a little more eau de toilette on her throat. Picking up a blanket and pillow for Georg, she left her bedroom and went back to the parlor, where Georg lay on the couch, snoring. Elisabeth sighed. He could have at least made it easier for her. She covered him with the blanket and threw the pillow on the floor for the time being. She went to the sideboard and poured two glasses of cognac and put them beside her on the table. Then she sat down on the edge of the sofa.

"Georg, I want to talk to you." She shook him gently. "It is important."

It took a while for him to come to. "Elisabeth?"

"Yes, it's me."

"What's the time?"

"I don't know. I tried to sleep, but I couldn't. I must tell you something, Georg."

He had trouble sitting up. Elisabeth bent down, picked up the pillow off the floor, and stuffed it behind his back. In doing so her breast grazed his shoulder, as if accidentally. She picked up the glasses, which she could hardly make out in the dark room, and gave one to her brother-in-law.

"I would like us to have a toast for our last night together, Georg," she told him.

"What do you mean?" He seemed to be slowly sobering up.

"I am leaving," she announced. "I must. I can't go on like this anymore."

"Leaving?" He sat up with a start. "Where are you going?"

"I don't know yet. But I cannot stay here any longer. I will tell Martha tomorrow morning." She clinked her glass with his. "Here's to staying as close as we were this evening and never forgetting this time."

Elisabeth drank, but Georg didn't share in the toast. He leaned forward and put the glass down on the table, coming very close to Elisabeth.

She put down her glass and moved as if to get up. Georg held her back.

"Please, Elisabeth, tell me where you're going."

"I really don't know, not yet. As soon as I've found something suitable for Martha and me, I will let you know."

"But why?" He held her by the shoulders.

She breathed heavily. "This evening with you . . ." She shook her head. "To see how wonderful you are and how you suffer nonetheless.

How you carry out your duty and work for the family without regard for yourself. You are a wonderful, strong man. A man somebody can respect." She covered her face with her hands. "I was so proud of you tonight, but that is what I ought not to feel. I cannot stay like this any longer, I don't want to. It's too much for me." She sobbed.

Georg leaned forward and took her in his arms. He held her for a while as she cried. Then he leaned back, holding her shoulders. "Please, Elisabeth, don't go! Everything I've achieved recently I owe to you. I'm strong with you by my side, confident, and can win people over. Please, Elisabeth, I need you."

She raised her eyes, slid his hand from her shoulder, and pressed it to her breast. "I want more from you than just being near you."

She moved his hand, sighed, threw her head back. Georg gulped hard, breathed more loudly, and pulled her toward him. They kissed frantically and intensely, and he seized her breast as she pulled the blanket aside and put her hand between his thighs. Georg groaned softly as he slipped off her bathrobe. Elisabeth stood and pulled her nightgown over her head, standing before him completely naked. He could just make out her slim well-shaped silhouette and saw that she was breathing heavily with desire. He stood up, took off his clothes, and was soon naked, too.

Elisabeth seized his erection, stroked it, and pressed him back onto the couch. Then she lowered herself down on him, letting him glide into her. She slowly moved up and down, again and again. She rotated her hips, took him fully into herself, dug her fingers into his shoulders, threw her head back, and moaned. He put both hands on her breasts while lifting his hips to meet her. Her movements grew faster, more demanding, as if she was trying to feel him even more deeply inside herself. They both gasped, yielding more and more to their desire. Elisabeth convulsed. She moaned and cried out, and in response Georg's passion came to a climax. Elisabeth's movements faded; she let her arms sink as she gasped for air and leaned against Georg's chest.

They stayed that way for a moment; then Elisabeth climbed off him, picked up her nightgown and bathrobe, and put them on. She bent down and gave Georg a long, passionate kiss. Then she left the room without a word. She washed quickly in the bathroom, went to her bedroom, and lay down on her bed. Everything had worked exactly the way she'd planned. She smiled and fell asleep a few moments later.

Chapter Eighteen

Vienna, Mid-October 1889

They met once a week, sometimes more. For Karl it was simultaneously the most wonderful and the worst time of his life. Florentinus sent him little notes in sealed envelopes that street urchins delivered to his office, mentioning just a time and place. Florentinus would not wait for Karl longer than half an hour. If Karl didn't come within that time, it meant the rendezvous was not happening. But that happened only once. They'd meet in different hotels, never arriving at the same time. Florentinus would reserve a room and then go out and around the corner where Karl was waiting. Florentinus would give him the room number, and then he would go up first, followed by Karl a little later. They would give themselves an hour, never much more, for making love. Then Karl would hurry back to the office so that Felix, his sole employee, would not be alone for too long.

Every meeting with Florentinus stirred Karl's emotions, making him euphoric, then despairing just as deeply. How *could* he do that to Therese, his beloved wife, who was so honest and sincere and loved him with all her heart? It often took hours for him to get hold of his fear of being discovered and to be able to fall asleep. Why wasn't he like everybody else? How often had he asked himself this question that never had an answer?

It had always been that way, as long as he could remember. When other boys would gaze after girls, he was never interested. He would feel excitement when he played with other boys and brushed against their bodies. Then he would lie in bed at night, touching himself as he thought about how it felt when another boy accidentally grazed him. It was confusing and didn't feel right, yet he indulged himself, bringing agony and pleasure at the same time. He hated himself for it. He had always hated himself for it. And yet he couldn't disavow it.

When he met Therese, he had hoped she would be the one who could bring about a fundamental change in his life. A woman who understood him, though he could never entrust her with his secret. The law punished men like him; he could even be imprisoned. Some doctors had conducted experiments to explain that homosexuality was a disease, which might make it possible to avoid punishment. But Karl could never have withstood the humiliation associated with it.

He was twenty-three when he had his first real encounter with another man. He remembered it as if it were yesterday—it had been after a party. Adalbert, a student like himself with whom he'd talked all evening, was going home the same way, so they'd taken a shortcut through the park. They were quite drunk, laughing, and on that warm summer night, they suddenly decided to go swimming in the little duck pond. Adalbert had suggested it, and for months afterward Karl wondered whether he had planned it from the start. They'd scarcely undressed and jumped into the pond when Adalbert had come very close to Karl and brushed against him as though by accident again and again as they swam around. Once they had gotten cold and climbed out of the pond, there were no towels, so they just brushed the water off. Karl began to put on his clothes when Adalbert laid a hand on his arm and stopped him. Karl didn't understand at first, but then Adalbert got down on his knees and took Karl in his mouth. Just like that, as if it were the most natural thing in the world. Karl gasped for breath, wanted to push Adalbert away, yell at him. But the feeling was so incredible, so exciting and overwhelming, that he closed his eyes and let it happen.

But afterward, burning with shame, he grabbed his clothes and ran, naked, away from the pond. He didn't stop until he was far away, and he looked to see if Adalbert was following. He quickly dressed and ran home. Everyone was in bed, so he didn't have to explain his agitated state to anyone. There had been a few other men, but Karl had despised himself so much every time that he stopped, unable to bear the distress it caused him. All that lay far back in the past, because when he met Therese, he truly believed she could change him. But he'd only made it worse and ran the risk of destroying what might have been his only chance at a real life.

He'd been on a ladder the day before, getting a box on the highest shelf, when the ladder had wobbled under his weight and he had to quickly grab the shelf so he didn't fall. And then something strange happened. It crossed his mind that it might be good if he let go. The shelf was just below the ceiling, a good twelve feet up. From that height a broken neck was not only possible but probable. Could he find peace that way? Felix came in at that exact moment to see if he could help, startling Karl out of his thoughts. He told Felix roughly to go back to the salesroom in case a customer came in. Then he'd taken the box and carefully made his way down, rung by rung. But the idea that it might be better for everybody—especially Therese—if he were dead had burrowed into his brain. He went to bed that night thinking about it, and when Therese rose the next morning, he hadn't slept a wink.

"Will you come to the café after work?"

At the kitchen table, Karl was distracted by his own thoughts. "What?" he asked, which earned him a blistering look from his wife.

"Don't tell me you forgot!" she said, arms akimbo.

"Quick, help me, it's too early to think."

"Herr Riemenschneider's coming today, the man who owns the building next door, who is thinking of selling."

"Oh yes, right, that's today."

"And I'd really like it if you were there."

"Of course. When?"

"He wanted to come at five. Can you make it?"

"Yes, I'll ask Felix to lock up."

"Good." She sat down at the table. "Sometimes I think I'm in a dream. Who would have thought a few years ago that my café would be too small?"

"It's extremely impressive, what you've accomplished."

"What you've done, too. You know, I think it's nice we are both excited about our work, don't you?"

"Yes, it is."

"Karl, what's wrong? You haven't laughed in a while and are always so distant. I feel as though you're not really here."

"Of course I'm here. Where else would I be?"

Therese scrutinized him. "Sometimes I think you don't love me anymore."

"Therese, stop it! That's ridiculous!"

"Yes, that's true. I know you love me. I know it deep down. But you've changed. Do you still want the life we have?"

He reached across the table to take her hand. "I most certainly do, my little sunshine. You're the most important part of my life."

"If it gets to be too much for you that I keep working and wanting to do more and more, then you must tell me. Are you listening?"

"I will. Count on it. But what could be better than having a wife who loves her work and brings home loads of money?"

She laughed brightly. "Well, it's not all that much, but I do think we can't complain. Your business is on everybody's lips, and the profits have increased remarkably."

"I'm satisfied, but I'd be happier if the volume were greater."

"Then talk to your brothers about it," Therese suggested as she had some coffee. "Of course, it's hard to do that with Robert, but you could send Georg a telegram." She paused. "No, not a telegram, a letter."

"Yes, I really ought to."

"Do you think there's a reason all the shipments still go through Hamburg?"

"I honestly don't know. Georg's last letter said he forwards the bulk of Robert's shipments to me right away, but I think he wants to feel that he's an important part of it all."

"And the good people of Hamburg still don't buy enough cocoa?"

"Precisely."

"Hmm. If you're right, you shouldn't address it too directly. Just let him know how much you can store, give the exact amount, explain that you have no objection if the beans are sent to you directly. If he still wants it to go through Hamburg, then leave it at that. There's no disadvantage for you, and it would be unfair to push him into a corner by demanding something."

"You know, whatever you suggest is always right, no matter the subject. I love that about you."

She shrugged. "I don't think one needs to hurt people. There's enough pain in the world without adding to it with thoughtless acts or stupid remarks that could easily be avoided."

"You're a wonderful person. I don't deserve you."

"Why not? You're exactly the same way, Karl. Or would you hurt me by doing something thoughtless?"

Karl swallowed hard. The doorbell rang, saving him from having to answer.

"Oh, is it that late!" Therese jumped up. "That must be Tino."

Karl choked on his mouthful of coffee and coughed. "Florentinus?" His wife was already at the door and returned with her brother in tow.

"Good morning, Karl."

"Good morning. I didn't know you were in Vienna."

192

"Just for the day. Therese asked me to sound out the seller of that building before the two of you see him. See if there are any bodies in the basement."

Therese looked carefully at Karl. "You're pale all of a sudden. Don't you feel well?"

"The coffee went down the wrong way, and I couldn't breathe."

"You haven't told your husband about our plan?"

"Oh, I meant to. But he's at work so much that we hardly see each other, and when we do, then one of us is too tired—or both of us are—to talk."

"I understand." Florentinus smiled.

"Besides, it's no secret, anyway," Therese said. "I just want to see if my old neighbor Riemenschneider is an honest man or will lie and promise me the moon. And you're a master at fooling people with your smooth talk, brother dear."

"Well, if you say so."

"Oh, I'm late. Stay here for a while, Tino? It would be suspicious if you showed up at Riemenschneider's when I've barely opened the café next door."

"Fine." Florentinus sat down in Therese's chair opposite Karl.

"I've got to be off as well," Karl said as he got to his feet. "I've got too much to do at the office."

"I could go with you and help instead of just sitting around here waiting."

Karl wanted to reject the offer, but Therese spoke up first. "That's a wonderful idea! Maybe my dear husband will make today's appointment on time and even be home before evening."

Florentinus stood up again. "Gladly. Of course, only if you've no objection."

Karl gave him a look that signified anything but agreement. "Of course not. Why would I?"

"Good." Therese gave Karl a kiss. "See you later—and don't forget: five sharp at the café. I'm relying on you."

"I'll be there."

Therese gave Florentinus a kiss on the cheek, grabbed her coat, and left. They heard her dance lightly down the stairs.

Florentinus took a step toward Karl.

"Don't you dare get near me in this apartment," Karl warned him.

"What's the matter? Have I done something?"

"I didn't know you were coming, and I can't say I like the surprise. This is where I live with my wife, your sister. It's almost as if you want her to find out."

"My sister asked me to come. That's God's truth. And she did because she hasn't the slightest inkling."

Karl opened his mouth and shut it. Then he leaned on his chair for support. "I'm sorry. My nerves are shot."

"I don't want her to find out every bit as much as you."

"I know. I overreacted. I'm sorry."

"Of course."

Karl put on his jacket, and they left the apartment for the office. Under different circumstances Karl would never have worried about what people might think about the two of them. How often he'd walked along Vienna's streets with Felix, Martin, Friedhelm, or another friend when they were on business or on their way home. But now, with Florentinus, he was overcome by the thought that everyone could tell by looking what joined them together. Karl felt completely naked and that everyone was staring at him.

Suddenly he couldn't breathe from one moment to the next. He felt a tightness pulling in his chest and gasped for breath.

"Karl, what's wrong?" Florentinus held him so he wouldn't fall.

Karl's eyes rolled back, and he looked about to faint. They were attracting some attention.

"What's happened?" a woman asked, looking at Karl with concern.

"I don't know. Just a minute ago everything was fine, and then suddenly . . ." Florentinus broke off.

They dragged Karl along the sidewalk and leaned him against the wall of a building.

"You must stay calm, do you hear?" The woman tried to look him in the eye. Then she said to Florentinus. "There's a pharmacy just ahead. Maybe they can help him there, or get a doctor."

Florentinus picked him up from one side and asked the woman to support Karl from the other. Karl felt everything spinning around him.

"Please help us," the woman said as they dragged Karl into the pharmacy.

"Good heavens!" the pharmacist exclaimed, rushing out from behind the counter.

He and Florentinus heaved Karl onto a chair.

"Wilma, quick, a glass of water and get Dr. Sulzbach!"

She came running with the water, put it on the counter, and rushed out to fetch the doctor.

The pharmacist looked at the lady. "Is he your husband?"

"No," Florentinus answered. "He's my sister's husband, my brother-in-law. This lady kindly helped us."

"What happened?"

"I don't know. We were on the way to his office when suddenly his eyes turned upward and he looked as if he was going to faint."

The pharmacist put his hand on Karl's chest. "His heart's beating too fast." He fanned Karl with his hand. "You must breathe slowly, do you hear?"

Karl swallowed hard, struggled to breathe, closed his eyes, tore them open again.

"Karl, don't worry! Everything's fine, it'll be all right." Florentinus put his hand on Karl's back, which only made him breathe faster.

"Dr. Sulzbach, thank God!" the pharmacist said when the doctor opened the door and came in.

"Stand aside, please." The doctor knelt in front of Karl and looked up at his eyes. "Can you hear me, sir?" He asked Florentinus, "What's his name?"

"Karl. Karl Hansen."

"Can you hear me, Herr Hansen? Are you in pain?"

Karl nodded, gasped for air, and bent over.

"It could be his heart," the doctor said. "What was he doing when it started?"

"We were walking on the street, that's all."

The doctor took out his stethoscope and motioned for the pharmacist and Florentinus to help the patient sit forward. Then he listened to Karl's chest. "Your heart's too fast, Herr Hansen." He turned to Florentinus again. "Was he running or overexerting himself?"

"No."

"Did anything frighten him?"

"No, nothing happened."

"Peculiar." The doctor laid his stethoscope down. "Herr Hansen, listen to me carefully. Listen to my breathing and follow my rhythm—it will improve immediately." The doctor inhaled deeply, stretched his back, and exhaled slowly. "And once again. In"—he breathed in—"and out. That's good, Herr Hansen. And in again"—he inhaled—"and out again."

They did this for a while until Karl was breathing in a regular rhythm and was visibly calmer.

"Now, Herr Hansen, stand up carefully. We can take a few steps together back and forth." The doctor helped him out of his chair.

Karl swayed briefly; then he regained his balance.

"May I have some water?" he asked.

"Certainly." The pharmacist handed him a glass.

Karl took a drink, breathed deeply, and exhaled slowly again. "It's getting better. Thanks to all of you."

"Are you sure? I'd like you to come to my office and let me examine you properly."

Karl shook his head. "That won't be necessary."

The doctor looked him over once more and put his stethoscope back into a leather bag. "You know yourself best."

Florentinus handed the doctor some money. "Many thanks for coming so quickly."

The doctor accepted his honorarium with a nod. "May I speak with you for a moment outside, Herr Hansen?"

"Yes." Karl followed him out the door, and they took a few more steps.

"Is this the first time this has happened?"

"Yes."

"Well, I suspect you know what caused you to react so violently?"

"I'm not sure."

"I'm a doctor, Herr Hansen. I obey a vow of silence. If you don't want to tell me, you don't have to. But you must make sure you keep your feelings under control. All indicators point to panic caused by fear of something or other." The doctor tried to look Karl in the eye. "You will know best what you were thinking or seeing when it happened. I can only urge you not to suppress that feeling. It will only get worse. You're a strong young man, but your heart can't handle these attacks. At least not if they occur frequently."

"Many thanks for your advice, sir. I will think about it."

"Do that. People often put off these considerations until it's too late."

Karl looked at him thoughtfully, very much as if he wanted to ask him something. Then he shook his head and offered the doctor his hand. "Thank you. I'll be able to manage now."

They said their goodbyes, and the doctor left.

Florentinus came out of the pharmacy, followed by the owner and the woman who had helped them. Karl shook her hand and the pharmacist's and thanked them for their assistance.

"So what happened?" Florentinus asked and tried to look Karl in the eye as they walked along.

Karl stared straight ahead. "I have made a decision," he said. "We will no longer meet, never again! Except when your sister's present."

"What? I don't understand. What's going on with you?"

Karl stopped. "I don't want to keep doing this anymore, do you hear? It's over."

"But . . . ?" Florentinus raised his hands helplessly.

"No buts, no maybes. What we did was wrong. Wrong and unfair. And this attack made that perfectly clear to me. I would like you to stay away from me, once and for all. Do you understand?"

Florentinus stood there as if turned to stone. Still stunned, he softened his expression. "I love you, Karl," he whispered, looking down at the ground.

"And I love your sister, and starting immediately, we will have the marriage that she deserves. I want to have children with her, many children. And if ever you come to visit, you will be nothing more than an uncle." Karl had started to move away but turned back to face Florentinus. "And if we have a son, I do *not* want you getting close to him, do you understand?"

Florentinus closed his eyes for a second. "I'll never forgive you for those words, Karl." He spun on his heel and hurried away without looking back.

Karl felt as if he had ripped his heart out of his chest.

Chapter Nineteen

Cameroon, End of September 1889

Luise could finally breathe easily. The tribe's chief decided that the Duala would continue to work on the Hansen plantation and would not move elsewhere. Robert had avoided a danger he didn't even know existed. It had been difficult for Luise to keep the promise she'd given Hamza about not warning her father, and she was glad the pressure was off. She watched with pride as the first sacks from the new harvest were loaded onto carts taking them the next day to the first Hamburg-bound ship. Everything was the way it always had been; the daily routine was reestablished.

Since the day Hamza told Luise that the Duala might move away, they'd been meeting every morning at sunup, sometimes talking, sometimes sharing the silence. Neither said it, but each of them felt something had made them inseparable. They did nothing more than hold hands while watching the sky's varying colors. But the day before, Luise had given Hamza a kiss on the cheek after he'd told her about the chief's decision. Presumably she should have been startled by her own reaction to the good news, but she wasn't. Luise felt their intimacy was right and good.

She'd come to realize that she was in love with Hamza. And she was just as sure she could never be with him the way other lovers were. But she would rather settle for sitting with him and holding hands for an hour every morning than lead her life with a husband she'd never love. The mere thought that someday the chief would order Hamza to take a Duala woman for a wife worried her. She decided to reject such a fate for herself. No matter how hard her father might push, she would never marry a man not of her own choosing.

"I can imagine Georg going over the manifests and rubbing his hands," Robert said as they watched two cartloads of beans depart for the beach.

"Hamza was right. We'll have a good harvest."

Robert put his arm around his daughter's shoulders. "What do you think? Shall we tell Georg to give Martha the money to buy you a pretty new dress? They could send it on the next ship."

"Why have a pretty dress here?" Luise laughed gaily. "No, Father, many thanks. I'd prefer a box of writing paper."

"You'll turn into a real author if you keep writing like this. What are you writing about, anyway?"

"Oh, mainly my thoughts. Occasionally I draw things I like. I've already made some sketches of the church and Mount Cameroon and one of our plantation and the view of the beach when the ship was pulling in."

"Would you show them to me sometime?"

"I'd love to."

They went back to the house.

"Tell me, Luise, do you ever miss anything?"

"What? In Hamburg?"

"Hamburg, the family, your friends, school."

"I learn more with Herr Weidorf than any of my classmates do in Hamburg. Sometimes I miss my friends, I suppose. But as for the rest . . ." She shrugged. "No, not at all."

"Not even your sister and mother?" Her father had hesitated in posing the question.

"I missed Martha at first, yes. But I got used to not having her around."

Robert waited for her to say something about Elisabeth, but she said nothing. "I'm wondering whether we ought to go to Hamburg for Christmas."

They reached the veranda and sat at the table.

"Do you think that's a good idea? I mean, you and Mother didn't part on friendly terms."

"At times it scares me how much you think like an adult," Robert confessed. "I'd be lying if I said all is forgiven. But she's my wife and your mother and Martha's. A family should be together for Christmas."

Luise shrugged again. "It's your decision, of course. But that would mean we'd have to leave before the end of November and wouldn't be back until the end of January. There's a lot of work to be done during that time."

Robert gave a loud laugh. "You're more worried about it than I am. Really, Luise, I think perhaps you've grown up too fast being here."

Luise was speechless at that.

"We also have to think of your future," he added.

"What about my future?" Luise had been leaning her head against the back of her chair but sat upright at once.

"Well, look at the facts. You'll be taking your final high school exams in a few years. Of course you can do that here with Herr Weidorf, but it would be better for you to be examined by a panel of teachers."

"That's a long way off, and we've several harvests to bring in before then."

"You sound like Malambuku," Robert joked. Then his expression grew serious again. "But we have to think beyond that. I've talked to your tutor, and he thinks you're gifted. You could become the highly respected wife of a prominent husband."

Luise rolled her eyes, sank back in her chair, and stared into the sky. "In a silk dress with ruffles? Father, must we have this conversation now?"

"Luise, I don't like your tone of voice."

She sat up again. "Sorry. I didn't mean to be disrespectful. But be honest. I didn't belong in society when we were in Hamburg. And even less now, for sure. I do not want respectability because of a prominent husband—I want to be free."

"Free to do what?"

"Free to live the way we do here."

"You don't want to live your young years entirely on a plantation in Cameroon, do you?"

"Why not? What's wrong with that?"

"What about having your own family? The number of younger Germans here is negligible. I'm afraid you'll regret it later, but later can be too late."

She frowned.

"Young Leffers seems to be showing some interest in you. What do you think of him?"

"Raimund? He's nice."

"Luise, don't make this so difficult for me! It's your mother's job to have this talk with you. But since she's not here, you'll have to put up with my clumsy attempts." He struggled to smile.

"Couldn't we postpone it until I've reached the point of becoming an old maid?"

Robert chuckled. "That's exactly what I meant when I said that later might be too late."

"I'm still young," Luise remarked laconically. "Malambuku compared me to a young antelope yesterday. If that turns into an old hippopotamus, then we'll talk."

"You're incorrigible, Luise." He guffawed. Then he noticed somebody behind Luise. "Ah, Hamza. Say, are there any hippos nearby? Luise would love to see one."

Hamza had walked onto the veranda and looked indecisively from one to the other.

Luise burst out laughing. "Don't listen to him, Hamza. I'm not at all interested in hippos."

Hamza didn't quite know what to make of the conversation, so he just told them why he'd come. "The last cart has been loaded and is on the way to the ship with the other two."

"Thank you, Hamza. Come, sit down and have something to drink."

Hamza was about to when they heard the sound of an approaching horse, and a few seconds later, Raimund Leffers pulled up in front of the house.

"Good day, Luise, Robert, Hamza."

"Good day," they responded.

"Luise, I wanted to ask you if you'd like to come with me to the race tomorrow. The Bele Bele and Deldo are going head-to-head in their canoes. It's supposed to be quite a spectacle and will surely be fun."

"You wanted to go, anyway, didn't you, Luise? Hamza told you about it." It was Robert who answered.

"Fine. Then I'll come by and pick you up."

Before Robert could respond, Luise quickly said, "We'll meet each other there. Thank you, Raimund."

The young man looked a little disappointed but nodded. "Fine. Until tomorrow, then. I'm looking forward to it." He spurred his horse on and departed as quickly as he'd come.

"He's making an effort with you. You might be a bit friendlier toward him."

Luise and Hamza shared glances after Robert spoke.

"I must get back to work," Hamza said, turning and leaving.

How could she explain to her father that she and Hamza had already made a date to go to the race together?

"Yes, Father," she managed. "I'm exhausted and would like to rest before dinner if you don't mind."

"Of course not."

She stood up, kissed him lightly on the cheek, and went into the house. The concerns of her father that she thought were so far away suddenly seemed frighteningly near, close enough to touch.

Hamza did not come at dawn to watch the sunrise with Luise. She would have liked to explain that she'd had no choice but to accept Raimund's invitation. What could she have said with her father there?

Hamza avoided her all the next morning, too. She was annoyed but wanted to resolve the issue as quickly as possible no matter what. She considered a quarrel needless and stupid.

"Can I please speak to you, Hamza?"

He was spreading the fermenting beans. "I must work."

Luise looked all around them. The other Duala didn't seem to be paying them any attention, or else she didn't notice.

"Hamza, please. Or would you rather I talked to you right here?"

Hamza did not look up from his work.

"All right, then. I don't know who else here can understand me, but I must talk to you," she began.

Hamza looked up in alarm. "I will come," he hissed at her, grabbing her arm, and leading her out of the shed. "Some of them understand your language," he said when they'd walked far enough away. "I can get in trouble if they hear you."

"Now see here!" Luise stopped with arms akimbo. "When your people are around you, then I'm supposed to keep quiet. But when it's my people, then I'm supposed to stand with you? You hypocrite!"

Hamza squinted. "That is something different."

"No, it's not. If you'd like me to tell my father I want to go to the race with you and not Raimund, I'll do it. Right now. And I'll ride over to Raimund's and tell him the same thing. You're welcome to come. Let the horrible gossip begin. I don't care!"

"I understand you, Luise."

She'd talked herself into a rage. "Oh, I don't think so. I don't think you understand how serious this is for me. Look at me!" She slid her hands down over her body. "I'm not a noble *nyango* who struts around in fine clothes. I am Luise Hansen. I harvest cocoa beans. I live on a plantation in Africa." She swallowed and then went on more softly. "And my heart belongs to Hamza. I don't care who knows it."

Hamza looked down at the ground, then raised his head and gave her a smile. "It hurt me to see him and know that you will go with him and not me."

"Me, too." Luise thought for a minute. "Couldn't you escort me to the race, anyway? I was so looking forward to it."

"I will take you there. But when Raimund comes to be with you, I do not know how I can stand to see you together."

"Of course." She sounded sad.

"I have to go back to work. They will ask questions. I will say I had to help you with the rabbits."

"Very good. Is everything fine between us again?"

Hamza looked at her and nodded. "It's fine, Luise."

The sad undertone in his voice was unmistakable.

Members of both tribes had come from all over for the canoe race. The men wore colorful face and body paint, the likes of which Luise had never seen. One side wore blue loincloths, the other red. For Hamza's sake she chose not to wear a dress, which would have meant she had joined the ranks of the Germans. Instead she wanted to demonstrate that she was closer to him than to her compatriots, so she wore her work pants and blouse. Apart from that she'd just trimmed her hair a little. And she had a further motive. Raimund was a nice man, and she liked him. But she didn't want him getting the idea that she was dressing up for his sake. She didn't want to send the wrong signal.

Hamza picked Luise up at the agreed time and brought her to the race, where Raimund was already waiting for her. After they'd said hello, Luise asked, "What's the point of this race?"

"It used to be just for fun, but eventually it turned into a real event," Hamza explained. "The families, with forty to fifty men in each canoe, want to see who's better but also to show off their wealth. It costs a lot to make a boat like this—they're sixty-five to ninety-five feet long. And look at the *tangue*, the hand-carved figureheads on the bows! They're commissioned by a rich patron and carved by specially trained artists. When a *tangue* is completed, the family keeps it as a gift."

As if on command, the two teams brought out the long canoes. Each had been dug from a single tree. Luise looked closely at the beautiful figureheads that were decorated with stylized animals and some European-influenced motifs like a cannon, a ship's bell, or a schnapps bottle—all shimmering in black and gold.

"The canoes and the equipment are the property and inheritance of the families, and the boats have their own names, even personalities. And there are songs about them. But"—Hamza pointed again at the figureheads—"the *tangue* are very special. They are guarded all year long by a *mutatedi*, a safekeeper, and only brought out for races. There used to be races between the families more often. But your kaiser wants them to take place only once a year, on the twenty-seventh of January, his birthday. But that hasn't happened yet."

Luise and Raimund listened in amazement as they watched the preparations, the brightly clothed canoeists, and the boats themselves.

"Does the winner get a prize?" Raimund asked.

"Not directly. It used to be that seers would use the race to predict the future, and that was an honor for the winning family. But look!"

Hamza pointed at the canoes. "It will begin any minute now." He was standing to Luise's left, Raimund to her right.

A horn blast signaled the start, and the two crews immediately stabbed their wooden paddles into the water. The boats had no keel and were too heavy to gain speed quickly. As the paddlers swung into a rhythm and paddled harder, the boats moved faster and faster. It became apparent that the blue team was stronger, as their canoe inched farther away from the red boat among shouts from the many hundreds of cheering spectators. In spite of a desperate effort, the red team couldn't catch up, and shouts of triumph greeted the blue boat and its team.

"I should have put money on it," said Raimund. "I said earlier the Bele Bele would win."

"Well, you'll just have to make do without all that money."

"Let's go to the Germans and have a drink," Raimund suggested.

Luise turned to Hamza.

"I wish you a good evening," he said. "I will now go to the Duala."

"Goodbye, Hamza."

Luise wondered if she would get a chance to talk to him later. She would have asked if he was coming tomorrow morning to their meeting place. She sighed and turned to Raimund. "Love to. Let's go."

"Luise, Luise," Raimund's mother scolded her. "You must wear something more suitable to an event like this, shouldn't you?" She looked at Luise's clothes with disapproval.

"Well," she replied, "actually, this was the best thing in my wardrobe."

Raimund laughed loudly.

"I did have the impression that your sister was more partial to the finer things in life" was Raimund's mother's reply.

Luise had a rejoinder on the tip of her tongue but didn't want to aggravate the situation needlessly. She didn't like Raimund's parents, but that was no reason to be impolite.

"You're right. Martha and I are very different when it comes to these matters. She loves beautiful clothes, and I feel comfortable in pants and a blouse." It sounded conciliatory.

"To each his own."

"Come on, Luise, let's go get a drink," Raimund spoke up.

Luise said goodbye to his mother and went with him. "I don't think we'll be the best of friends," she said, laughing.

"I rather think not," Raimund laughed, too.

Raimund got some fruit juice, and they clinked glasses. Several young people joined them, and it indeed turned into a jolly evening, though Luise would rather have passed the time with Hamza. She was surprised that her father came as well; he generally avoided such gatherings on account of the constant questioning about Elisabeth. It was getting late when Luise said she'd like to say goodbye and return home, whereupon Raimund immediately asked if he might take her home.

"That won't be necessary. My father's here, so I can go back with him."

Raimund saw Robert was talking with a group of men and having a good time. "It looks like he won't be leaving soon."

"I know my father," Luise countered. "He's got to get up early tomorrow and won't be staying long."

"Why are you so reluctant to be with me?" Raimund attempted to make eye contact.

"Oh, I'm not." Luise felt very comfortable with herself.

"But you avoid me, and constantly. Doesn't matter whether I offer to take you home after church or suggest we get together. You didn't even let me escort you here and came with Hamza instead."

Luise searched for the right words. "I wouldn't wish to offend or hurt you, Raimund. I like you. And I'm not avoiding you. I don't want to give you the wrong impression. But I just don't want . . ."

"You just don't want me to accompany you regularly."

"That's right. I hope you don't hold it against me for being so direct."

"Why, no. But I thought we understood each other well. You're pretty, clever . . ."

"And the selection here in Cameroon is negligible."

"Well, you got right to the heart of it."

"You see, that's my point. I wouldn't want to be the best among a group of poor choices. That's not good enough for me."

"I understand what you're saying. And to be honest, I don't want that either. So"—he held out his hand—"friends?"

"Friends."

Raimund did take Luise home shortly afterward, but she no longer felt uncomfortable about it. Their relationship had been clarified, and she was relieved beyond measure. Their goodbyes were neither forced nor uncertain.

"Goodbye. See you Sunday!"

"Goodbye, Luise. I had a lot of fun today. And now that everything is clear between us, I'd like us to do things together more frequently."

"We could do that," Luise replied. "Goodbye for now, Raimund."

"Good night, Luise."

Luise went into the house and straight to bed. She lay awake for a while but eventually dropped off to sleep and woke at the usual time. She looked out the window. Would Hamza be waiting at their rendezvous? What did he think about yesterday evening?

She put on her bathrobe, tied up her hair, and crept downstairs as she did every morning. She was nervous when she turned the bend before the tree. Hamza was already there. As she approached, he turned around and smiled.

Chapter Twenty

Hamburg, End of October 1889

Georg paced restlessly back and forth in his office until the boy finally arrived to tell him the ship from Cameroon had just moored at the quay. He was relieved. Karl had sent a third telegram urgently requesting another shipment, but their warehouse was as good as empty. He still had plenty of coffee, but not a single cocoa bean in stock. The Hamburg market had stabilized a little, and if things kept going like that, it would soon make the office a happier place.

Everything had basically gone in his favor. True, his personal situation was anything but straightforward. He'd never have imagined he'd deceive his wife someday. But was it really cheating if he merely got from someone else what he would never get from her? Vera's condition was neither better nor worse. Elisabeth, however, had become his lover and a dependable partner as well, sacrificing herself for his and the firm's interest.

Richard had left the villa weeks ago. He'd graduated and was at the university in Heidelberg. Now it was critical to find eligible bachelors from good families for Frederike and Martha, and it was equally important to use these alliances to firm up business contacts. He could safely delegate that task to Elisabeth. She had an exceptional talent for such things and had his complete confidence.

The question of what his life would become crossed his mind more and more frequently. At last he had a woman who supported him and whose ambition surpassed his by far. He desired Elisabeth, especially because she turned out to be an imaginative lover. Even before leaving the office, he could hardly wait to be back at the villa, though time there would pass agonizingly slowly while Frederike and Martha were awake. But when everybody was in bed, and he should have been sleeping beside Vera, he would sneak over to Elisabeth and let her pamper him.

Yes, he loved that woman. He loved her like a predator loves the smell of blood. He desired her in a way he'd never desired Vera. There was an air of danger about her; she sated her desire with him and then drew out his climax for so long that it was simultaneously torture and delight. From the moment he crept into her bedroom, she was in charge. His experiences with her fascinated him. Did she do similar things with Robert? He could hardly imagine so. Wouldn't his brother have been happier with her all those years if she'd satisfied him in that way? For Georg, at least, it was fulfillment. He yielded to her at night; during the day she was once again his capable sister-in-law who praised his business skills and took her assignments seriously—and supported him so he could wholeheartedly focus on making money.

He wondered how this could go on if Robert were to come back to Hamburg. Elisabeth and Georg agreed that Robert must not find out about it no matter what. A divorce would harm the family and the business, so it must be avoided at all costs. On top of that, Georg couldn't even begin to imagine Robert's reaction if he discovered the manner in which he'd been betrayed.

Georg put on his coat and left the office for the harbor. He walked slowly, reflecting on the previous night and the conversation he'd had that morning. The ambitious young man who had come to see him intended to start up a coffee shop in Hamburg modeled on the Viennese café. It was to feature baked delicacies, especially chocolate ones. He wanted to collaborate with Peter Hansen & Sons. Though Georg had his doubts that the young man could achieve his plans, he'd assured him of their cooperation. After all, the business could only win.

There was music coming from somewhere, and it accompanied his steps until he'd reached the harbor quarter. It was odd, but his personal situation imbued him not with the fear of being discovered, but rather with strength and the self-confidence that he could accomplish anything he put his mind to. But what was to happen to Vera? Her bad days were now strung together like pearls on a string. She hardly left her room, no longer took meals with the family, and essentially had contact with only Anna, who saw to it that Vera ate something regularly. Georg didn't care anymore. His feelings for her were extinguished; it was Elisabeth he wanted.

The October sun blinded him, though an icy wind was blowing. It was too cold for the season; winter appeared to be arriving earlier that year. But oh well, they were North Germans after all. So he flipped up his collar and braved the cold. He observed with satisfaction the goodly number of sacks bearing the label *Peter Hansen & Sons* that were being piled on the quay, one after another. Some of the cargo was for others, but the lion's share was his.

The captain and some of the crew were disembarking. Georg had known Rupert Gerlach since he'd been a boatswain, and had followed his career right up to his captain's hat.

"Georg!" the captain shouted. "I've got a letter for you from your brother!"

"Rupert, welcome home!"

They shook hands, and the captain handed him several letters. "And some more for the family."

"Thank you. Did you have a good voyage?"

"An old sea dog like me? I'm unflappable, come what may. But I'm looking forward to a few nights in Sankt Pauli before going back out."

"Take care of yourself, Rupert." Georg put the letters in his coat pocket and nodded at the captain.

"Good luck with the business, Georg!"

The captain tamped some tobacco into his pipe and stuck it in his mouth without lighting it. Then he strolled off toward Sankt Pauli.

"Should I ask Mother if she'd like to come downstairs and listen?" Frederike offered. They were sitting around the table shortly before dinner. Georg had summoned Elisabeth, Martha, and Frederike to a reading of Robert's letter.

"You're welcome to ask, Frederike. But I don't know if she's strong enough," Georg replied.

Frederike stood up and pushed her chair back in. "Excuse me for a minute. And don't begin without me."

"Of course we will wait," Elisabeth assured her.

She wasn't gone long before she walked through the door, shaking her head sorrowfully. "Mother won't be coming," she reported, disappointment showing on her face.

Georg waited for his daughter to sit down before he read the letter:

Cameroon, September 27, 1889

Dear family,
Luise and I are doing really well. As you have seen, we were able to bring in another excellent harvest and will continue doing so for the next several weeks. There was a fire in the adjacent forest, but our plantation was unscathed. Malambuku said the fruits had protected the beans, and he was absolutely right.

213

We've gotten used to life here. Harvest time is arduous and yet fulfilling. We work hard and understand more and more what is essential for working a plantation. The natives say that Mount Cameroon—they call it Fako—is threatening to erupt. But we're not in any danger. The distance the lava would have to travel to reach us is too great.

Meanwhile we're learning the local language better and better, but I have to admit that we're not half as capable as Hamza, Malambuku's son. He's learned to speak our language fluently, and almost without mistakes, so that you might think he'd learned it at an early age.

Life here is simple, but Luise and I are happy. She's sitting beside me and sends her greetings. She'll write you shortly, but at the moment she's busy with the harvest.

We've discussed possibly spending Christmas in Hamburg, and we hope very much that you will be pleased with the thought. In any case we have to wait to see if everything keeps on going smoothly so we won't risk the possibility of having lower yields while we're away.

These words will reach you at the end of October, but we'll let you know in our next letter if you can include us in your Christmas plans.

We hope you're happy and healthy, and we're looking forward to hearing from you soon.

Fond wishes from

Robert and Luise

Georg laid the letter on the table in front of him.

"Mother, did you hear that?" Martha exclaimed enthusiastically. "They want to come home for Christmas!"

"That is not yet decided," Elisabeth responded coolly.

Georg and Elisabeth's exchange of glances betrayed their concern. Martha seemed disappointed. "Aren't you happy they're coming?"

"Please stop being ridiculous, Martha," Elisabeth said, as if giving her a slap on the wrist.

Anna opened the sliding door. "If sir, madame, and Fräulein Martha and Frederike are ready, might I serve dinner?"

"Yes, Anna, please do," Georg answered.

The housekeeper nodded, disappeared, and returned with their dinner.

"Has my wife been given her dinner yet?" Georg inquired.

"Yes, sir."

"Good."

Not much was said over dinner. Frederike told her father about an afternoon tea to which Elisabeth had taken her and Martha. Georg only half listened with an occasional nod of feigned interest. But his mind was elsewhere. Robert intended to come home for Christmas, which would put his affair with Elisabeth to the test. He could only hope their visit would be brief and that Robert would return to Cameroon immediately after the holidays.

◆ ◆ ◆

Cameroon, End of October 1889

Robert was surprised when a ship brought him a letter. The first shipment of beans had just arrived in Hamburg. The letter would certainly not be a response to his latest one. The family must have written him this letter before that, which both delighted and unsettled him. He hoped that nothing terrible had happened.

He opened the envelope with the familiar printed words: *Peter Hansen & Sons. Coffee Merchants since 1850.* He didn't realize right away that it was an old envelope, because "coffee" was crossed out. He could not have been more taken aback when he saw that Vera and not Georg had written him:

Hamburg, September 21, 1889

Dear Robert,

I am appealing to you from the depths of despair since nobody else can help me. If you receive this letter, it is because Anna, that faithful soul, helped me smuggle it out of the house and took it in person to a ship bound for Cameroon.

What I must tell you will be an awful shock. It's about Elisabeth and Georg. I hardly know how to say this because it's so incredible and repulsive that words fail me. But the long and short of it is your wife has become my husband's lover!

I know this must shock you terribly. It did me when Anna told me, and I later watched them several times when they were together. I was at a loss for what to do, so I've done nothing until now. Because— Robert, I hope you don't think I'm mad!—I believe they are trying to poison me!

I had been ill for a long time, so the doctor I consulted at Elisabeth's urging prescribed a sleeping drug. But very soon after, I became sluggish all the time and was hardly myself. I suspect that Georg and Elisabeth have mixed something with my food along with my prescribed medication. Even after I stopped taking it, I felt feeble and tired and could only sleep. Ever since Anna began to throw out the meals Elisabeth brought me and make me new ones, I've been feeling better.

But I dread what might happen if Georg and Elisabeth find out that I'm onto them. I fear for my life, Robert, quite apart from the pain of their adultery and the terrible scandal this affair means for us. And they've managed to turn the children against me, so now I'm absolutely alone except for my faithful Anna.

There's only one way to clean up this terrible business. Please come and take your wife away from here! She has no right to destroy our family. She and Georg disgust me most deeply. They are adulterers, and if my suspicions are correct—and everything points toward it—they are making an attempt on my life!

Please, Robert, you are the only one who can save me! Come and help me, I implore you!

In profound solidarity,
Your sister-in-law Vera

Robert dropped into his chair and tried to clear his head. Elisabeth and Georg! He could hardly believe it. He'd never have imagined his brother could do such a thing. It struck him that he'd only thought of his brother; Elisabeth's betrayal didn't really surprise him. He just wouldn't have guessed that his *brother* would do it. The letter was still in his hand; he looked at it again without actually reading it. Elisabeth and Georg—the people closest to him—had betrayed him.

But that wasn't all. What did Vera say? That they were making an attempt on her life? Was that only the suspicions of an angry, betrayed woman, or could he believe that his own brother was capable of such a thing? No, it couldn't be. Maybe Vera's claim was intended to underscore the seriousness of her situation and pressure him to do something about it.

He put down the letter. But what should he do? What *could* he do? He was in Africa, and home was thousands of miles away. It was harvest time—he couldn't just drop everything and go back with Luise. That simply wouldn't work. He rubbed his tired eyes as thoughts tumbled in his head. What was it Georg had said on their day together during his last visit? That he was looking for meaning in his life? Damn that son of a bitch! Robert had scarcely turned his back and Georg betrayed him two seconds later. He balled up the letter and threw it angrily into the corner just as Luise came into the room.

"What's happened?" she asked when she saw the grim look on her father's face.

"We're taking the next ship back to Hamburg." He stood up. "Take only what you need most. We're going to bring your sister and your mother back here immediately. We won't be spending Christmas there."

"What?" Luise was stunned.

"Pack your things and don't ask questions," he snapped, and stormed out of the room.

Luise watched him in bewilderment. She'd never seen him act like that. What had happened? Her eyes fell on the crumpled paper he'd thrown as she came in. She picked it up, smoothed it on the tabletop, and began to read. After just a few lines, she was horrified and jerked her hand up to her mouth so she wouldn't scream. Now she definitely had to sit down.

It took a while for her to comprehend what this letter from her aunt meant. Tears ran down her cheeks, and she momentarily closed her eyes. She got up from her chair and slowly went upstairs. As she passed her father's room, she knocked on the doorjamb, though the door was open. He was packing his suitcase.

"How are you feeling?"

"I don't want to talk about it, Luise. And I can't tell you what's happened."

She held out the crumpled letter toward him. "I already know. I read Aunt Vera's letter."

Robert hesitated for a moment before he went back to packing. "So you know. Well, I can't change that, though I wish you hadn't read that letter."

"Me, too."

"Now go to your room and pack. Malambuku will find the next ship."

"I don't want to go with you, Father."

Robert looked daggers at her. "We both know I've heard those words before, and they came from your mother's mouth. And we know where that's led. So you are coming, and I'm not going to discuss it."

"I don't want to be there when you two meet." Luise began crying bitter tears.

Robert had been exasperated, but the sight of her moved him. He laid down his shirt, went over, and took her in her arms. "I'm so, so sorry that you have to go through this."

"I don't want to go to Hamburg for a whole month and watch my parents fighting. Please, Father, let me stay here! I'm old enough. Malambuku is here and will take care of me if there's any trouble."

Robert sat back on the bed, undermined. "I feel like everything's slipping away from me. If you don't come with me now, the family will be torn apart once and for all."

"It already was, a long time ago," Luise said bitterly.

"Yes, that's true." It looked as if Robert would burst into tears any second, but he pulled himself together. "I do understand why you don't want to come," he conceded. "But I've definitely got to go."

"Of course. I'll be here when you come back."

"Even if I travel as fast as possible, I won't be here for your birthday, Luise."

"That's all right." She nodded at him.

He put his hands to his face. "I'm miserable. I'm sorry you have to see me in this state."

"I hate Mother for what she's done to you." Luise bit her lip.

Robert dropped his hands. "I will get this settled."

"What will you do when you get to Hamburg?"

"If you weren't my daughter, I'd say I'd go to the villa and beat the hell out of my brother." He snorted. "But because you're my daughter, I'll say I will talk to your mother and bring her and Martha back to Cameroon."

"And then?"

"And then *what*?"

"What will happen? It certainly wasn't easy when she was here before. Do you think it's going to be any better after all that's happened?"

"No." Robert shook his head. "It won't. But I have to do something."

Luise hesitated before asking her next question. "Do you think Aunt Vera's right about Uncle Georg and Mother trying to poison her?"

"No, I don't. Vera must be exaggerating. No, Luise. Your mother may not have been the woman I wanted for your mother and my wife, but she would never make an attempt on anyone's life."

His answer was a relief to Luise.

"I'll take care of the harvest while you're away."

Something struck Robert when she said that. "Yes, do that. But don't send anything to Hamburg."

"No?"

"No. If there's the slightest bit of truth in what Vera claims, I won't be working with Georg from now on."

"But the firm needs our beans," Luise argued.

"Yes. But partnerships are based on trust and honesty. If this is true, Georg won't get one single, wretched bean from us again."

"But who will we sell to?"

"I'll see to that," declared Robert, who was starting to think ahead. "Karl has the Vienna business. We can ship to him directly. And if he'd prefer to stay out of it, I'll find new clients. Believe me, Luise, we'll be fine. But if Georg has done this, I'll see to it that he's ruined."

Luise saw a transformation in her father. Though he'd just been shocked and was desperately disappointed, his growing rage gave him strength to make plans, even if they were designed to harm his brother.

Robert finished packing, and they went downstairs.

Malambuku had just come through the door and looked at them expectantly. "Where to, *sango?*"

"I must go to Hamburg, Malambuku. Luise will be staying here. Promise me you'll watch out for her."

"Promise to protect *nyango* like a daughter."

"Thank you, Malambuku."

"Hamza will sleep in house until *sango* return so *nyango* is never alone."

Robert looked at him. "Excellent idea, Malambuku. What do you say, Luise? Let's have Hamza sleep here. I'd be pleased."

"Why, yes, that sounds fine," she replied, feeling a little overwhelmed. Hamza with her night and day? She didn't know what to think. But she'd have been lying if she'd said she wasn't excited at the thought.

"When's the next ship, Malambuku?"

"Today, *sango,*" Malambuku stated. "Not the ship that takes the beans. Smaller."

"Can I still make it?"

"By horse, yes, if not, no."

Robert turned to Luise. Their goodbye came sooner than expected. He hugged his daughter tightly.

"You know the ropes. There's money enough upstairs where I showed you. If you've trouble making a decision, ask Malambuku for advice."

"Yes, Father, I'll manage."

He kissed her on the forehead. "I'm so sorry I can't be here for your birthday."

"If you don't leave this very minute, you will be!" She gave him a big hug. "Take care of yourself!"

"You, too." Robert hugged her back. Malambuku had ordered a horse while they were saying their goodbyes; the suitcase was already tied onto it, and Robert rushed off.

Luise had tears in her eyes as she waved goodbye. She asked herself what she would do if he didn't return, if something were to happen to him. She'd be all alone. She brushed the thought aside. Father would come back—she could rely on that. But the anxiety wasn't completely dispelled.

Chapter Twenty-One

Vienna, Mid-November 1889

Karl scanned the full shelves in his warehouse happily. It wasn't filled to capacity, but Georg's latest shipment would last a good while. And more was expected in two weeks. Karl hoped Robert could ship enough to fill his warehouse so stock wouldn't get as low as it had last year before the next harvest.

He'd been working until near exhaustion recently, hoping to drive Florentinus and their affair out of his head. There wasn't a day that went by that he didn't wonder whether he ought to write to Florentinus and try to explain why he'd said those terrible things and how sorry he was. But Karl knew that would be a mistake. Things were fine the way they were; any rapprochement would have been accompanied by a danger that Karl wanted to avoid at all costs.

It had proved hard to be a better husband to Therese and forge a life befitting a real man. He still had to summon images in his mind in bed at night so he could perform, but he justified it by telling himself it served a greater purpose. He could feel how pleased Therese was that he was more attentive to her, and he showed her as often as possible how desirable he found her. Yes, everything was as it should be.

He just mustn't dwell on Florentinus anymore. When they met again—unavoidable, given their family ties—time would have healed his wounded feelings. But Karl knew that this wouldn't apply equally to his love. He loved that man as he'd never loved anyone before, or would again. It was a cruel fate that the two people he'd give his life for were, of all people, brother and sister.

Karl heard a customer come in and speak with Felix. Karl recognized the man's voice but couldn't place it, so he put down the bag he was packing and went out front.

"I still find the taste slightly bitter. Is there something else I could try?"

"Good day," Karl greeted the customer, preempting Felix's answer.

The customer seemed to think for a minute before his face registered recognition. "Good day."

"I'll take it from here, thank you, Felix. If you could just finish the sorting back there." He turned to the customer. "How nice to see you here as a customer, Doctor."

"I had no idea this was your company, Herr Hansen. It is Hansen, isn't it?"

"Quite right."

"You're looking better. Is it going well?"

"Yes, thank you. Fortunately I haven't had another attack, and my heartbeat is calm and regular."

"I'm glad to hear it."

"Did I hear you have a question about the beans?"

"Yes, indeed. When I have hot chocolate in a café, it's sweet and not at all bitter. But when my housekeeper makes it at home, it has a kind of bitter aftertaste. Can you tell me what might cause that?"

Karl breathed an inward sigh of relief. For a brief moment he feared the doctor had come for another reason. Maybe, he thought, the doctor had suspected something about his relationship with Florentinus and was now, armed with this knowledge or at least a suspicion, going to confront them with the fact that they both were liable to prosecution.

"Yes, I've had the same experience," Karl said. "It's very possible that your housekeeper is roasting the beans too much. It's best to roast them slowly on a low heat."

"The heat. Yes, that's possible. She's always in a hurry when roasting the beans."

"And that ruins the beans. The roasting process takes time. Tell your housekeeper to have a little more patience. And let me know if it still tastes bitter the next time you come."

"Many thanks for your advice, Herr Hansen. I would like a quarter pound, please."

"With pleasure."

Karl adjusted the weight on the scales and poured the beans into a bowl on the other. Not until he heard the weighted side move up did he stop pouring.

The doctor looked pleased, paid for his purchase, and picked up the paper bag.

"I will let you know if this works," he promised. "Goodbye—and stay healthy, Herr Hansen."

"And a very fine day to you, Doctor . . ."

"Sulzbach," he reminded him. "Doctor Ludwig Sulzbach."

"I'll not forget your name next time, I promise."

Dr. Sulzbach left the store, and Karl stared at the door, lost in thought. He must stop his constant worrying and anxiety over every encounter or harmless remark. Seeing the doctor again was the proof. Karl vowed to work day by day to rid himself of the fears and doubts he was disposed to. He knew he could manage to do that much. The door opened again, and a pleasant-looking woman entered. He greeted her politely, and she asked for cocoa beans to make her own chocolate, just as Dr. Sulzbach had.

"I want very badly to learn the secret," she said.

"What do you mean?" He became anxious again.

"Your wife's secret." She pointed a finger at Karl. "I've seen you together several times. You deliver the cocoa, and your wife makes them into the most delicious chocolate in all of Vienna." She smiled. "They're the same beans. Eventually I am going to find out what's in it, why your wife's chocolate tastes so good."

Karl returned her smile. "Well, you won't get anything from me." He pretended to lock his mouth with a key.

They chatted until the lady took her bag and left. Karl shook his head at himself. Once again, he'd recoiled in horror just because somebody used the word *secret*. This must stop! Once and for all! After closing the office for the night, he looked in on the café to see if Therese was working late, as she'd been doing every evening in recent weeks. Renovating the space next door had paid off but demanded its tribute. Therese was working even more, and a question that hadn't concerned Karl before was now foremost in his mind: What would happen when she became pregnant?

He rapped on the window. "Therese! It's me!"

She was wiping the tables and looked up when she heard his knock. A smile brightened her face, and she let her husband in.

"Good evening." He gave her a kiss. "You look exhausted, my little sunshine."

"I am. But happy." She turned around and swept her hand around the room. "Just a bit more to do, then everything's the way I want it."

"Can I help?"

"No, it won't take long. But if you want to wait, we could go home together."

"You're probably the only woman in the world who works harder than her husband."

Therese laughed. "No, my dear. Not by a long shot. It's that men have a remarkable ability to *not* see the work their wives do—except you."

"You sound like those Englishwomen talking about women's rights."

"To tell the truth, I've read about them," Therese acknowledged. "They're demanding that women get the right to vote, did you know that?"

"I've heard about it," Karl replied. "But honestly, I don't think their struggle stands a chance."

Therese became serious. "So you're against it?"

"No, I didn't say that. If every woman were as clever as you, it would be a crime not to let her vote. Clever minds are needed. You might not want to hear this, Therese, but very few women are like you. If I think about my sisters-in-law, for example . . ."

"What about them?"

"Well, how shall I put it: things like work and responsibility are completely foreign to them."

"Doesn't sound like I'd like them." She looked around. "But we can discuss that some other time," she declared. "Or we'll never get out of here." She picked up her rag and went back to wiping the tables.

"Speaking of my family, I wanted to ask you something."

"Yes?"

"I got a letter from my brother Georg with the last shipment, and he tells me that Robert and Luise will likely be in Hamburg for Christmas. What do you think: Should we seize the opportunity to go there for the holidays so you can meet my family?"

"I'd hoped we could go to my parents' like last year. It was the first time I truly enjoyed Christmas there."

Karl shuddered at the thought of meeting Florentinus there. The atmosphere certainly wouldn't be as jolly as the previous year's was for him. "But you haven't met anybody in my family."

"You're right." Therese moved on to the next table. "Though I think we should take into account that the café brings in the most money before and after the holidays, and I'd have to close it for such a long time."

"You don't want to meet my family, do you?"

"Not so." She turned around, gave him a quick look, and hurriedly wiped the next table. "Well, maybe I'm a little afraid they wouldn't like me."

Karl walked over and laid his hand on her back. "How could you even think such a thing?"

She sighed and straightened up. "I think your family might be just as stuffy and conservative as mine. That I just won't fit in."

He took her in his arms. "Just like me, my little sunshine. And that's why we're such a good match." He kissed her tenderly and took the cloth out of her hand. "Tomorrow's another day, and now we're going home. Agreed?"

"Agreed."

She took his arm and leaned her head against it.

Karl finished closing up, and they strolled through the city streets to their apartment.

"I've been thinking," Karl reopened the conversation. "We do want to have children?"

"Yes."

"But how are we going to manage?"

She shrugged. "Other people do."

"Only because the women stay home and don't work."

"Do you think this is the right time to discuss it? After all, we've just expanded the café."

"That's exactly why I'm talking about it. We should be prepared if you were to get pregnant."

"What exactly do you expect from me?"

"Nothing, Therese. Quite the opposite. I'd like to help if I can."

Therese was quiet for a while. Then she said, "I'm afraid I'm too tired to think about it now. Can we put this conversation off until later?"

"Of course. Just let me know when you're ready."

They'd come to their apartment, and Therese turned to look at her husband. "I thank you, Karl. I mean it truly. There can't be many men as kind as you."

He unlocked the door, leaned over, and gave her a kiss. "My pleasure!"

"Tell them we're coming."

"What's that?" he asked, letting Therese lead them into the apartment.

"Your family," she explained. "Please tell them that we'll come for Christmas."

"Thank you," he responded, happy to have escaped Christmas at the Loisings' villa.

Therese worked the next few weeks until she was near collapse. Her café was now keeping pace with the great cafés of Vienna thanks to the expansion. She had kept her style, but in the new section, all the tables and chairs matched, presenting a uniform appearance—unlike the original space next door. And she noticed something peculiar: most customers preferred the old section. The new area only filled up when all other seats were taken.

Therese observed this for a while and then had Frieda help her change everything so that in both areas there was a merry hodgepodge of furniture. The consequences were immediate: the customers used both rooms equally. Therese laughed to herself because what was originally a stopgap solution coming from a lack of money was now her signature style, and a brilliant success. She discovered that it didn't matter about being the best; it just had to be something that felt comfortable. Her customers were perfectly in tune with her own way of thinking.

But she hadn't found time to talk with Karl about the issue he'd raised: What would happen if she became pregnant? Her workload pushed that thought into the distant future. She was happy with the way things were. She got along with Karl better than ever, her staff was made up of devoted people, and she had hired two new waitresses and another person in the kitchen. In spite of the increase in expenses, there was enough money in the till at the end of the day for her, with her modest demands, to lead a carefree life. Everything was exactly as she'd always wanted it.

But she'd noticed a change in herself the last couple of days, which brought the subject of children into focus. She'd felt nauseous in the mornings and more tired than usual during the day. Aside from that, she sometimes felt a strange pull in her stomach. Might she actually be pregnant, or was it something else? A visit to the doctor brought certainty: she was pregnant.

Her first impulse after seeing the doctor was to go back to work at the café, but she decided against it. Frieda could teach the new waitresses what to do and ensure that everything ran smoothly. So she took some time to walk along the Danube. She wanted to clear her mind and think about what the baby would mean for her life. Two or three months ago, it would have been the most wonderful news she could have imagined. But now she had doubts. Would she be a good mother? Could she really manage the café and still raise children? She couldn't come up with any good answers to these questions.

She waited for Karl at home that evening, sitting comfortably on the sofa when he came in.

"There you are," Karl said as he came in. "I dropped by the café, but Frieda said you'd gone home early. Are you all right?"

"Come in and sit down," she replied. "Yes, everything's fine."

He took off his coat and hung it up before sitting down on the edge of the sofa beside her. "So what happened?"

"Nothing. Well no, that's not exactly right. There's something I have to tell you." She took a deep breath. "I'm pregnant, Karl. We're having a baby." She gave him a big smile.

"What?" Karl needed a second or two to understand what she'd said. His eyes sparkled. "You're pregnant?"

"Yes, Karl. I'm pregnant."

He leaned forward, pulled her toward him, and held her in his arms. "You're having a baby!" He laughed loudly, looked at her, and drew her to him once more. "We're having a baby, Therese, a baby!"

"Yes, Karl. We're going to be parents."

He sat up again and looked at her searchingly. "Tell me, are you happy?"

"But of course I'm happy. I . . ." She searched for the right words. "Oh, Karl, I'm afraid." She leaned on his chest, his arms around her. "I don't know why. I've been hoping all this time. But now it's finally happened, I feel this terrible anxiety."

"Oh, Therese, that's completely normal." He stroked her back tenderly. "It only shows how seriously you take your responsibility. Don't worry! We can do it."

Therese couldn't hold back her tears any longer. "Really?"

He held her tightly. "Really!"

"What about the café?"

Karl waited a moment. It was clear what his wife was afraid of. Could he blame her? She'd built it up all by herself. To put it in someone else's hands would be a terrible loss for her. And even though it wasn't how he'd been raised to think of an upper-middle-class family, he found he wasn't bothered. "We'll find a way for you to keep running the café and still take care of our baby."

"Promise me?"

"Yes," Karl affirmed, "I promise."

Maybe that would in some way make up for the wrong he had done her.

Chapter Twenty-Two

Cameroon, November 1889

The first few days her father was away were hard for Luise. She missed him more than she'd anticipated: at breakfast and at work, but especially in the evening when they would discuss the day's events. Hamza spent as much time with her as he could. They still went to the tree together every morning and often talked until it was time to get to work.

Luise had instructed the workers to store the sacks of beans in the large shed until she'd received word from her father to resume the shipments. She was worried about the course of recent events. The plantation was running well and making a good profit, which was so crucial to the business. But if Vera was telling the truth, would her father refuse to work with Georg ever again? What would happen to the business, and what would Uncle Karl do? Her grandfather came to mind. Would any of this have happened if he were still alive? Luise didn't think so. He'd been a real head of the family. There's no way he would have permitted such goings-on. But everything was off kilter since he'd died.

Luise noticed she hadn't even asked herself whether her mother was capable of adultery. The answer was clear, and not very flattering for the woman who'd raised her. Luise had searched deep within herself to find out what her mother meant to her and her life, and she felt it all depended on the news her father would bring home. *Home.* Yes, Hamburg was not her home; she used the word for Cameroon. And she ardently hoped her parents' conflict wouldn't have repercussions for her future in the colony.

The sun was up, and Luise and Hamza were sitting on the tree trunk, holding hands.

"A penny for your thoughts?" Luise asked.

Hamza deliberated. "I wonder why your father did not take you to Hamburg." He looked at her and paused. "Do you want to tell me? You don't have to."

She thought for a minute because she was sure her father wouldn't approve of her sharing confidential family matters.

"Oh, I'd like to tell you, but I don't want to go against my father's wishes, and I don't think he'd like it."

"I understand. I won't ask again."

"Thank you, Hamza."

"Do you think about going back to Hamburg?"

"No, never. I will stay here as long as I live."

She looked over at Mount Cameroon, surrounded by dark clouds while the sky brightened to rose pink.

"What happens when the time comes for you to choose a husband?"

"What happens when the time comes for you to choose a wife?"

"That's already decided. I am to marry Jala."

"What?" Luise leaped up. "You tell me that by the way? You want to get married?"

"No, I don't want to. But I can't go against the chief's decision."

"When?"

"No date yet. And Jala likes me as little as I like her."

"Then you surely cannot get married."

"It is an obligation, as you say in your language. But I'll think of something." He looked at Mount Cameroon as he pondered some more. "Many people believe that our ancestors answer our prayers and help our wishes come true if we ask them enough."

"And what do you ask for?"

"I ask for moments like this one. I ask that nobody in our village gets the fever. I ask that . . ." He broke off.

"What?"

"I ask that I can choose you, and you me."

Luise lowered her eyes. "Yes, I wish for that, too."

"The chief says *sango* comes and harvest the fruits. And then go to another country and harvest there. This is not their home."

"It is mine, Hamza."

"Yes, you are different." He tightened his grip on her hands. "What happens with your people when someone has chosen?"

"Do you mean a spouse?"

"Yes."

"Well, I think it's like now. They hold hands."

"And then?"

"Then they kiss." Luise gulped, staring into Hamza's eyes.

He unhesitatingly leaned forward and gave her a tender, brief kiss on her mouth. "And then?"

"Then they embrace."

Hamza put an arm around her shoulder and pulled her toward him. She nestled against him and closed her eyes. They stayed for a while until they had to go back to the house, before Malambuku or anyone else came to begin their work for the day.

The days went by in their usual rhythm. Three weeks had passed since her father left; he'd arrive in Hamburg before long. Luise could only imagine how he must feel and the thoughts ranging through his mind. Had he figured out a plan to confront Georg and Elisabeth with what he knew? What would he do? Luise didn't know, couldn't even guess.

She could do nothing more than work her hardest every day and show her father on his return that he could rely on her. At the very least she didn't want to disappoint him.

◆ ◆ ◆

Hamburg, November 23, 1889

He pulled his hat down over his face after the ship had moored and he'd disembarked. Robert didn't want to be recognized; though he'd been away for a long time, he wasn't entirely unknown in the city. It wasn't yet noon. Children were still in school, and Georg was doubtless in his office, assuming he wasn't taking his pleasure with Robert's wife. Robert decided to go by the office and hope he wouldn't be seen. He hated all this secrecy. He'd have preferred to burst into the office and confront his brother with Vera's accusations. But he wanted to make sure first. He intended to catch Georg and Elisabeth *in flagrante delicto* and leave no room for doubt.

A boy ran past and grazed his pant leg. "Sorry," the boy shouted, and scampered on. Robert went around the corner and caught sight of him disappearing into the Hansen office. Surprised, he stopped and waited to see what would happen. Shortly afterward the boy emerged with Georg in tow. Robert pressed himself against the wall to avoid being seen. He was alarmed to see they were coming straight for him. He pulled his hat down at once and quickly crossed the street, walking away from the office. Georg didn't see him, though he passed only fifteen feet away. Robert looked around cautiously. Georg kept rushing on. Where was he off to in such a hurry?

Robert followed him and soon figured it out. The boy had presumably informed him that a ship from Cameroon had arrived. Georg was waiting for the next shipment because it was already two weeks overdue. Robert felt schadenfreude rising in him when he saw that he was right. Georg spoke to a few sailors after they disembarked. One shook his head, which made Georg wave his hands about wildly. The sailors just left him there and went off on their shore leave.

"Yes, brother mine, a shock, isn't it? Why didn't I send the beans?" he murmured softly to himself.

Georg hesitated uncertainly, turned and looked at the ship again, and then went back the way he'd come. Robert refrained from following him. He waited a few minutes before finding a carriage and had himself dropped off near the villa. He walked through the park where they'd played as children; he knew it like the back of his hand. Was the old shed still standing? He didn't want to arrive at the villa before nightfall; Georg and Elisabeth must think they were absolutely safe.

Robert was relieved to reach the shed and find the roof in more or less good repair. He wasn't properly dressed for the cold, not to mention the fact that his body had adjusted to the climate in Cameroon, and he was freezing terribly. It wasn't long before his teeth started chattering. He yearned for the warmth and comfort of the villa, where there was sure to be a fire in the fireplace. He flipped up his collar and rubbed his arms. It wasn't even two o'clock. He'd have to wait seven or eight hours in order not to jeopardize his plan. Damn it! He paced back and forth and jumped up and down several times to warm up. Finally he sat down and huddled up against the wall. His anger was fueled by the cold.

"I'm beginning to worry." Georg was at dinner with Elisabeth, Martha, and Frederike. "I should have received a new shipment from Robert weeks ago, but there was nothing for us on the ship that came from Cameroon today."

"Did he write?"

"No, that, too. There was no letter for me."

"That is peculiar," Elisabeth said. "But it *is* harvest time in Cameroon."

"It is. We can only hope that the plantation hasn't been damaged by another fire or that something else has happened."

"Have any ships gone missing?" Elisabeth looked at Georg, worried.

"I thought of that, too, so I made inquiries. Every one of the ships has come into port."

"Do you think something might have happened to Father and Luise?" Martha asked uneasily.

Georg shook his head. "No, we'd have heard about it from the German envoy in Cameroon if something had happened. No, you mustn't worry."

"What will you do now?" Elisabeth asked.

"I will write him. It's hard because Cameroon isn't developed yet. If they only had a telegraph station there! Then we'd have news in a few days. But right now a letter takes almost a month."

"It will come in good time, you shall see. Even for us Germans it's not easy to civilize an entire country."

"Have you any news from Mother?" Frederike asked, hoping not to be reprimanded for asking.

"She is well and gaining a little strength every day." Elisabeth smiled at Frederike. "Good of you to think of her."

Frederike gave a faint smile and went back to her meal.

After they'd finished, Frederike and Martha went to their rooms, Georg to his study, and Elisabeth to the parlor. The girls soon wished everybody good night and went to bed.

Georg was still in his study, going through his papers, when Elisabeth came in and stood behind him. He leaned his head against her breast, relishing the way she massaged his shoulders.

"You're more worried than you want to admit, aren't you?" Elisabeth asked after a while.

"It's distressing. After all, I've made promises and rely on those shipments to keep them. The amounts Karl alone needs . . ."

"Anything I can do?"

"No, unless you find a way to get a telegraph station into Cameroon."

She leaned down and kissed his forehead. "How long will your supplies last?"

"I can't say. Depends on a lot of factors."

She massaged the back of his neck. "You won't be able to do anything more tonight. But you're badly in need of some relaxation."

"Go upstairs. I'll have a quick look to see if the girls are asleep. Then I'll come to you."

"No" was Elisabeth's answer. "I will wait in *your* bedroom. I think my place is there now that Vera's not here."

Georg wavered. He wasn't comfortable with the idea of Elisabeth completely taking his wife's place. After all, she would be coming back some day.

"As you wish," he nonetheless relented.

Elisabeth kissed him and removed her hands, sensing she'd won another victory.

Georg went to Frederike's room, then to Martha's to make sure they both were asleep and would not wake. Then he went to his bedroom, where Elisabeth was waiting for him in bed.

She smiled at him and pulled the covers down on his side. "Come here."

Georg undressed, but he didn't experience the pleasurable anticipation he usually felt when his sister-in-law beckoned him that way. There was too much on his mind, but he didn't tell her that. He didn't want to provoke an argument and add another thing to his worries.

Robert had watched the lights as they went off and on and noted in which rooms. Now the house was in complete darkness. He hurried across the lawn to the front entrance and reached under the third flowerpot, where there was always a key. Nothing had changed since his childhood in that respect. Robert unlocked the door.

He entered the house silently and was greeted by a virtually intoxicating warmth. It hadn't been raining, but the evening mist had made a damp film over his clothes, which felt clammy and cold, as did his skin. He was tempted to go to the parlor and warm up a little, but he was too anxious to see what might be awaiting him in his bedroom.

He crept up the stairs as quietly as possible, avoiding the sixth step, which had creaked for as long as he could remember. He made it to the hallway, tiptoed to his bedroom, and opened the door as softly as he could. He listened hard, trying to make out any sounds, unable to see anything in the dark. His eyes gradually adjusted, and he saw that the bed was untouched. He exhaled audibly, turned, and left the room.

He stopped at Georg and Vera's bedroom door and listened for a minute. He could hear sounds, soft and muted, but nonetheless distinct. He hesitated. What if Vera and his brother were in there? He dismissed the thought. Why would Vera have written him in desperation if the two of them were still sharing a bed? No, it didn't make sense. He pressed the door handle as gently as he could and opened it. He could sense some movement on the bed in the dark. He wondered what time it was; the electricity was turned off at eleven o'clock. He wasn't sure how long he'd stayed in the park, but he would bet it wasn't eleven yet. So he reached for the light switch.

Elisabeth, sitting on Georg, let out a shrill cry, quickly rolled off her lover, and held up the sheet over her bare breasts. Georg sat up with a jerk and stared at Robert as if seeing a ghost.

Robert gave them a cold, disgusted stare. "What a delightful surprise after such a long journey!"

"Robert, we can explain . . ."

"Oh? I'd absolutely love to hear that," he retorted, folding his arms across his chest.

There were footsteps in the hallway. Frederike and Martha appeared in the doorway. Both of them put their hands to their mouths, aghast.

"Father," Martha said in confusion as she looked at Robert. Then she looked back at the bed. "Mother?"

Elisabeth looked away, humiliation written all over her face. "You two, leave!"

"Why? So you can put on a dress? Just stand up and show them what you are: a whore."

"Robert!" Georg croaked. "Don't talk to her that way!"

"Don't tell me how to speak to my wife! She's a whore, and you're a rotten scoundrel."

"Oh, please don't!" Frederike implored and started to cry.

Robert struggled to get himself under control. "Martha, Frederike, this has nothing to do with you. Go back to your rooms until I call you."

"But I—" Martha tried to object.

"This minute!" Robert commanded.

Frederike and Martha looked at each other, distraught, then ran back down the hallway into Frederike's room.

"I'll wait for you two downstairs. I think we have some things to discuss." Robert slammed the door behind him and went downstairs.

"Herr Hansen, sir!" Anna stood in the hallway in her bathrobe and looked at him with relief. "You're home?"

"Indeed I am. Good evening, Anna. My sister-in-law's letter told me you'd helped her. Where is she, anyway?"

The housekeeper pressed her hand against her mouth, unable to hold back her tears. "Herr Hansen and your wife sent her away."

Robert came closer. "What do you mean—they sent her away?"

"She's in a clinic for people with nervous disorders."

"Nervous disorders?" he asked, flabbergasted. "Vera's not sick!"

"I know," Anna agreed as the tears ran down her cheeks. "Oh, if only you hadn't left, sir!"

"What's the clinic called?"

"I don't know, sir." She sobbed. "I just know that she's in Berlin."

"Berlin?" he asked in disbelief and thought for a minute. "Does Dr. Arnsberg know about this?"

"Yes, sir. He was the one who committed madame. But only because he was told lies." She sobbed again.

Robert looked up as Georg appeared and proceeded calmly down the stairs. Anna took one look at him, curtsied, and ran off like a frightened animal.

"I'm sorry, Robert. This wasn't at all planned."

Robert looked at his brother, pulled back his arm, and punched him in the face with all his strength. Georg staggered and fell on the stairs, remaining there.

"I deserved that." He wiped the blood from the corner of his mouth and grimaced with pain.

"You deserve a hell of a lot more than that, but I don't want to get my hands dirty. I despise you, Georg."

Georg looked up at him. "I love you, Robert."

"Wonderful. You can keep that damned bitch for yourself!"

"Don't talk about her like that!"

"I'll talk about her any way I want. And you as well, you monster! I'll never, ever forgive you two!"

"Robert, do let me explain, please."

"No." Robert stopped him short. "There's nothing you can say in your defense. I trusted you, Georg. Your betrayal hits me harder than hers."

"I don't know what to say. I . . . She's . . ."

"I left everything and went to Cameroon to save our family from being ruined. And this is the thanks I get!" he spat. "God knows you deserve each other!"

Georg looked away and gave up any attempt to explain himself.

"I feel nothing but contempt for you, *brother*." Robert emphasized the last word with scorn. "I promise you're going to regret your adultery.

You and your whore who sneaks into your room." He pushed past Georg and ran upstairs.

Georg watched him go. He felt powerless, unable to go after him, but somehow he managed to pull himself to his feet.

Robert went straight to Frederike's room. He knocked and carefully opened the door. "May I come in?"

Frederike and Martha were sitting on the bed, crying.

"Of course," Martha managed to say.

"I'm so sorry you had to see this."

"We didn't know anything about it, honestly!" Tears kept streaming down her cheeks.

Robert sat down beside them. "Of course not. And you couldn't have done anything if you had," he said in a calm, sympathetic voice.

"When did you come back to Hamburg?" Martha asked.

"Today."

"And Luise?"

"She stayed in Cameroon," Robert explained. "I must go back. I know it's a horrible situation for both of you. Of course you can't stay in this house. Not as long as those two are here."

Frederike and Martha wailed loudly.

"But where will we go?" Frederike sobbed.

"To your uncle Karl. I'm sure he'll care for you until I've straightened things out in Cameroon."

"What do you mean?"

"I have to talk to Uncle Karl first," Robert said. "After that I'll know exactly what will happen."

"What are we to do?"

"Pack up a few things. You're coming with me. We are leaving this house right now."

Frederike and Martha exchanged a look of tacit agreement. They got up and each took a suitcase from the closet and began to pack.

Robert waited in the doorway in case Georg or Elisabeth tried to intervene, but neither of them did.

When the three of them came to the stairway, Robert saw that Georg was no longer there. He carried the girls' suitcases downstairs and asked Anna to have the carriage driver hitch up the horses.

"Where are you going?" Georg shouted as he and Elisabeth emerged from his bedroom. The right side of his face was swollen.

"I'm taking the girls away from here."

"I can't stop you from taking your daughter, but Frederike stays here."

"I'm sure I'm acting as their mother would wish by taking them with me. And they want to come."

"I'm her father, and I will not permit you to take Frederike with you."

"Father, please, I want to stay with Uncle Robert," Frederike begged.

"Take your suitcases and go outside," Robert said calmly to Martha and Frederike, who obeyed instantly.

Robert took a few steps toward the staircase. "She's your daughter *and* my niece, and I won't allow her to live in a degenerate household any longer. You can forbid me to take her—but you can't prevent me."

Georg came down the first two stairs, but Elisabeth held him by the arm. "Please, Georg, don't!"

"Yes, Georg, better listen to your lover. If you try to stop me, I can't guarantee what will happen. You never won a fight with me when we were children. And now I won't stop just because you're pleading for mercy." He looked at his brother coldly.

"Georg, we will clear this up. But not this way. I beg you. He cannot take your daughter away. At least not for good," Elisabeth implored.

Robert waited for a moment to see if Georg would come down. When he didn't move, Robert tossed his head up scornfully, turned around, and went to the door.

There he turned back again.

"You two will rue this—I swear it!"

Chapter Twenty-Three

Berlin, November 24, 1889

They had spent the night in a simple lodging near the train station before taking the first train to Berlin, arriving at about four in the afternoon. They took a carriage to the Charité, the famous hospital where the clinic was housed.

Robert was a bit on edge. He didn't know what lay before them but was determined not to leave the clinic without Vera. In Hamburg he'd considered seeing Dr. Arnsberg, who had been the family doctor for many years, and asking why he'd refer Vera to the clinic. Robert had always thought him a man of integrity who took his oath seriously. But Robert didn't know who was trustworthy, and he couldn't risk having the doctor contact Georg and Elisabeth and so upset his plan.

"You know what to say if anybody asks?"

Martha and Frederike nodded in unison.

"Good. Let's go."

They went into the hospital, and Robert addressed the first person they met.

"Good day. My name is Georg Hansen. I would like to visit my wife."

"Hansen? What's your wife's illness?"

"She's in rehabilitation, recovering from exhaustion."

"Of course. That's a different wing. Down the corridor, then left into the adjacent building."

"Thank you." Robert tipped his hat. "Good day."

They followed the directions, coming to a locked door, where Robert rang the bell.

A moment later a stout, friendly lady of about forty opened the door and asked, "What can I do for you?"

"Georg Hansen. And these are my daughter and niece. We would like to see my wife, Vera."

"I don't know if Frau Hansen is allowed visitors."

"I beg your pardon? Who will stop me from seeing my wife?"

"Oh no, I didn't mean it like that. Our patients need special care." She opened the door wider. "Please come in. I'll ask the professor."

"Thank you."

"Have a seat over there," she said. "I'll be just a minute." She left the room.

They exchanged glances and sat down. Robert rubbed his thighs several times; he was nervous, almost visibly so. But he had to get a grip on himself. If he wanted to fool a professor of neurology, he'd have to concentrate fully.

After a while the nurse came back with a man Robert estimated to be about fifty. He rose to his feet.

"Herr Hansen?" the man asked. "Professor Helmut Hoffmann."

"Good day, Professor Hoffmann." Robert gestured toward the girls. "My daughter and my niece."

The professor welcomed the girls and asked, "What may I do for you, Herr Hansen?"

"I should like to see my wife, Vera."

"*Your* wife?" The professor furrowed his brow. "I'm astonished."

"I can imagine why. You think my wife's husband is another man, don't you?"

"I do."

"I'm afraid I have some explaining to do. I, sir, am a coward."

The doctor looked puzzled. "What do you mean?"

"When my wife came here, she was with my brother and his wife."

"They introduced themselves as her husband and sister-in-law."

"Because I asked them to." He took the professor aside as if not wanting the girls to hear. "Vera and I have had significant problems over the past few weeks, no, months. We quarreled, and I'm afraid I put her under too much pressure. We needed distance from each other, and she needed care, and I knew this clinic could help. But I didn't feel I could bring her here myself." He raised his arms in a gesture of helplessness. "And I was afraid there might be problems in admitting her if her brother-in-law and not her husband signed the papers. I ask your forgiveness for that. I've regained my composure now and would like us to be a family once again."

"I understand, Herr Hansen. And I thank you for being so candid."

"How is Vera?"

"Well, she's calmer. But I'm afraid there is still much work to do." He cleared his throat. "I shall be as frank as you were, Herr Hansen. Your wife believes that you are having an affair with her sister-in-law."

"That is my fault. I did indeed let Elisabeth come too close in my despair over my wife's condition. But please do not think anything untoward happened. I merely asked her for support and advice, when I should have asked my wife. But I'm certain that Vera and I can set our problems aside if I can just see her."

"I understand your wish to see her. I will ask the patient if she would like to see you."

"Thank you, Professor."

"Please wait here."

He left, and Robert sat down next to the girls again.

The professor returned after a brief while.

"I'm sorry, Herr Hansen. She refuses to see you."

"I could just look into her room. I know she would change her mind."

The professor considered it.

"I'm very sorry."

"What about Martha and Frederike? Would she like to see them?"

"The patient became very agitated when she learned you were here, Herr Hansen. I'm afraid I cannot allow her to become agitated again. She said I should tell you, word for word, that you and your"—he looked at the girls and decided not to quote Vera exactly—"that you and your sister-in-law can go to hell. Then she collapsed in tears."

Frederike jumped up. "I want to talk to her just for a minute. Please tell her that!" she urgently asked.

"All right, I'll ask her."

He left the room again. When he came back he said to Frederike, "She will be happy to see you."

"Thank you."

Frederike glanced at Robert and nodded before following the professor. He knocked at the patient's door. "Frau Hansen, your daughter is here."

Frederike poked her head through the doorway. "Hello, Mother."

Vera was so overcome that she held a hand to her mouth, stood, and ran to her daughter. The two embraced and wept.

"I'm so happy to see you," Vera cried as they separated themselves, and she caressed Frederike's cheek.

"Me, too."

They both went over to the bed.

"May I be alone with my mother for a minute?"

"Of course. I'll close the door and wait in the hall."

He was barely out the door when Frederike seized her mother's hands.

"Please listen carefully. It's Uncle Robert who's here, not Father. You were right. Father and Aunt Elisabeth were betraying you. Uncle

Robert told us on the train that you wrote to him for help. That's why we're here. We want to take you with us, Mother. But Uncle Robert was afraid they wouldn't discharge you unless they believed he was your husband."

Vera gasped and put a hand to her chest. "Robert? Oh my God!"

"Yes, Mother. That's why you must pretend he's your husband. So we can get you out of here."

Vera nodded firmly, stood up from the bed, and went to the door. "Professor Hoffmann?"

"Yes, Frau Hansen?"

"I would like to speak with my husband now."

The doctor peered past his patient and gave Frederike a stern look. "You mustn't let yourself be influenced by anything, Frau Hansen. That would compromise your recovery."

"It was an old anger that came back when I heard my husband was here. But it's passed. I would like to speak with him. Please fetch him, Professor."

"All right. As you wish."

Frederike and her mother waited in silence. They were too tense, too nervous to utter a single word. They heard footsteps in the corridor, and the professor came in with Robert and Martha.

"Martha," Vera welcomed her niece first and hugged her. Then she looked at Robert. "Georg! Thank you for coming."

Robert walked over and hugged her. "Vera, you look recovered! How do you feel?"

"Perfectly fine, thank you."

"Well, well. So your time here has helped you."

"Yes. I know I was against it at the start. But you were right to insist I come here."

"I'm so glad you see it that way. Now I believe we can only solve our problems together. If you want to, I'd very much like you to come home with us."

"One moment," the professor interrupted. "It's not that simple."

"What?" Robert asked in surprise.

"Well, I explained it to your brother—when I assumed he was you—during the admission process. Your wife was referred by Dr. Arnsberg, and we've signed a contract. Of course, it was your brother-in-law who signed your name, but the contract is valid."

"As far as I can see, this is a clinic and not a jail. If my wife wants to leave and I, her husband, agree, I don't know on what grounds you can keep Vera here."

"The length of stay that was agreed must be adhered to," the professor insisted.

Robert thought quickly.

"*Now* I see, Professor. Of course the contract will be honored in full." He paused because he didn't know whether his brother had paid everything in advance or there was money owed. "My brother said the cost of treatment has been paid."

"That is correct."

"My wife and I are most grateful to you for your help. It was worth all the money in the world. Consider our payment as compensation. Naturally, we will forego a refund."

"It's not just that," Professor Hoffmann protested.

"I am a businessman, Professor Hoffmann. And I understand financial interests. I understand that a business contract must be honored. You can assign my wife's room to someone else immediately. If that brings you twice the income, so much the better. And now please be so kind as to fetch someone to help my wife pack. We would like to leave for Hamburg right away."

The four of them were on the train in a matter of hours, going not to Hamburg but Vienna. Robert was exhausted. He'd hardly slept at all for the last two nights, and his thoughts and worries swarmed around in his head like hornets.

He thought of Luise and wondered how things were going. His gaze fell on Vera and Frederike, who held hands as though mother and daughter had finally found each other after many years of separation. He'd never seen the two of them so close. He felt all the sorrier for Martha. After what she'd just been through with her mother, she'd never see Elisabeth in the same light again. His wife had destroyed everything. Not only their marriage but also the respect the girls had for her. He felt no pity for Elisabeth, only for their children; the kind of life they'd led up to that point was gone forever.

He wondered what Karl would think. And Richard. What would *he* think when he came back for the holidays and found nobody in the villa except his father and his aunt as lovers. Robert decided to write him in Heidelberg so that he wouldn't be unprepared on his return home.

He looked at Martha, who stared ahead, lost in thought. He took her hand and kissed it. His daughter smiled in return. Then Robert leaned his head back and was lulled to sleep by the train's regular motion.

◆ ◆ ◆

Vienna, November 25, 1889

The train came into the station, hissing and whistling. Robert helped Vera and the girls down from the car and found them a carriage.

"We would like to go to Landskrongasse. Do you know it?"

"Certainly, sir. Please have a seat."

The driver—or Fiaker, as they are known in Vienna—brought the horses to a gentle trot, their hooves striking the paving stones with a regular rhythm.

"I'm most curious to see the look on Karl's face," Robert ventured, trying to lighten the tension.

Vera laughed uneasily.

"Do you think he'll take it well?" Frederike asked.

"He'll be delighted, I'm sure."

They were silent for the rest of the ride.

When the carriage stopped, Robert stepped down before the driver even left his seat, looked up at the storefront, and whistled at the size of the building and its sign, *The Hansen Company*. "Well, have a look at this, would you!"

The others craned their necks.

"I didn't imagine it would be so large," Vera said, astonished.

"Come on. Let's go in and see what the owner has to say about our arrival."

A bell over the door announced them, and a friendly looking young man emerged from the back and came to the counter.

"Good day, ladies and gentleman. What can I do for you?"

"We would like to speak with Herr Hansen. Is he here?"

"Yes, he is. May I say who wishes to see him?"

"Four more Hansens," Robert replied with a smile as he offered him his hand. "Robert Hansen. My pleasure."

"Felix Mursch. It's an honor." He shook Robert's hand and bowed his head slightly to the women. "I'll fetch Herr Hansen right away. Just a minute, please!" He went through the door to the back.

It was no more than two seconds until they heard rapid footsteps, and Karl appeared in the salesroom.

"I don't believe it! Robert, Vera, Martha, Frederike!" He spread his arms wide and hugged one after the other. "I thought Felix hadn't heard properly."

"Karl, it's great to see you again at last!"

"What are you doing here, anyway? Why didn't you tell us you were coming? Therese and I could have made some preparations for your visit."

Felix came back into the salesroom.

"A few days ago, even we didn't know we were coming," Robert said with a wry smile.

"Has something happened? Something about Georg." Karl looked worried.

"He's not hurt. But you guessed right, something *has* happened. Could we go somewhere and talk undisturbed?"

Karl looked at his assistant. "Felix, take a half-hour break."

"But I've already had a break."

"Take another."

Felix hesitated, then took his coat and left.

"I've got a warehouse of cocoa beans here, but nothing to offer you," Karl apologized.

"Doesn't matter. We'll eat at the hotel later."

"I'd invite you to stay at our apartment, but it's quite small."

"We didn't want to put you and your wife to any trouble, and I prefer a hotel," Vera said.

"As soon as Felix is back, I'll bring you to a hotel near our apartment," Karl said. "But please do tell me what's happened."

"It started when Elisabeth, as you already know, refused to go back to Cameroon. She and Martha stayed in Hamburg while Luise and I returned to the plantation," Robert began, and then, assisted by Vera, Martha, and Frederike, told Karl what had happened in Hamburg. "And we came directly from Berlin to here," he said as he finished.

Karl braced himself against the countertop and shook his head in disbelief. "I think I've got to sit down. If you weren't standing here before me, I wouldn't believe it. Georg? Really? Our older brother, the constant, reliable, moral head of the family?"

Vera nodded. "I'd never have believed him capable of it. And Elisabeth. I can't say with certainty, but I believe they wanted to harm me. It was only after Anna threw out the food Elisabeth brought me and made me meals herself, bringing them to me in person, that my head became clear again. There were times when I was incapable of getting out of bed."

"I feel so badly because I thought you just needed to be stronger and then you'd be fine," Frederike said to her.

"Me, too," Martha piped up in a feeble voice.

"Don't be hard on yourselves. Even I had no idea what was going on. How could you two have known?"

"What are your plans?" Karl asked Robert.

"That's one reason we're here." Robert took a deep breath. "I will not run the firm of Peter Hansen & Sons with that man."

"I understand," Karl said.

"You and I, we make up a majority. Unless"—Robert hesitated—"you side with him?"

"I'd never dreamed I'd have to choose between you two." Karl's expression was serious. "But after what you've told me, there's no doubt about which brother I'll continue to work with."

"Thank you, Karl. I believed that's what you'd decide, nothing less."

"What do you think we should do now?"

"I gave it a lot of thought on the train. My first idea was to return to Cameroon, keep working the plantation, and send the beans exclusively to you or others—but not to Hamburg. But that way I would still be in business with him, so I threw out that idea."

"Which means?"

"I'll look for a steward to oversee the plantation instead of me. I, or rather we, will tell Georg that we no longer want him in the business and pay him a third, minus outstanding debts, and send him on his merry way."

"Suppose he refuses?"

"Then *we* bow out of the firm, and he'll have to pay us off, which he certainly can't afford."

"So he has no choice."

"No, he doesn't." Robert raised his head. "He gets one third of everything, including the value of the villa. And then he is to disappear. I will take over the Hamburg office and restore the firm to its former glory."

Karl looked worried. "I haven't the slightest doubt that you'll pull it off. That *we* will pull it off. It will ruin him, you have to recognize that."

"I do."

"It won't be easy for me. After all, he's still my brother."

"He was my brother until he slept with my wife."

Karl sighed. "That's right. It's unforgivable."

"And what will happen to us?" Vera chimed in.

"Martha stays with us. I'll never allow her to live with *that woman*"—he spat out the words with contempt—"again," he said. "You and Frederike can choose wherever you want to live. You're family, and Karl and I will provide for you."

Karl nodded his strong support. "You have my word on it."

"I'll make sure that Georg and Elisabeth leave the villa as soon as possible. Then we'll all move in again: Vera with Frederike, and I with Martha and Luise."

"I'd never have imagined the day would come when we brothers were divided."

"Me neither," Robert concurred. "But we're not to blame, only Georg."

The bell over the door jangled as Felix returned. "Am I interrupting?"

"No, Felix. Good you've come. Can you please lock up tonight? I have to see to my family."

"Yes, Herr Hansen."

Karl showed them to a hotel near his and Therese's apartment. They agreed that the travelers should freshen up while Karl went to the café to tell Therese about their unexpected visitors.

They went out to a restaurant for dinner, where the rest of the Hansens met Therese for the first time. They took to one another immediately. Maybe it was because Karl had told Therese in advance about what had happened in Hamburg. At any rate she felt she had real, honest people around her who were devoid of the upper-class arrogance and aloofness that she'd secretly anticipated. In spite of the unhappy circumstances, it turned into a hearty, informal evening, and Therese looked forward to spending more time with her husband's relatives and getting to know them better. When she and Karl announced toward the end of the evening that they would soon become parents, the warmth between Therese and Karl's family was assured.

Therese could not know how valuable that cheerful evening was for the Hansens from Germany, and how much strength they gained from their brief time in Austria with her and Karl. It meant the most to Vera, who'd suffered the hardest and knew that many trying days were ahead, until she restored some faith in her future. It meant almost as much to Frederike, who felt guilty about not standing up for her mother and being deceived by Elisabeth, and whose father had permanently forfeited her devotion and respect with his transgressions. And Martha, of course, who'd seen her mother in such a disgusting situation and who had heard her distraught father call his wife a whore. None of those three would ever forget the past few days. But they left dinner with the hope that their life in Hamburg would get back on the right track.

And of course, his brother's support meant a great deal to Robert. He had suffered a profound betrayal—thanks to his wife *and* beloved elder brother. But his obligations to the business and responsibility for his family—along with his deep hatred of Elisabeth and Georg—would carry him through the next few months.

The next day Robert wrote to Luise about the recent events and his decision to hand over the plantation to a steward. He knew his daughter would not be pleased; she had no choice but to accept it. He also said he didn't know exactly when he would make a final voyage to Cameroon to organize things *in situ* and return with her to Hamburg. He suggested she ask Raimund Leffers to see if he might be willing to administer the plantation. After all, he hadn't any actual function there, a fact that likely weighed heavily on the clever young man.

Robert and Karl walked together discussing the steps for their split with Georg.

"I've spoken with Therese," Karl began. "She asked me to suggest that I go with you to Hamburg and that Vera, Martha, and Frederike stay in Vienna until things are cleared up. They've already been through enough."

"Do you *want* to come?"

"I think it's for the best. Georg should see us united, side by side, to let him know we're serious."

"Thanks for that, Karl."

"I don't know what I'd have done if I'd been in your shoes."

"Do you know what's the worst thing about this whole business?"

"No."

"I feel that the blame is all on me because I brought that poisonous snake into the family."

"Nobody forced Georg to sleep with her," Karl objected. "Not even Elisabeth. It was his decision and his alone, and now he's got to face the music."

"Luise will hate going back to Hamburg. She's really blossomed in Cameroon."

"Luise is young. She'll be sad for a while, but give her time, and she'll find that Hamburg's still a beautiful place."

"I hope you're right."

Karl and Robert left for Hamburg two days later. Frederike decided to help Therese in the café while they stayed in Vienna, and Martha would attend to Vera, lending her loving support.

Therese was happy to have found something to occupy Frederike at least. She couldn't understand why Martha refused her offer. She was convinced it would be better for Vera, too, to find some meaningful activity rather than spend the time dwelling on her broken marriage and her husband's betrayal. Apart from that, Therese would have found it utterly boring to spend the day the way Vera did: going for walks and reading a book at the hotel. But she resigned herself to the fact that her sister-in-law and she were two very different people.

Chapter Twenty-Four

Hamburg, Beginning of December 1889

Robert had borrowed a winter coat from Karl but still felt inadequately armed against the cold. Or was it anxiety at the thought of what would play out in the next few hours or days?

During the trip, they rehearsed every possible response to any move Georg might make. They felt well prepared as they walked from the station to the firm to confront their brother.

Fräulein Denker looked at them with astonishment when they came in.

"Good day, Fräulein Denker. Is our brother in the office?"

"Good day. What a surprise to see you! Shall I tell him you're here?"

"We'll just go on up," Robert replied.

They mounted the stairs and stormed into Georg's office without knocking, startling him by flinging the door open.

"Robert? Karl?" His eyes jumped from one to the other as he stood.

"Skip the welcome." Karl waved him off. "Robert told me what's been going on, so there's no point to false friendliness."

Georg sank back down as Karl and Robert sat on the other side of his desk.

"I wish you'd given me a chance to explain," Georg said, turning to Robert.

"And why? Why should you have a chance, when you behaved like a swine, cheating on your wife and with mine, for God's sake?"

Georg was about to say something sharp, but caught himself in time. "I understand it's useless. However, I would like to apologize sincerely for my behavior, Robert. We never wanted to hurt you."

"Save it. We didn't come here to forgive you."

"So why did you?"

"We want you to quit the firm." Karl came unceremoniously to the point.

Georg sat bolt upright. "What did you say?"

"You heard me. We no longer want to work with you."

"The very idea! I may have committed a personal transgression, even a serious one. But to demand I leave the firm because of it—that's ridiculous. They are two separate things that have nothing to do with each other."

"They do for us," Karl retorted. "We can't trust you anymore, Georg."

"I have never taken one cent out of the business without your knowing."

"Oh no? Then how did you pay the clinic when you wanted your wife to disappear?" Robert asked with a grimace.

Georg's eyes widened.

"Don't take the trouble to go to Berlin. Vera isn't there anymore. We're taking care of her now."

"She's ill! You don't have any right to do that. And I took the money out of my share of the profits."

"Justify it all you want," Karl objected. "Though after all I've heard, I wonder if you're still in *your* right mind."

"Are you so blind that you can't see where Elisabeth's taking you? You deceived your brother, locked up your wife, lied and lied some more, and don't see that you'll be left with nothing in the end."

"Leave Elisabeth out of this! You never appreciated her."

Robert shook his head. "Think of her what you will. But let me ask you one thing, brother dear: After you tell her you don't have a penny to your name, how long do you think she'll stay?"

"Elisabeth loves me!" Georg banged his fist on the table.

"This is going nowhere," Karl said, putting his hand on Robert's arm to calm him down. "We're here to take care of the formalities."

"There's nothing to take care of." Georg snorted. "I will continue to be the head of the company, and that's that!"

"And where will you get the beans from?" Robert said, mockingly.

"If you don't supply them, I'll find others who will."

"And how will you pay them?"

It seemed as if Georg still hadn't gotten it. "The firm's in good shape. I don't need you two."

"Oh? That's what you think?" Karl countered. "Robert and I have discussed it thoroughly. You can have the Hamburg office. But you'll have to pay the two of us our shares."

"That would bankrupt the business, and you'd be left with nothing!"

"Wrong!" Karl exclaimed. "It doesn't matter whether the sacks coming to Vienna are labeled 'Peter Hansen' or 'Robert Hansen.' The Hamburg office turns a modest profit—but only because of coffee sales. To keep it going would cost Robert and me more than it does to shut it down. That's the bitter truth."

Georg looked rapidly back and forth between them. "You can't do this."

"We can and we will. We're offering you the only way out. Take it or leave it."

"What is it?"

"We will pay you your share of the firm's total value less your portion of the outstanding debts. On top of that, you will receive payment for one third of the villa."

"The villa?"

"Yes. We can't let you keep on living there. Accept our offer, Georg. Otherwise we turn off the flow of money at the spigot, and you'll be insolvent in less than two months."

"The business is just recovering. If I leave now, I'll barely have enough to live on for a year, even with the villa thrown in."

"Then it's time you started working on finding a new income."

"How? There'll be gossip all over Hamburg. I won't stand a chance here."

"Perhaps you ought to think about leaving Hamburg." Robert shrugged.

"I need time to think this over."

"No." Karl contradicted him firmly. "The instant we leave this room, we're going straight to Palm and making arrangements. And he will get *either* instructions from us to calculate our current value including debts *or else* news that Robert and I are leaving the firm, which will result in the business defaulting on the debt. Say how you want it."

"You two are thugs!"

"Think whatever you like. So? We need a decision."

"Elisabeth won't want to move out of the villa."

"Believe me, Karl and I couldn't care less what Elisabeth does or does not want. You wanted that woman, and now you've got her."

"But we're brothers. Let's talk this over."

Robert stood up. "Let's go, Karl. There's nothing more to say. It seems he doesn't want to accept our offer."

Karl followed him toward the door.

"Fine," Georg shouted as they reached the doorway.

Robert turned and looked straight at him. "We'll have the papers drawn up. We'll be here tomorrow with the notary."

With that they left the office and didn't see Georg collapse in his chair in tears.

It took five days to have the contracts signed and the villa and the business transferred to only the two brothers. Robert was surprised how relentless and calm his brother Karl was during the negotiations. Apparently Georg's deceitfulness vis-à-vis Robert had hit him harder than Robert had thought.

"I shall *not* move out of here," Elisabeth announced emphatically. "And no one can force me to." She shook her head vigorously.

"You will, believe me," Robert responded in a calm voice.

"I am still your wife."

"I'll see to that part later," Robert announced. "I'm sure I can find a judge who will find your *attachment* to other family members repulsive enough to grant me a divorce. The question of guilt has plainly been laid to rest, and you know it. Consider yourself lucky that I'm putting divorce aside for now and sparing you, for the time being at least, the humiliation associated with it."

"And if I do *not* leave?"

"You don't think I can find a way to encourage you to move out immediately? Perhaps I should have a word in confidence with a few good friends in Hamburg society? You obviously don't know me very well."

"You wouldn't dare!"

"*I* would," Karl butted in, which flustered her.

"Please, Elisabeth," Georg pleaded, "let's pack and go. They're right. The villa's theirs now."

"Because you gave in," she scolded. She held her head up stiffly. "If my daughters will be living here, I have an equal right to stay."

"You know, Elisabeth, there were times when I appreciated your ability to come up with new ideas, even admired it. But those times are gone."

Still furious she suddenly changed her expression. "Where am I to go?"

"I've found something that will do for a while until we get back on our feet," Georg said in a feeble voice.

"I shall not live in some wretched hole in the wall!"

"Now I've had enough!" Robert took a step toward her. "You have one hour to pack and get out. Otherwise, I hereby swear, Karl and I will push you out the door ourselves. Do you understand?"

Elisabeth said nothing, just stared at Robert.

"Aha, you've understood," Robert said. "Karl and I are going up to the study and will wait there. One hour and no more. By that time you'll both be out of the house. Let's go, Karl."

"And don't think about taking the silver, it's included in the villa's evaluation," was Karl's parting shot.

Georg tried to take Elisabeth by the arm.

"Don't touch me!" she hissed.

Karl and Robert couldn't hear anything else because they'd closed the door behind them. They had a few glasses of Danziger Goldwasser and a cigar. They went downstairs exactly one hour later.

There was no sign of Elisabeth or Georg—and the silver was gone as well.

◆ ◆ ◆

Cameroon, December 1889

Luise stared at the letter from Vienna in disbelief. It couldn't be! It mustn't be! She had to read her father's words five times to understand what had happened in Hamburg. The events seemed monstrous, and at the same time, Luise didn't want to accept that they meant she would have to leave Cameroon.

Her sixteenth birthday had passed recently, and nobody had given it a thought, including Malambuku and Hamza, of course. She didn't hold it against them. Celebrating birthdays was not a custom in their culture, and Malambuku had certainly forgotten that it was a year since her family had sent her the rabbits. She admitted to herself that she was sad not to have received good wishes from a single person on that day.

Several days after the letter arrived, Christmas was upon them. Impossible for her father to be back by then. What was she to do? Go to church? Sundays she had to run a gauntlet now since everybody kept asking when her father would return and expressed their concern that she was alone on the plantation with all those Africans. On the other hand, she couldn't stay away from church at Christmastime. It was a dilemma. Worse than the uncertainty about her father's return was that it would immediately end their life in Cameroon. The very thought brought acid into her throat. What could she do to avoid going back to Hamburg?

In her desperation she'd read Hamza the letter right away. Since then the feeling between them was one of foreboding. Hamza was disappointed that Luise couldn't keep her promise to stay in Cameroon all her life. But what could she do? She was sixteen but couldn't possibly go against her father's will. Her despair drove her to contemplate momentarily having an affair with Raimund Leffers. If he were to take over the plantation, she could use that to try to stay in Cameroon. But her father would never permit it, aside from the fact that Luise didn't want to give herself to any man but Hamza. The price was too high. But it was urgent to come up with something if she didn't want to lose him and her life there. But what?

She'd cried so much the last several nights that she was too tired to watch the sunrise with Hamza. She did her daily chores listlessly and without smiling; at night she cried herself to sleep. After not seeing her at the tree for four consecutive days, Hamza came at sunrise on the fifth day into Luise's room. She was asleep in bed and didn't wake up.

"Luise." He touched her shoulder gently. "Luise, the sun is coming up."

"I'm too tired."

"Soon you will be gone. Then we will have only memories."

Luise blinked at him. "I'm so tired. I've no energy. I can't get up."

Hamza thought for a minute before lifting the sheet and crawling into bed with Luise.

"What are you doing?"

"I would like to be with you and hold you as long as it is possible."

At first she didn't know how to feel, but soon she snuggled up to him. They both went to sleep, and Hamza didn't tiptoe out of Luise's room until just before he had to go to work.

The next day Luise invited Raimund Leffers over, and he accepted. Luise summarized for him what her father had written.

"So I would be in your father's service?"

"I suppose so." Luise shrugged.

"Why do you want to leave Cameroon?"

"I don't want to leave," she protested. "Most definitely not. But there were changes in the Hamburg office that require my father's personal attention."

She liked Raimund, but she didn't want to tell him the truth about the awful mess her family was in.

"I understand. And he thinks I'm up to the task?"

"Well, I've managed it for the few weeks he's been gone. Mostly without Malambuku."

"And Hamza?"

"Yes, and Hamza."

"May I ask you something, Luise?"

"Please do."

"Are you in love with Hamza?"

Luise blushed instantly. "What are you talking about?"

"Nothing. Forget it."

"What made you say something like that, Raimund? I thought we were friends."

"I oughtn't to have asked. Please, forget it."

His question annoyed her. Was he trying to provoke a reaction? And if so, why?

"Maybe it's better if you left. You can consider my father's offer."

Raimund got to his feet. "I will. Please forgive me if I offended you. That wasn't my intention."

"Why did you ask? To accuse me of something?"

Raimund shook his head. He wavered, wrestling with himself, and finally said, "Because *I* am in love with a girl from here and had hoped to talk about it openly with you. I thought you had feelings for Hamza and might understand me for that reason."

Luise looked at him, taken aback.

"I urgently request that you not tell my father. He'd probably give me a whipping."

"Raimund, please, sit down?" Luise asked, regretting her reaction. "I misunderstood you, please excuse me."

"I shouldn't have said anything."

"Raimund." She pointed to his chair. "Please."

He sat down again reluctantly.

"I reacted that way because it's true, and I felt vulnerable," Luise explained.

A smile flickered across Raimund's face. "I'm relieved, Luise, really. I've suspected you were fond of him. But you objected so strongly I thought you found the mere idea of loving an African repugnant, so you couldn't understand my feelings."

"I understand them. Too well." She sighed. "I can't imagine a day without Hamza. But my father will force me to give up everything here. And I'll never see Hamza again."

"What if you didn't go?"

"You know yourself, I have no choice. I'm sixteen and a woman. No German father would permit his daughter to live in Africa by herself."

"Have you ever thought about escaping?"

"What do mean 'escaping'?"

"Simply running away when your father comes back. You can leave him a note saying you're all right but will stay away until you're old enough to make decisions about your life on your own."

Luise gave a hollow laugh. "You've got to be joking!"

"No, not at all. I'm thinking about it myself."

"Really?" Luise's pulse quickened. Was it possible that Raimund had a way out for her?

"Yes. There are villages in the British colonies where white immigrants live with Africans. That's where I'd like to go with Suna."

"Your girlfriend's name is Suna?"

"Yes. She isn't actually my girlfriend. Not yet. She feels the way I do. But she'll soon be given in marriage to a man from her tribe."

"The way that Hamza's supposed to marry Jala."

"It's remarkable how similar our stories are."

"Those villages in the British colonies, nobody cares?"

"It definitely won't be easy there. But it's different from the way it is here. I must get away from my father above all if I don't want to get beaten to death."

"Is it far from here?"

"Well, yes, it's several days."

"You've planned to leave for quite some time, haven't you?"

"Yes. And that's why I can't accept your father's offer."

"Doesn't matter. He'll find somebody else. But that village . . . I mean, what do I do if I want to go there with Hamza, too?"

"So you're thinking about it?"

"Yes. But it would have to be fast. Father's coming back soon."

"It will work even when he's here. We'd leave at night. But you mustn't say a word about this to anyone except Hamza, do you hear?"

"Yes, of course."

"Here's the plan. I'll let you know when I've got everything ready. If your father returns in the meantime, send me word. I'll let you know the next possible time, and then the four of us will leave."

Luise's heart beat wildly. "Yes. Let's do it, Raimund."

"Don't you want to talk to Hamza first?"

"I'm sure he'll agree."

Raimund stood up. "Good. Then let's do it. You'll hear from me in the next few days."

"Or you from me."

Luise didn't sleep a wink that night. When first light finally broke, she hurried to Hamza's room to take him to the tree. He was happy, if somewhat surprised, to see her cheerful for the first time in so long.

As soon as they got to the tree, she shared what Raimund had told her. But Hamza's reaction was not what she'd expected.

"You're saying no?"

Hamza looked at his hands. "I can't abandon my village and my tribe, Luise."

"You mean you don't *want* to!"

"No, I mean I *cannot*. My family is dependent on my support. What would happen to my brothers and sisters if my father got sick and couldn't work anymore? Who will take care of them?"

Luise didn't know how to respond. She was sad and furious at the same time. "You'd rather accept that we'll never see each other again?"

Hamza looked at the ground and took her by the hand. "I don't want to lose you, Luise."

"But that's exactly what will happen if we don't go." Her voice cracked. "When my father comes back, he'll arrange everything in a few days and then take me back to Hamburg. It won't be hard to find one of the Germans here to be a steward on the plantation."

"So we'll get a new master?"

"Yes, presumably. I don't think my father will turn over all the responsibility to your father."

"Then that is how it will be."

Luise began to cry. "Please, Hamza, let's go to the British colony."

"And what kind of life will we have?"

"I don't know. But at least we'll be together." She snuggled up to him. "Don't you want to be with me?"

"You know I want to."

She pressed against him more closely, kissed his cheek, then his neck. Hamza turned to face her. Their lips met. They clutched each other like drowning people. Their kisses became more demanding. They held each other tighter and tighter, kissing and caressing, slipping off the tree trunk down into the grass. Hamza's hand slid under Luise's bathrobe, and she opened his fly. Hamza pulled her nightgown up, let his hand play over her breasts. Luise felt everything spinning around her. They'd never touched like this, never felt such passion. Luise tugged his pants down, and Hamza took them the rest of the way off. Then Luise stroked his thigh until she touched his erection. She didn't have any idea what to expect, how it would feel, hadn't given it any thought until then. Touching him there now excited her to the core. Hamza stroked between her legs, and Luise sighed, gasped for air. She exhaled loudly and spread her legs. Hamza braced and placed himself on top of her, and penetrated her. It hurt briefly, but then it was wonderful, beautiful. Luise's heart raced, she arched up against him. Hamza lifted himself up, and shortly afterward his movements died away. Gasping, he laid his head on her breast, to slow his breathing.

He raised himself up on his elbows and looked into her eyes. "You're crying?"

"No." She smiled at him. "They're tears of joy."

He kissed her mouth, rolled off her, and lay holding her on the grass for a long while. Neither of them said another word; there were too many feelings for them to speak. They parted in front of Luise's room with a tender kiss. Then Luise sank down onto the bed. Though her heart was still beating rapidly, she was asleep in a second.

It was Christmas Day, and Luise went to church with the rest of the Germans. She smirked because the hymns were exactly the same and in the same order as last year. When they came to "Silent Night," Luise was grateful. She hadn't been able to concentrate on what the pastor was saying and just as little on the carol. After the service some of the congregation asked her to come celebrate with them instead of being on the plantation by herself. Luise had refused with thanks and was about to leave when Raimund came up beside her.

"Everything's ready," he said.

"Really?"

"Yes."

"Good. I'll tell Hamza and send you word. I'd like to go after my father comes so I can see him one last time."

"But don't give it away. You know what that would mean for all of us."

She shook her head. "I'll be careful, I promise."

It was December 30, 1889, when the *Erna Woermann* anchored off the coast and Robert Hansen returned to Cameroon.

While she was working, Luise smiled at the memory of the previous night, which she'd spent by Hamza's side just like the preceding ones, blissful through and through. They didn't go to the tree anymore; he came directly to her room long before sunrise, and they would make love. How wonderful it was! Downright intoxicating! She raised her head when she heard him running up behind her.

"Your father," Hamza shouted up to her. "He's back."

They exchanged glances. They knew that the time had come for them to leave. Luise nodded at Hamza, and they ran to the plantation together.

The Duala crowded around Robert, welcoming him back.

"Father!" She ran up to him.

"Luise!" He spread his arms and hugged her. "My Luise, oh, how I missed you!" He held her as if he would never let her go.

"Were you able to get everything settled?" she asked.

"Yes. Come and sit down. I've so much to tell you." He looked around. "I see everything's the same. I admit I'm not surprised. I knew you'd keep everything in good order."

"Good day, Herr Hansen." Hamza bowed shallowly. "It is nice to see you again, and well."

"Hamza." Robert shook his hand and clapped him on the shoulder. "Your German has improved. You speak like an educated young German man."

"Thank you very much, Herr Hansen. That's kind of you to say."

Luise took her father's arm and went to the veranda along with Malambuku.

"It's good to be back," Robert said, stretching his legs.

"I'm happy you are, too. You look exhausted."

"That I am," Robert confessed. "The last few weeks were difficult."

"What's happened since your last letter?"

Malambuku came with drinks, and Robert took a big gulp.

"Thank you, Malambuku."

"Good you're back again, *sango*."

"I'm glad to be back, too."

271

After Malambuku had left, Robert said, "Your mother's no longer living in the villa; neither is your uncle Georg."

Luise nodded and kept silent.

"Vera, Martha, and Frederike are delighted you're coming home, and we'll all be living there together. Your uncle Karl and your new aunt Therese came for Christmas. Therese is pregnant, by the way. She's a charming woman—you'll like her. They'll have gone back home long before we arrive, but there'll be time for you to get to know her."

Luise faced him squarely. "Please tell me why we must leave Cameroon."

"You know why. I'll be running the Hamburg office from now on, and Karl will work out of Vienna."

"But I love living here!"

"I know, Luise. But there's no other way right now. Maybe one day. But not now." He took another drink. "Did you speak to Raimund Leffers?"

"Yes. He has other plans," she said curtly.

"Too bad. But I'll be able to find somebody."

"I could stay, of course." Luise smiled wanly, knowing her suggestion wouldn't be taken seriously but wanting to have at least said it.

"Oh, my dear Luise." He shook his head. "No, I certainly can't leave you here. But I appreciate your offer."

"Will you and Mother divorce?"

"I don't know. A procedure like that isn't simple, though I'm sure any court in the land would determine that to prolong the marriage would be unreasonable. But it's not a priority at the moment. What's important now is that we head for calmer waters. Grandfather's death threw everything off track. But the fog's slowly lifting, and I'm confident we'll be able to lead a normal, respectable life in a matter of months."

Luise wanted to say that life in Cameroon was normal, too, and beyond that, it was magnificent, and she enjoyed every minute of it. But she knew she couldn't change his mind.

"When do we leave?"

"In three days."

"So soon?" Luise was wide-eyed. It was all coming so fast now. In just three days, she'd leave her life completely behind. The thought scared her.

They had a light meal together, and Robert went to lie down after his long voyage. Luise went to her room and wrote to Raimund to let him know they'd have to leave the night of January 1 at the latest. She gave it to a Duala man to deliver and watched him leave, letter in hand. Luise felt she was a traitor to her own father.

The first of January, 1890, arrived—the day Luise Hansen was to turn her back once and for all on the life she'd led. She'd spoken with Hamza that afternoon. They agreed to meet at the tree and go from there together to meet Raimund and Suna. Luise had noticed how quiet and withdrawn, even despairing, he was. She'd asked him why, but he hadn't wanted to talk about it. She was afraid for a moment that he wouldn't come. But no. Hamza would never do that to her.

The ship that was to take Robert and Luise to Hamburg had been at anchor for a day. Robert had seen that the beans had been loaded onto carts and, along with their personal luggage, were already on board. Luise was sorry that she could only take a few things to the colony, but she couldn't risk arousing her father's suspicions if she didn't bring all that she owned on board. So she resigned herself to taking little more to the British colony than what she carried on her. It pained her most that her father had the rabbits sent on board so they wouldn't have to carry additional baggage with them the next morning. It was terribly difficult for her to say goodbye to them, but she couldn't have taken them with her, anyway.

Robert told the ship's captain that he would be pleased if the ship left as early as possible. That was fine by the captain since the cargo was already on board. It allowed Robert to say farewell to Hamza and the rest of the Duala at the end of the previous workday. He'd see Malambuku the next morning since he'd slept in the farmhouse that night so he'd be on hand for their early departure.

Luise and her father said farewell to the natives she'd known for more than a year, who'd increasingly occupied a place in her heart each day. She smiled at Hamza and squeezed his hands while saying farewell. He lowered his eyes and looked at the ground. Suddenly Luise felt anxious. Would her lover not come? Or was he just sad to have to leave his people behind? She attempted to drive away those dark thoughts, put on a happy smile, and promise the Duala she'd be back. One day, she said, they would see one another again.

Evening came, night fell, and then finally the first light of day broke through the clouds. Luise hadn't slept. She'd been sitting in bed, completely dressed, and waiting. At first light she rose, picked up the small bundle containing her diary and portfolio, and tiptoed down the hallway and stairs to the front door. She looked around for the last time. She'd probably never see that place again. Tears welled up in her eyes.

"Forgive me, Father," she whispered.

She walked across the plain to the fallen tree, *her* tree, where she'd sat almost every morning for more than a year to greet the sun. How terribly she'd miss it! But she hoped that in the British colony, there'd be steppes and landscapes and that she'd discover a good view for enjoying the sunrise. The main thing was that she'd be there with Hamza, the man she loved with all her heart. Yes, it was the right decision.

She took out her diary and read some passages about her feelings when they'd first arrived in Cameroon and what motivated her to write them down: a deep longing paired with the sentiment that everything that had happened since then felt incredibly right.

The sky was slowly turning brighter pink. Luise looked around, smiling. Hamza wasn't there yet, but he would be at any minute. She looked again at Mount Cameroon before her: a huge black shadow rising above the surrounding landscape. She dwelled on it for a while, then gazed up at the sky. Pink still dominated, but gradually distant tints of orange appeared. She turned to look behind her once more. Hamza was late, much later than usual. What was keeping him? It was almost time to set out and begin their new life. Was he slow taking his leave of his brothers and sisters, maybe looking at them once again as they slept, for one last time?

She stared at the mountain for a few seconds longer before turning around—she didn't want to miss seeing Hamza emerge from the brush. Suddenly a strange feeling crept over her. Could it be that he wasn't coming? Never, she concluded. Never. He'd never do that to her. She'd given herself to him. They'd vowed their love for each other. It couldn't be—he wouldn't hurt her that way. Even if he found it difficult to bid farewell to his family and friends in the village, he'd told her, *promised* her, that he'd chosen her and a life with her.

The pink in the sky disappeared, the orange grew stronger and stronger until it turned into a warm yellow. Luise turned around again, looking at the mountain as tears ran down her cheeks. She didn't know how long she sat there. It must have been hours. Hours during which the realization that he wasn't coming had permeated her body like a cancer. Then she heard familiar footsteps but didn't turn around.

"There you are. I was getting worried. Are you saying goodbye?"

She nodded without looking at her father. "I'll probably never be here again."

Robert put a hand on her shoulder. "Oh, Luise, who knows what will happen over the years?" He bent over to kiss her hair. "Let's go. There's still time if we want to get something to eat."

"I'm not hungry."

"Neither am I, to be honest, and Malambuku has packed us enough so we won't starve." He touched her arm. "Well now, let's go."

They walked back to the house. Luise didn't want to go inside but to leave at once. As she and Hamza should have done. She choked up at the thought.

She went over to Malambuku and gave him a hug. "I'll never forget you, Malambuku. Never, as long as I live."

"Malambuku hopes to see *nyango* someday again."

"No, Malambuku. I don't think I'll ever come back. Farewell!"

She raised her head and looked once again into his warm, familiar eyes. They were Hamza's eyes, too. She smiled, turned, and walked over to her horse. Robert and Malambuku exchanged a few more words before her father came to her; they took their leave.

He tried several times to strike up a conversation, but her responses were curt. So he left his daughter in peace and gave her time to put Cameroon behind her.

Reaching the beach, they found less commotion than there would be later in the day. That was fine by her. They thanked the men who helped them into the boats. They boarded the ship that would bring them to Hamburg.

Luise stood at the rail, which offered a fine view of Mount Cameroon. She would miss everything here. But after what Hamza had done, it was no longer the place she wanted to live. He had broken her heart terribly.

It wasn't long until the captain gave the order to weigh anchor, and the engines hummed to life. Slowly and sedately the ship slid out of the bay. Luise looked toward the beach again, scanning it back and forth. Then she turned away from the rail, went to the saloon and its comfortable armchairs, and turned her back on Cameroon for good.

So she missed seeing, at that moment, a young man who limped onto the beach, wildly waving his arms, and then collapsed, weeping, onto the sand as the ship sounded its horn in farewell.

About the Author

Ellin Carsta is a pseudonym for Petra Mattfeldt, the German author of thrillers, crime novels, and books for young adults; she also writes historical fiction under the name Caren Benedikt. Her many novels include the bestseller *The Secret Healer* and its equally popular sequel, *The Master of Medicine*, as well as *The Draper's Daughter*. Her historical novel *Grapes of Gold* made the short list for the 2017 Skoutz Award.

She lives with her husband and their three children near Bremen. More information about the author can be found at www.petra-mattfeldt.de and www.instagram.com/ellin_carsta.

About the Translator

Photo © 2019 Nina Chapple

Gerald Chapple is an award-winning translator of German literature. He received his doctorate from Harvard University and taught German and comparative literature at McMaster University in Hamilton, Ontario. He has been translating contemporary German-language fiction, poetry, and nonfiction for more than forty years. Among his seven translations for AmazonCrossing are four novels of suspense by the Swiss-Canadian author and journalist Bernadette Calonego: *The Zurich Conspiracy, Under Dark Waters, Stormy Cove,* and *The Stranger on the Ice.* He lives in Dundas, Ontario, with his wife, Nina, and can often be found studying birds, butterflies, and dragonflies; reading; listening to classical music; or enjoying his children and grandchildren in New York.